between departures

LOVE IN TRANSIT SERIES

K.V. THORN

THORN PUBLISHING HOUSE

between departures

Published by Thorn Publishing House

ISBN 979-8-9938308-4-1 *(paperback KDP edition)*

ISBN 979-8-9938308-2-7 *(paperback edition)*

ISBN 979-8-9938308-3-4 *(ebook edition)*

author's note

This book explores family dynamics, feelings of neglect, and sibling relationships. It also follows a love story with a significant age gap and some sort of power imbalance.

Along the way, you'll find sensual/sexually explicit scenes. Please be mindful of that if it's something you're not comfortable with.

As always, please take care of yourself while reading. Your well-being is more important than finishing a chapter.

With all my heart, K. V. Thorn

also by k.v. thorn

Never Not Yours

To all those women who ran away trying to find happiness, I hope you found the best versions of yourselves.

spicy chapter guide

Chapter 9
Chapter 13
Chapter 16
Chapter 18
Chapter 20
Chapter 21
Chapter 24
Chapter 25
Chapter 26
Chapter 27
Chapter 28
Chapter 29

the playlist

Cherry, Lana Del Rey

The Bolter, Taylor Swift

Motion Sickness, Phoebe Bridgers

Delicate, Taylor Swift

Adore You, Harry Styles

Dress, Taylor Swift

Earned It, The Weeknd

Slow Hands, Niall Horan

Do I Wanna Know?, Arctic Monkeys

Paris, Taylor Swift

I Like Me Better, Lauv

between departures

CHAPTER ONE

Sam

THE THING about my life is that every day holds a *maybe*, a what if.

Every trip I take, it's a clean slate. Every city that I visit gives me the chance to be someone new, someone different, someone lighter.

And that's why I love flying.

I don't need to be Samantha Hayes. I don't have to be the daughter of a man who built a global empire. I don't need to be part of a family that *loves* living in tailored suits, is well used to boardroom stares, and has people meddling in their lives. I don't need to be the 'heir' who is supposed to cash out a trust fund that's been sitting in a bank account for over twenty-five years.

I get to be whoever I want to be.

"Do you ever think that we're just like… cosplaying adulthood?" Rose asked, interrupting my daily crisis, as she entered my bedroom with coffee for both of us.

"Honestly? All the time," I admitted, taking the coffee from her hands. "But hey, we've got hardwood floors, an espresso machine we barely know how to use, and a yoga instructor. Feels like we're doing more than cosplaying it." She rolls her eyes at me, laughing, because she knows it's true.

We've been living together for a few years now, since that chaotic, wine-soaked layover in Madrid where she'd drunkenly offered me the spare bedroom. Back then, she was living in a tiny apartment in one of the worst areas of the city. The right answer to that proposal was obviously no. Which is why I said yes, without even knowing her last name.

Now, we live in a *very* overpriced apartment with amenities we don't use, a butler who has seen us drunk more times than I would like to admit, and has certainly seen a lot of visitors. But hey, we're just living life. It should've been a disaster back then. Instead, it turned out to be the most solid relationship I'd ever had. She is the best person I know in every sense that word can hold.

We share everything, and when I say everything, I mean *everything*. From the whole skin care routine, to secrets and, of course, tears, lots and lots of them. She knows when I need a distraction and when I need silence. And she never, *ever* asks why I flinch when people ask about my last name. She just respects me, and that's all you can truly ask for in a best friend.

"The car will be here in fifteen," she said as she disappeared into her room, and I turned back to finish my half-packed suitcase.

This is why I chose movement over stillness, temporary over permanent. Not because I've lived my life running. Okay, maybe I've been running a little.

But hey, the view will always be nicer at 35,000 feet than in a glass boardroom.

By the time we got to JFK, the terminals were buzzing with that organized chaos that only international flights can create.

There are rolling suitcases everywhere. A few screaming toddlers, whose parents are losing their minds, and people sprinting in heels like they are chasing the planes down the runway.

Rose and I move through it like professionals, which, to be fair, we are. We've done this routine hundreds of times. Hair tied up, glossy lips, fresh-faced in that barely trying, but very curated kind of way.

We have matching navy blazers, not-too-long, not-too-short skirts, and roller bags that look sharp and are way too organized. "I swear, if I don't get pistachios and sour gummies in the next five minutes, I'm going to bite someone," Rose muttered as we passed the Sun Valley News stand.

"Oh, that's very wellness-core of you," I said, grabbing a protein bar, a bag of almonds, and an emergency chocolate bar for the emotional support I'll need after this flight. "You joke, but I saw a girl saying that the key to beating jet lag is sour candies and electrolytes."

"I believe her," I say without a doubt, because everybody has the right to cope with things the way they think they should. And I respect that. "You don't even know who I'm talking about."

"It doesn't matter. I bet she's right."

We paid, shoved everything into our bags, and made our way through crew security, cutting past the endless lines of passengers, tired families, and one man loudly explaining crypto to someone who clearly didn't ask.

Sometimes I forget how weird our life might look from the outside. The blazers, the badges, even the ease with which we float through the stress of everyone else's travel day. We aren't just in transit, we *are* the transit. The calm in the chaos, the smiles before takeoff.

Everything that happens between departures.

We stepped into the lounge, which was quiet and tucked away from the fluorescent terminal glare. We slide into a booth near the back, away from the coffee machines and the clink of champagne flutes. Rose grabbed a green smoothie and a mini sandwich. I went for a matcha and a croissant, which I absolutely didn't need but obviously wanted.

I lean back, sipping my drink, watching the room.

Business travelers typing furiously on laptops, a honeymoon couple taking selfies by the floor-to-ceiling windows, a group of pilots laughing too loudly by the espresso machine. Assholes.

I've always thought that airports have a funny way of blurring reality. Everyone here is between something. Between meetings, between countries, between relationships. And that's what I like about it, I think.

Nobody expects *permanence* in a place like this.

Our phones buzzed in sync.

Boarding call, minus 25 minutes.

That's enough time to reset, refresh, and slide into flight attendant mode like slipping into armor. "Ready?" I asked. "I was born ready, babe," Rose replied, fixing her lipstick in the reflection of her phone.

We stood, pulling ourselves together. Okay, here we go. Lip gloss, check. Crew badge, check. Smile that doesn't quite touch the eyes, check. At the gate, the energy was already shifting.

Our flight hasn't started boarding yet, but people are already in line. I don't know why people rush to get into the plane when they're going to be there for the next eight hours.

"Sam," a voice called out behind me. "Hold up a second."

I turned to see Marla, one of the senior flight

attendants on the roster. Red bob, heels that had seen three decades of transatlantic crossings, and eyebrows that could silence a grown man. She was flipping through a clipboard as if it were a weapon.

"Maya called out sick. You've been reassigned to First Class for this flight," she said, not looking up.

"First?" I repeat, waiting for her to clarify.

"Yes, first. You look surprised."

Of course, I look surprised. I *am* surprised. I didn't plan for this. I haven't worked first class in over two months. "I just—I haven't been scheduled in a while, so I didn't think—."

"Well, now you are. Congrats, honey. You'll be handing out Dom and Whiskey instead of Diet Coke." I glanced at Rose, who gave me a half-smirk. "Look at you, Miss Champagne Cart."

"Don't act like you're not jealous," I shot back jokingly, though my stomach flipped a little.

Yes, first class can be intimidating, and while I'd worked it before, it has its own rhythm. It's more luxurious, there's more service, more scrutiny. It's filled with people of status, and they are the kind of passengers who don't just board flights. They expect to be catered to like gods in leather seats. They are the kind of people I ran away from.

"You'll be up front with me," Marla added, finally glancing up. "Don't let them talk circles around you. They smell fear."

"Copy that," I said, adjusting my blazer. "No fear.

Just foie gras and forced charm." Rose gave my arm a quick squeeze as she passed.

"Text me if someone famous boards." I rolled my eyes, but a small laugh escaped.

As I walked down the jet bridge toward the aircraft, I felt that shift again, that little click that happens every time the real world falls away and you're about to step into the sky. The jet bridge door hissed open, and the first wave of First-Class passengers stepped onto the aircraft like they owned the sky. I greeted them with practiced ease. A smile, a nod, and brief eye contact.

Most were absorbed in their phones or already annoyed by seat assignments. This is routine for them, as it is for me. They are all used to this.

Then *he* boarded.

Seat 1A

Tall, tailored, and annoyingly calm. The kind of calm that isn't practice.

You inherit that shit.

Charcoal coat, white shirt slightly unbuttoned at the collar, no tie.

He has that look people try to recreate in fashion campaigns. Effortless and expensive. But there is something else too, something unguarded around his eyes that didn't match the rest of him. He offered me a polite smile as he stepped into the cabin, one hand casually tucked into his pocket, the other gripping a carry-on that seemed brand-new but scuffed just enough to look used.

"Good evening," a man said as he stepped into the cabin. I looked up from the galley cart.

"Hi, welcome aboard."

I always try to make people feel comfortable, maybe a little joke here and there. Something to lighten the mood, but also something to make sure they aren't assholes to me for eight hours.

"Looks like you are in my section today," I said with a smile.

"Lucky me." I gave a polite nod, motioning toward his seat. "Can I take your coat?"

"Sure," he said, slipping it off and handing it to me. He moved easily, unbothered, with no need to perform for anyone. I stowed it away and returned with a tray. "Would you like something to drink before takeoff?" He glanced up to face me. "Do you happen to have Jack and ginger?"

"Yes, we do." I gave a small smile.

"Great. I'll take one if it's not too much trouble."

"Not at all." I headed to the galley, fixed the drink, and returned a few minutes later. He was settling in, one arm draped casually over the armrest, watching the quiet bustle of boarding.

"Here you go," I said, handing him the glass. He took it carefully from my hands and then looked up at me again.

"Thank you. You're very efficient and fast." I let out a short laugh. "Well, that's a way to describe my job." He laughed a little.

"You seem like you've got it down to a science."

"It's more like muscle memory at this point," I said, then asked him, "Do you fly often?"

"Way more than I would like," he said, taking a sip. "Usually business. But, this one's a mix." I nodded.

"So, Paris for both business and pleasure, huh?"

"Well, technically just work, but I'm hoping for a quiet night or two while I'm there." I didn't press. Passengers said all kinds of things. Some wanted to talk, some didn't. He seemed like the kind who didn't mind a good conversation but wouldn't want to waste his words either.

"Well, let me know if you need anything else," I said.

"Will do," he replied, then leaned back and looked out the window. That was my cue to notice the conversation had just ended.

I moved on to the other passengers and kept serving some drinks. To be first class, there was nothing unusual happening, nothing worth remembering.

No famous people to tell Rose about.

CHAPTER TWO

theo

THE ICE CLINKED SOFTLY in my glass as I opened my laptop and *tried*, once again, to finish the welcome email I'd been rewriting since last night. At least I have the subject line.

Excited to join the team.

And I have a draft. Just three paragraphs of corporate-safe bullshit, all hollow by the way.

I stared at the blinking cursor, my fingers frozen above the keys. This isn't just another trip. This is the end of a version of my life and the beginning of something that, quite honestly, I'm still not sure I've earned. Or want.

I take a slow sip of the Jack and ginger. It's good. Way stronger than I was expecting. So was the flight attendant, now that I think about it. She was calm, sharp, and quick with clean replies. No fluff, no forced smile.

She was just… present.

That's rare. Most flight attendants don't care about you, or care too much. And I get it, they're doing their job, some of them go above that, and some of them just stand out. Like she did. She didn't ask for my name, but I guess she could see it on her little tablet as I ordered the drink.

I glanced up for a second, looked around the cabin, and spotted her behind me on the aisle, tucking a blanket over an elderly woman a couple of seats back. She looks like the kind of person who can make even the most chaotic thing easy.

I look back at the screen.

I'm honored to step into this new chapter at Hayes International, and I look forward to…

Nope.

Delete.

My body is in this seat, but my mind is back in every boardroom, every strategy meeting, every well-meaning conversation about legacy and vision that has landed me here. I sigh louder than needed, and the person next to me gives me a judgmental look.

I hadn't had a vacation in years. Not a real one anyway. Not one where I wasn't sneaking emails under the table or running numbers between sight-seeing stops. The last time I truly unplugged, I was drinking rum from a pineapple on a beach in Tulum for my honeymoon. Six days in paradise. She picked the destination, and I picked the hotel. It was a nice balance.

That was before everything imploded. Before the

late-night fights, the cold shoulders, and the truth that surfaced in the form of a text message from one of my oldest friends.

This trip isn't technically a vacation. But it's the closest thing I've allowed myself in years. A couple of nights in Paris before the transition starts. Just one breath before I stop being Theodore Jones, the guy who built his own tech company from scratch to become the face of someone else's empire.

Hayes International.

The name itself makes something in my chest tighten. It sounds so big, old, and powerful. This is the kind of company that comes with a lot of pressure and a whole lot more politics. Which I've spent most of my career avoiding. But it is also an opportunity, a shift, a challenge I couldn't turn down, even if a part of me wished I had.

Outside the window, the last bit of sunlight dipped below the horizon. The flight attendant passed by, checking trays, moving smoothly between rows. She didn't look my way this time.

I reopened the laptop and stared at the blank email again.

I'm honored to step into this new chapter…

No, too stiff.

Excited to join the Hayes team…

Way too eager.

I rub my temples trying to take the stress out of my mind and body. How is it harder to write a paragraph opening for a corporate welcome email than it was to build a product roadmap or convince investors to give me millions of dollars?

"Hi," she said, holding a leather-bound menu and getting me out of my head, which I'm thankful for.

"Just wanted to go over your meal selections."

"Sure," I said, tilting down the laptop's screen. "Let me guess, chicken or pasta?" She cracked a small smile. "Not quite. Tonight's dinner options are short rib with horseradish-mashed potatoes, roasted salmon with fennel, or butternut squash risotto. You'll also want to choose an option for breakfast, oh, and a snack, so we don't have to wake you up mid-flight."

I took the menu from her, glancing over it quickly. "You are really good at this, aren't you?" She shrugged lightly.

"You figure out the rhythm after a while. Dinner, snacks, breakfast. Keep the cabin calm, keep the coffee hot, try not to spill red wine on anyone's white shirt."

"That's practical," I said. "And poetic, in its own way."

That earned a short but real laugh. "Poetic isn't usually in the job description." I looked up at her again. She was standing easily, her weight slightly shifted to one side, her hands resting in front of her. Confident, but not stiff. Professional, but not cold.

There was a flicker of something in her expression, amusement? Interest? Or maybe she was just doing her job really well.

I tried to remember what it felt like to be good at

reading people. That used to be my thing. Now I wasn't sure whether I was picking up on someone being flirty or just imagining it.

"I'll do the short rib, the fruit and cheese plate, and the egg sandwich for breakfast," I said, handing the menu back.

"Solid choices. The short rib's a favorite."

"Good to know." She hesitated just half a beat before adding, "Would you like another Jack and ginger?" I met her gaze, trying to read something in it, tone, body language, anything that would tell me if this was standard or… more. I nodded. "Sure. One more."

She gave a small smile. I wasn't sure if she was flirting. I wasn't sure if I cared at all. I'm just seeing things to distract myself.

That's it.

"Here you go," she said, setting the Jack and ginger on the tray table with a practiced grace. "Thanks," I replied, adjusting the glass. She gave a light nod, then did another sweep through the cabin.

The lights dimmed. The captain came on to announce expected turbulence over the Atlantic.

I leaned back in the seat, sipped the drink, and stared at the blinking cursor again.

Subject: A Note of Introduction

Yes, that's better. It's clean, looks professional. Not too casual, but not too formal either.

Then, finally, the paragraph came.

I'm honored to be joining your team and look forward to

getting to know each of you over the next few months. Though this is a new chapter for me, I'm stepping into it with deep respect for the company's legacy and excitement about the road ahead.

That was it. It was simple and safe. With just enough sincerity to sound like I meant it.

I hit save.

The cabin lights softened to a warm glow. Most of the passengers were already reclined or fading into their noise-canceling headphones. First Class had a way of making people disappear fast, one glass of wine and a good pillow, and half the cabin looked like a hotel lobby at midnight.

I kept my headphones in and worked quietly. One spreadsheet open on one side of the screen, the draft email on the other. It wasn't exactly a 'rest', but it was the closest I got.

A little over two hours in, the galley curtain rustled, and there she was again. "Dinner is here," she said quietly, placing the tray on my table. "Short rib, and here are your utensils."

"Thanks," I said, removing my headphones. "Still working?" She glanced at the screen before I shut it. "Yeah, trying to finish something before we land."

"Something important?" I shrugged.

"It's an introduction email. I'm starting a new job next week." She tilted her head slightly. "Oh, is it Paris-based?"

"No. But I have a meeting there, and I could use a break before everything starts."

"That's smart. Most people wait until they're already burned out to take time off." I smiled faintly.

"Yeah, that's right. Most people don't even realize they're burned out until it's too late."

She stayed beside the seat a moment longer, glancing toward the rest of the cabin. A few passengers were already stretched out with blankets over their laps, eyes closed, wine glasses half full on their trays. One was softly snoring.

"It gets quiet up here fast," she said. "Once the meals are out and the lights go down, it's like a different flight."

"Not complaining," I said. "I need the quiet." She looked at me for a second, assessing me. "You look like someone who doesn't get much of that." She's not wrong. But before I could respond, she added, "I'll check on you again in a bit. Let me know if you need anything."

I turn back to my food, still thinking about the way she said it. Like she'd seen something in me I hadn't meant to show. Not that it mattered. We'd be in Paris by morning. And people like her didn't remember the passenger's name in seat 1A.

The tray was cleared, the lights dimmed again, and for a while, I worked in silence. A few more emails. One calendar sync. Half an article I didn't finish reading.

Eventually, I leaned back, stared at the ceiling panel, and pressed the small button above my seat. The chime was quiet, barely noticeable, but a few minutes later she appeared, hair tucked neatly behind one ear, with that same calm expression, though her posture was more relaxed.

"Could I bother you for another drink?" I asked. "Of course," she said with a quick smile, then disappeared behind the galley curtain.

When she came back, she held the drink with both hands and leaned in slightly as she placed it on the tray table. "Double Jack and ginger," she said, tapping the top of the glass gently with her finger. "On the house."

I looked up at her, a little surprised. "I thought they were all included?" She shrugged, mouth tugging into something between a grin and a smirk. "They are. But it sounds cooler when I say it like that."

"Nice one," I laughed more than I meant to.

She lingered a bit longer this time, resting her hand lightly on the seat, leaning just enough to make the proximity feel intentional. Or maybe that was the drink talking. Still, the angle of her hip, the way her gaze held mine a little longer than necessary… it felt like something.

"Do you spend much time in Paris?" I asked, in a tone way more casual than what I was feeling. "Here and there," she said. "It's one of our more regular layovers. Depends on the schedule. You?"

"Not since college," I said. "This time's more of a rest stop than a vacation destination." She nodded.

"That's one of my favorite things about traveling. Sometimes you go because you want to see something.

And others, you go because you need to leave something behind."

I didn't reply right away. Instead, she effortlessly shifted the conversation. "Got plans while you're there?" I shook my head. "No agenda. Just walk around, eat something good, and drink. Pretend I'm not starting a whole new life in seventy-two hours."

Her smile softened. "Sounds like a decent plan."

We were talking about everything and nothing at the same time. Airline stories, favorite cities, terrible hotel coffee, good croissants, weird passengers. She told me about a rainy layover in Dublin where she and her best friend accidentally got locked out of their hotel room barefoot, and I told her about the time I lost my passport in a Lisbon bar and still managed to get back to the States without anyone noticing.

And when I finally glanced down at my screen, I realized we'd been talking for over fifteen minutes. She blinked, like snapping out of a daze.

"Oh, God. I should— sorry, I should check on the other passengers."

"Oh, no worries." She gave a quick nod, then pushed off the divider and moved back down the aisle, pausing briefly to adjust a blanket for someone before vanishing into the galley again.

It had been a long time since I talked to someone like that.

I must have dozed off for a while, because the next thing I remember was the gentle tap of a tray being set on my table.

"Breakfast," she whispered. "And a coffee. Thought you might need the help." I sat up straighter. "You read me too well."

She smiled. "You're not my first."

My breakfast was simple. An egg sandwich and some fruit, but the coffee was perfect. Probably the best thing I'd had in days. It wasn't like regular airplane coffee. This was better. She didn't linger this time. She just gave me a polite nod and moved to the next row.

Two hours later, the captain announced our descent into Paris.

The window shades lifted, seats started to be adjusted, and sleepy passengers blinked into consciousness.

And the flight was over.

CHAPTER THREE

Sam

I STOOD near the galley door, smiling on autopilot, thanking passengers as they got off one by one.

Some of them were clearly in a hurry. "Have a great day," I said to a businessman who didn't look up from his phone. How rude.

"Thanks again," a woman mumbled, balancing three bags and a neck pillow.

Then he appeared. He really took his time putting his stuff away and getting ready to step out of the plane. He looked freshly awake, hair a little tousled, shirt slightly wrinkled in the best way, bag in one hand, coat in the other.

Now that I really see him, he is tall, at least 6'2", and moves with that easy confidence some men just have without trying.

His skin is a bit tan, and he has brown hair that curls slightly at the ends. A very well-trimmed beard, and hazel eyes that somehow look golden in this morning light. He is muscular, but not in the gym-obsessed kind, more like strong in a way that looks natural.

"I'll give the short rib a solid eight out of ten," he said, stopping in front of me.

I raised a brow. "Only an eight?"

"The ginger wasn't quite spicy enough," he added with a faint smile.

"Oh well, that's tragic."

"Yeah, but the service definitely made up for it." I gave him the smallest smirk. "We aim to please."

There was a pause. Not long, but not nothing either. It was like he was thinking about saying something else, but he didn't. "Well," he said, adjusting the strap on his shoulder, "thanks for making the flight feel a little less like a flight."

"Anytime." He nodded once, the corners of his mouth lifting a little bit, then turned and walked up the jet bridge. He definitely was the most interesting part of my night.

I let out a slow breath and turned back toward the cabin.

First Class was quiet now, abandoned, crumpled blankets and empty glasses the only signs of life left. I started my routine, moving methodically through the space. I start fluffing the pillows, tossing the linens into the bin, and resetting the seats to their pristine, untouched positions.

It was strange how fast people disappeared. One minute you're handing them a drink and listening to them talk about croissants and restarts, and the next, they're just gone.

Still, I liked this part. The clean-up. The quiet. There was something comforting about putting things back in order, physical order, at least, even when the emotional kind was messier.

I tossed the last blanket into the cart, checked every seat one last time, then I grabbed my things from the jump seat, slung my tote bag over my shoulder, and headed to the back of the cabin, where Rose was already waiting, arms crossed, hair in a low bun that somehow still looked perfect.

"Finally," she whispered. "If I don't inhale a croissant in the next ten minutes, I'm going to pass out."

"Please, I need one the size of my head," I said, falling into step beside her. "With a coffee strong enough to reset my life."

"Followed by a nap," She smirked.

We laughed under our breath as we stepped off the plane and into the jet bridge, our steps syncing without effort. My hair is frizzy, the makeup is half-worn, but we still walk like we own the terminal.

* * *

By the time we got to the hotel, I was running on fumes and caffeine ambition.

But the second I stepped into the room, I felt like I could rally. The smell of clean sheets, the feel of blackout curtains, and that rainfall shower definitely give me hope.

Rose and I always book connecting rooms with

double beds, but the doors between them stay open the entire trip, unless we have *visitors*, of course.

We move in sync, shoes kicked off, bags dumped, uniforms unzipped and tossed in a pile that future-us would deal with. "I need a ten-minute shower, or I will actually cease to exist," Rose called out from her room.

"Make it five, and I'll let you use my leave-in conditioner," I yelled back, already halfway into the bathroom.

We had one real rule during our layovers. Quick showers. That was it. A shower just long enough to rinse off recycled air, sweat, and whatever soul-sapping energy clings to you after an eight-hour flight. The water hit hot, and I breathed out slowly as mascara traced little rivers down my face. I didn't even wash my hair, just twisted it into a low bun and let my skin breathe.

Within twenty minutes, we were out the door, oversized sunglasses on, glossy lips, sneakers clean enough to count as cute. Ready for coffee, croissants, and a couple of hours of pretending we live here.

"I saw you talking to a hot passenger," Rose said as we stepped out onto the cobblestone street. "Tall, tan, business class energy, but with first class face." She continued as I gave her a look.

"That's not a real scale." I shot back.

"Well, let me tell you something. It should be," she muttered, adjusting her sunglasses. "He looked like he reads on purpose and probably orders whiskey without blinking."

"Jack and ginger, actually."

She grinned. "And you remembered it."

"It's my job."

"No, Sam. That's not your job. Your job is to make and deliver the drinks, not to remember the drink order after the flight."

"So?" I shrugged. "He was nice. We talked a little, nothing major." Rose gave me a side glance. "You were smiling. And not in your 'here's your hot towel, sir' way." I shook my head. "You're imagining things."

"Am I? Because I'm also pretty sure Captain Morris a.k.a. Captain Flirt in 38C was giving me eyes." I laughed. "Wait, the guy with the navy sweatshirt, and the smug smirk?"

"Yep. He's one of the relief pilots for the return leg. Said he's deadheading but might 'see me around.'"

"Oh, he absolutely meant that in the 'i-want-to-be-part-of-your-layover kind of way."

"Obviously, but he's an asshole, and he's the type of man that has every flight attendant on a choke-hold, and probably a text away from his bed."

"Well, it's not his fault that he is hot, and some of us are desperately in need of... well, companionship during layovers." She rolled her eyes at me and made a joke about it.

We turned the corner toward a café we found last year on a similar layover, gold bistro chairs, tiny pastries, and the best espresso on this side of the Seine. "This is why we do it," Rose said as we slid into a sidewalk table.

"Ten hours of recycled air, crying babies, and fragile egos... for this."

"For buttery carbs and men who flirt and make eye contact like it's a sport?"

"Exactly." We ordered two coffees and a basket of fresh pastries, letting the city buzz around us.

This was the part of the job that felt like a reward. The part people only see on social media. The soft mornings, the stolen hours in a new place, the friendship you create along the way, and of course, the freedom.

By the time we drank our coffees and ate too many mini pastries, Rose was yawning behind her sunglasses like a cat in the sun. "I'm heading back to the hotel for a quick nap," she said, stretching as she'd just run a marathon. "If I don't sleep now, I'll crash during dinner."

I sipped the last of my espresso and stood, tucking my scarf into my coat.

"Go. I'm wired. That coffee hit harder than expected." She narrowed her eyes. "Promise me one thing."

"No Eiffel Tower without you?"

"Yep. You know me so well."

"Scout's honor." She kissed me, spun on her heel, and disappeared down the street like a very glamorous Parisian woman.

I walked for a while, no destination, just following the rhythm of the streets. The city was soft this time of day. Locals on bikes, dogs wearing sweaters, the occasional tourist trying to figure out where their taxis vanished to. I loved this part. Being alone, but not lonely.

Unknown in a beautiful place.

Eventually, after losing track of time, I slid into a seat at a little bistro with red awnings and menus printed in French cursive. The waiter barely blinked when I asked for a glass of wine; it wasn't even noon, but apparently, I looked like someone who'd earned it. After all, I had already had breakfast, so this was closer to my lunchtime.

And if they're serving it, I'm drinking it.

I set my tote bag on the table, pulled out my phone, and opened the browser without thinking too much about it. Call it curiosity. Something has been crawling around the back of my mind since we landed.

Theodore Jones.

I typed it quickly, expecting maybe a LinkedIn profile. A press photo, if anything. But what I got instead were headlines.

"Tech Visionary Appointed as New CEO of Hayes International."

"Theodore Jones Named Successor to Max Hayes."

"Theodore Jones to Lead Global Expansion of Hayes International."

I could feel how my heart stopped when I read that. My hands got sweaty, and I almost choked on my wine. *Tech Visionary Appointed as New CEO of Hayes International.*

I read the second headline as if it's going to give me more clarity. *Theodore Jones Named Successor to Max Hayes.*

Oh no. Fuck.

He is the new CEO of *Hayes International*? What are the fucking odds. I blinked and read it once again. *HAYES INTERNATIONAL?* As in my Hayes? I blinked at the screen for the fourth time, and I kept scrolling until I found another picture. But this time it was a glossy photo of him in a suit, shaking hands with my father.

Oh fucking fuck, kill me now.

I sat there for a full minute, maybe more, the wine untouched, and the screen burning into my retinas.

Hayes International.

Then I called Rose. She didn't answer, so I called her again.

"Sam?" she answered groggily on the third ring. "What— are you okay?"

"I need you to get up." She must be so confused right now. "What?"

"Get up. Right now. Throw water on your face. I don't care what you need to do, but I need you to come meet me."

"Where even are you—?"

"I just Googled 1A." She paused. "Okay… and? What's the matter?"

"And he's the new CEO of Hayes International." Silence. "Wait, wait. Hayes International… as in your Hayes International?" I stared out at the street, trying to slow my heartbeat. "Yes, as in my Hayes."

"Oh. My. God. Hang on, I'm putting on pants. I'll be there in a bit."

Ten minutes later, I saw her walking down the street in jeans, sunglasses, and a trench coat. She slid into the chair across from me as she'd just been briefed on a crisis.

"So," she said, catching her breath. "What the actual fuck?" I handed her my phone without a word. The headline was still open. Her eyes scanned it. Slowly. Once, then twice.

"Holy. Shit."

"Yep," I said, making an unnecessary emphasis on the p.

"Theodore Jones is the new CEO of Hayes International?" she repeated, voice low but intense. "Yep." She looked at me. "Your Hayes."

"Unfortunately."

We sat there for a moment, my glass half full, hers untouched. I wasn't really ready to say anything. But I also knew if there was one person in the world I could say it to, it was Rose. "I know you don't like talking about them," she said gently.

"I don't." I traced a finger over the rim of my glass.

The thing about my family is that they don't do small. Or soft. Or optional. They do legacy. They do strategy. They have expectations that feel like contracts signed in blood.

My sister, Naomi, embraced it early. She was valedictorian in her class. The business school's top student. She went for corporate law, and was second in her class. But if you ask her, she was the first.

She was practically born in a pantsuit. And of course, now she works for the company, some shiny corner office at Hayes International HQ, doing God knows what for God knows how much money. And, I was supposed to follow.

We both were. That was the plan. Max Hayes' daughters, one CEO, one COO, maybe CFO, depending on our career path. Those were the dreams my dad laid out for us like fine China. Very carefully, and very expensively.

But even as a kid, I didn't want any of it.

I didn't want the boardroom, the brunch meetings, or the fake smiles at shareholder galas.

I wanted stories, color, a mess. Things that didn't have to be profitable to matter. So, I majored in Art, History, and Languages. I double-majored on a full scholarship. I graduated with honors. And when I got my master's, they still held on to hope, like I'd wake up one day and suddenly crave a corner office and a twelve-hour corporate workday.

Instead, I became a flight attendant.

At twenty-four, I walked away from the family and

toward something entirely mine. I've been flying ever since. I know I'm smart. I know I could've crushed a career at Hayes International. I could've run the place blindfolded with a latte in one hand and a PowerPoint in the other. But that life? That world? It just… didn't feel like mine.

I looked at Rose, whose brow was furrowed like she was trying to piece it all together.

"He has no idea I'm Samantha Hayes. I didn't even say my name." I said finally.

"What are you going to do?" I stared into my wine glass like it might have the answer.

"I have no idea. I mean, it's not like I'm seeing him ever again."

CHAPTER FOUR

theo

THE SHOWER WAS HOT, almost too hot, but I let it burn the stiffness out of my shoulders. Ten hours in a suit jacket has a way of making you feel older than you are. I step out and slowly towel off, letting the quiet settle.

No email notifications, no texts from my former co-founder, no calendar pings. Just the hum of the city outside the window and the drip of water off the tile. My first real night off in, I don't even know how long.

I gave myself twenty minutes for a power nap. Not a second more. Just enough to reset my brain without slipping into deep sleep and waking up with a headache and regret.

Then the emails started. Most were onboarding logistics. Transition docs, HR briefings, and a formal announcement draft I still hadn't approved. I typed a few short replies, scheduled a call with Max Hayes for later, and flagged a dozen things to ignore until Monday.

CEO of Hayes International.

Even now, it didn't feel real.

Ten years ago, I was pitching investors in coffee shops and coding backend features in my friend's garage. I was the first in my family to make a million, quietly, without a ceremony. The first to own property. The first to make it to Forbes.

I built something from nothing. And I was proud of that. But I sold the company six months ago. Stepped down before the next round, passed the torch. People thought I was gearing up for something bigger, another startup, maybe a fund.

I bet they aren't expecting it to be... *this*. The Hayes offer came fast. Quiet dinners, boardroom meetings behind closed doors. Max Hayes had already made up his mind by the time I was sitting in front of him.

Said his daughters weren't ready. Said he needed someone who understood both growth and loyalty. His advisors had floated two names. Mine stuck.

The salary was way more than what most CEOs earn. Equity on a five-year plan. Perks most people wouldn't believe if I said them out loud. It was enough to make me a billionaire. So why did it still feel like I was borrowing someone else's life?

I pulled my laptop closer and opened a browser. I hadn't been to Paris in over a decade, not since college. I scrolled aimlessly through blogs, some posts, and a few local foodie pages until one spot caught my eye. Marée Noire, a restaurant-slash-lounge with great food, a deep wine list, and a subtle transition into live music and late drinks.

Not too flashy, not too dead.

Perfect.

I tossed on a clean button-down, charcoal slacks, and a dark wool coat. Not overly polished, but not tourist-y either. European casual, the kind of effort that looks like none at all.

Before I left the room, I paused at the mirror. My hair was still damp. My eyes were tired, and I looked like shit.

But I was in Paris.

The hostess seated me near the window, with a soft hum of music, linen napkins, and stoneware plates.

Nothing pretentious at all, but really well done.

I ordered a bottle of red wine from Bordeaux after asking the chef for recommendations. The waitress smiled and brought me a handwritten insert with a few off-menu specials. I picked a slow-roasted duck with fig glaze, not because I was craving duck, but because I didn't have to think about it. The menu was right there, and she swore it was the best dish.

Tonight was about not thinking too much. It was about enjoying the city and myself.

By the third glass of wine, I was back in one of my oldest habits, watching people. Not in a creepy Edward Cullen reading minds kind of way, but in that quiet, curious, what's your story kind of way.

There was a couple, two tables down, mid-40s, arguing softly in French. They didn't look angry, just worn out. The woman kept checking her phone between bites, and the man barely touched his food.

Across the room, two younger guys were clearly on a business dinner that had turned into a posturing match, with too many hand gestures and not enough food eaten. And me? Sitting alone in Paris, drinking good wine, eating better food, and pretending like I wasn't starting over in a way that scared me more than I cared to admit.

The waitress returned as I was finishing the last bites of my dinner. "Puis-je vous éclairer?" she asked in French with a soft accent. I don't know why she assumed I spoke French, but I didn't want to disappoint her.

"S'il vous plaît, faites," I said, handing her the plate. "And could I take the rest of the wine to the bar?" I knew French, but not enough to maintain this conversation. Or any really.

"Of course." She said now in English, and gave me a knowing smile, half 'enjoy your night', half 'don't do anything stupid in my bar', and disappeared with the tray. I brought my glass and the half-finished bottle to the long, polished bar. The crowd was growing, soft jazz shifting into something with a beat.

The place would be a full-on lounge in an hour, but for now, it still held that in-between energy. It felt relaxed, a bit warm, but buzzing with possibility.

The bartender was a tall brunette with sharp cheekbones and a sex appeal she wasn't even trying to have. She poured me a fresh glass and then leaned in a little too close, "Avez-vous besoin de quelque chose d'autre?" She has been flirting with me for a while. That much I could tell.

I shook my head, didn't flirt back, not really. But I didn't shut it down either. I never did. Not since the divorce. I wasn't interested in anything more than a night, and most people could tell. Which was fine by me.

I liked sex. I liked the simplicity of something physical, uncomplicated, without expectation. It was honest in a way most things weren't.

"First time in Paris?" she asked, fingers grazing the bar. "In a while."

She smiled. "Welcome back then." I nodded, taking a sip of the wine.

The place was crowded now, layers of conversation, coats being shrugged off, music pulsing under the chatter. But something about the motion at the front caught my eye. A woman stepped in first, petite, with dark red hair pulled into a messy knot, wearing heels that made her legs look impossibly long. Pretty, in that obvious way. The kind of pretty you're meant to notice.

But then, right behind her, I saw *her*… The flight attendant.

She looked completely different.

Same face, same posture, but no blazer, no bun, no polite, practiced smile. Her hair was down. She has long, dark brown hair, a little messy in that effortless, slept-in way. She wore jeans and a fitted top with a long jacket, casual but clean, and the curve of her hips under the denim caught more than one glance as she stepped further inside.

Light makeup. A spark in her eyes I hadn't seen on the plane. And then those blue eyes met mine. Like, even though she looked around the room, it was me who stood out to her.

Our gaze held, just for a second too long. And suddenly, the wine, the bartender, the quiet in my head, all of it vanished.

Because now I wasn't alone in Paris anymore.

She whispered something to the redhead as they entered, a little smirk tugging at the corner of her mouth. Whatever she said made the redhead glance my way, just once, before she kept walking with the rest of their group— three women, two guys, all headed toward a high-top table near the back.

But her? She started walking towards the bar.

I straightened just slightly on the stool, not trying to look eager but suddenly hyper-aware of my posture, my shirt, and whether I still smelled like duck and red wine. She slid into the open space next to me, her body angled just enough toward mine to feel intentional.

"1A," she said with a lift of her brow. "Ditched the Jack and ginger already?"

I smiled. "Couldn't let the Parisian wine go to waste." She leaned her elbow on the bar. "I was hoping you'd be a whisky loyalist. I like consistency."

"You'll be disappointed with me, then," I said, watching her closely. "I'm a fan of options."

Her smile curled a little deeper. Playful, teasing, but there was a new energy in her now. Off-duty, unfiltered, the version of her I hadn't met yet. "I'm Theo," I said, offering a hand. She looked at it, then shook it with just enough pressure to make it feel like a statement.

"I'm Sam. But I like 1A more."

"Is that a flight attendant thing?"

"Oh no, that's a me thing." God, she was good at this game. "Can I get you a glass?" I asked, nodding toward the half-bottle still sitting between us.

"I thought you'd never ask." I poured it for her and slid the glass her way.

She took a sip, then let out a quiet, appreciative hum. "Okay, I forgive you for abandoning whiskey," she said.

We settled into easy conversation. We talked about the restaurant, the food, the way the music had changed since the early crowd started trickling out, and the night energy rolled in. "A place like this is perfect for layovers," she said. "Low tourist density, strong drinks, dim lighting."

"You forgot the overpriced duck." She laughed. "Right. The full Parisian experience." We talked about traveling. Light stuff, favorite routes, weird passenger habits, the best and worst airport food in Europe. She was sharp, funny, and completely present.

"Do you always talk to passengers after you land?" I asked, curious. "Only the ones who drink Jack and ginger and ask polite questions about breakfast options," she said. "I was polite?"

"For a first-class man? You were practically a saint."

She was close now, just enough that our arms brushed every so often when we reached for our glasses.

CHAPTER FIVE

Sam

The wine between us was almost gone, but it wasn't really about the wine anymore. It was more about the ritual, the small act of filling and refilling, of staying in the moment. Of saying without saying, 'I'm not ready to leave yet'.

He tilted the bottle, trying to pour the last of it into my glass, and raised his brows when only a couple of drops fell out. I smirked. "Well, that's tragic."

He looked over at the bartender. "Should we?" I leaned in, just enough to feel the tension shift. "I guess we'll have to share another one. It would be rude not to."

He chuckled softly, flagging the bartender with a small nod. "Rude is definitely not my brand." When the new bottle arrived, he poured each of us a fresh glass. The night felt easy now. The bar was full, but our corner felt like its own orbit.

"So," I said, resting my chin lightly on my hand, "earlier you said this trip was your reset before something big. What's the big thing?" He hesitated, just slightly. Not enough to be suspicious, just enough to feel careful. I need him to say it. "I'm taking on a new role," he said. "It's corporate. A very well-established company. It's not my usual pace, but… it was time to make a change."

"Let me guess." I sipped my wine. "You used to be a start-up guy. Who dressed up with hoodies, was addicted to cold brew, and had fifteen-hour days?"

He laughed. "Guilty. Though I always liked button-downs. Even in the hoodie years." I tilted my head. "What kind of company?"

"Tech. We built software for real-time inventory tracking. Exciting stuff, I know."

"But you made it work?"

"Yeah. We scaled. Sold. I stepped down last year."

"And now you're, what, bored?" He shrugged, but I saw the flicker in his expression. "Not bored. Just… ready for something bigger. Or maybe just different."

Different. Right. Something like Hayes. I nodded, letting silence stretch just long enough to make him shift in his seat. "Sounds like you've been busy for a while."

He looked down at his glass. "For way more than a decade. I turned thirty-eight this year, and I haven't had a real vacation since my honeymoon, which was almost eight years ago."

That stopped me. Not because it was dramatic,

but because it was honest. I don't want to ask about his marriage, but I don't see a ring, not even a tan line on his finger.

Anyway, I don't care about that.

"Yikes," I said. "I don't even remember the last time I stayed in one city for more than a week, let alone a relationship." He gave me a sideways look. "You travel that much? Outside of work, of course?"

"Every month. My life basically fits in a carry-on. If you don't count my shoes."

"And you like it that way?"

I smiled. "I like not being expected to sit still." He nodded, slowly. Like he understood that more than he let on.

Then he looked at me, eyes warm. "Can I ask you something without sounding like an old man?"

"That's a dangerous opener."

He laughed. "How old are you?"

I gasped theatrically. "Oh my god. You're thirty-eight, and you still don't know you're not supposed to ask a woman her age?"

His expression tightened in mock guilt. "Noted." I swirled the wine in my glass, grinning. "I'm twenty-six."

"Good age."

"You make it sound like I'm a cheese."

He really laughs now, "I mean that in the best way."

I took another sip of my wine, letting the flavor settle on my tongue. The wine was smooth, deep, and warm. Like this night, unexpected, but settling in all the right places. And I couldn't stop thinking about the headline burning into my brain.

Theo Jones, CEO of Hayes International.

He didn't know who I was. And I wasn't planning on telling him either. He took another sip of wine, watching me over the rim of his glass. "Okay, your turn."

"My turn for what?"

"To tell me what you studied before you decided to become a professional city-hopper." I smiled, setting my glass down. "I majored in Art, History, and Languages."

His brow lifted. "Double major?"

"And a master's." He blinked. "Alright, over-achiever."

"I contain multitudes."

"So… history, art, Italian, French, maybe even German? And now you hand out hot towels in the sky." I gave him a look. "Hey, those towels are a luxury experience."

He smirked. "So, why the flight attendant thing?"

"Because I didn't want a desk job. Because I love airports. I like seeing the world and leaving before it gets too complicated." I paused. "And maybe because doing something completely different than what was expected felt… liberating." He didn't press, but I could tell he understood. "What about you?" I asked. "You said your last vacation was your honeymoon."

He nodded. "Yeah. I got married pretty young. Didn't last long."

"May I ask, what happened?" His tone didn't shift. He didn't dodge the question or make it dramatic. He just… said it.

"She cheated," he said simply. "With someone I used to consider a friend. We were already falling apart, but that was the final straw."

My fingers paused around the stem of my glass. "I'm sorry, that's awful." He shrugged. "It's okay. It was a long time ago. I don't regret it, I learned a lot. But I wouldn't do it again."

"So what do you do now?"

"Now I date when I want to. I keep it simple." Emotionless, yes, but not cold. Just factual, and a bit too honest. It was like he'd practiced holding truth without weighting him down. Not a lot of people could do that. I didn't know whether to admire him for it or feel sorry.

"And you?" he asked, tilting his head slightly. "What does your love life look like?"

I smirked. "You are a very curious man."

"I'm thirty-eight. It's allowed."

"It's messy," I admitted. "Fun, sometimes. Nonexistent, other times. I mean, being in a different city every few days doesn't exactly scream emotional availability."

"That's one way to avoid drama."

"I don't *avoid* drama. I just like to pick the kind I

can walk away from when it gets too much to handle." He chuckled. "That's fair."

There was a pause, not long enough to feel awkward, but long enough to make me hyperaware of how close we are.

His hand brushes his glass, mine brushes mine. The air between us felt warmer now. Then the bartender appeared in front of us with a perfect, untimely smile. "Need anything else?" she asked, her eyes trained directly on him. Theo looked up. "We're good for now, thanks."

She gave him a slow, unnecessary smile before walking off, one last look over her shoulder. I tilted my head toward him. "She's definitely interested." He blinked. "What?"

"The bartender." He glanced at me, then looked back down at his glass. "I hadn't noticed."

"Oh, you're such a liar." He smirked. "Would it matter if she were?"

"Not really," I said, leaning in a little. "But, I was about to order dessert, and now I feel like I'm competing with someone who knows how to use a corkscrew."

He laughed, the sound deep and low. "You've got nothing to worry about."

"Good," I said, clinking my glass lightly against his. "Because I don't like to share bottles or attention."

"But we're sharing a second bottle..." Our eyes held just long enough for the mood to shift again.

Now a bit lighter, maybe even a bit bolder, a little more dangerous. "To be fair, we've been sharing only this one. The other one was yours," I added.

I flagged the bartender for dessert, crème brûlée for me, nothing for him, and we kept sipping the wine like we had nowhere else to be. I mean, I don't know about him, but I didn't. Rose was with some flight attendants and the pilot, whom she swears she hates, so I was free.

The bar was quieter now. Most of the groups had moved toward the lounge or spilled onto the street. Our conversation had wandered, places we loved, flights gone wrong, the weird things people do when they think no one's watching.

Then the bartender returned.

She placed the dessert in front of me, then slid a folded napkin toward Theo with a casual smirk. "I'm off the clock," she said, tapping it with one red-painted nail. "In case you get bored later. My apartment is two blocks away." Before she walked off, she looked at me, then back at him. "You can bring her too," she said so casually that I nearly choked on the first bite of the brûlée.

Theo let out a short chuckle, picked up the napkin, and tucked it under his glass, saying thank you to her.

I gave him a look. "Are you this open to sleeping with strangers?"

He shrugged, calm as ever. "What? Who said I'm open to sleeping with her?"

"Well, you said thank you," I say, playing with what's left of the dessert.

"I was being polite," he said, but he had a very quirky smile on his face.

"The invitation included me, and you didn't even ask. That was rude." He laughed, like actually laughed, and I found myself grinning in spite of it. "I'm sorry, do you want an invitation?" he asked, eyes catching mine.

"To her bed, or to yours?"

"Well," he said, finishing his glass, "I can't offer hers. She already did. And besides, I only extend invitations to my bed."

I swirled the spoon in the melted sugar, meeting his gaze. "So, are you extending one or…?"

His voice was low, steady. "Do you want me to invite you to my bed, Sam?"

The way he said my name. It did something to me.

I felt the heat between my legs and down in my stomach. I held his gaze for a beat, let the tension stretch just long enough to feel it settle in my chest.

"I'm flattered," I said, soft but playful. "But I don't sleep with my passengers."

"Good thing I'm not one anymore."

"I'm not cleared for technicalities." He smiled again, slower this time. A bit measured. Like he knew exactly what he was doing.

My phone buzzed against the bar. I glanced down.

Rose: We're heading to the tower, come sparkle with us

I smiled and looked back at Theo, still tracing the rim of his wine glass with one finger, like he wasn't in a rush to be anywhere else. "Wanna go watch the Eiffel Tower sparkle?" I asked, casually, like I wasn't fully expecting a polite no. He looked at me like he was recalibrating. "When?"

"Erm… right now?" I grinned.

He paused, then nodded. "Sure."

I blinked. "Really?"

"Yeah. Let me grab the check." He slid his card onto the bar and looked at the bartender. "Can we take a bottle to go?" She blinked, surprised, but nodded. "Sure." He turned back to me and winked at me.

"Figured you weren't done judging my wine preferences yet." I shook my head, smiling as I grabbed my coat and the dessert spoon one more time for good measure.

We met the rest of the group just outside the station. Rose spotted me first, practically bouncing in her boots.

"Yay, you came!" she waved, then narrowed her eyes at Theo beside me. "And …you brought—"

"Rose," I said with a grin, interrupting her, "Meet 1A. Or well, Theo." He gave a small wave, warm but cool. "Nice to meet you."

Rose's eyes flicked to me, amused. "You're taller outside the plane."

"So I've been told," Theo said, ever the diplomat. We didn't linger too much. We just shared a few smiles, brief introductions, and a little awkward shuffle as the rest of the crew clocked in on who he was and how closely we walked.

But no one asked about it.

We strolled toward the Tower, passing glowing streetlamps and couples wrapped in scarves and nighttime plans. The bottle of wine was tucked under Theo's arm, and when I glanced up at him, he looked… relaxed. Lighter.

Just two people, in Paris, waiting for the sparkle.

CHAPTER SIX

theo

We said goodbye under the shimmer of the Eiffel Tower.

She didn't make it something bigger than it needed to be. Neither did I.

Just a warm smile, a thank-you-for-tonight kind of look, and then I walked her back to her hotel. When we turned the corner, I realized hers was just across from mine. But I didn't say anything. She didn't need to know.

She slipped inside with a wave and a, "Good night, 1A."

And that was the end of it.

I turned toward my own hotel, my hands in my coat pockets. I pulled out my phone and the napkin the bartender had given me earlier.

You still up?

I typed, stared at it, then deleted it. Almost

I don't know why I did that. She was a good-looking woman, she had a great sense of humor, and she wanted me. Well, she wanted both of us, but I know that if I showed up alone, it wasn't going to be a problem.

Who am I kidding?

I know why I didn't text her.

When I finally got to my room, I took a quick shower.

It was meant to be functional, just enough to rinse off the city and the night. But it didn't work the way I wanted. Because while the water hit my back and steam fogged the glass, she hit me harder.

The way she laughed, the way she leaned into her wine glass when she asked questions, as if she already knew the answers. Her ocean blue eyes were sharp and soft all at once. That damn uniform didn't do her body justice at all.

Do you want me to invite you to my bed, Sam? I'm flattered, but I don't sleep with my passengers.

Fuck. I was getting hard, just remembering her. I changed the water to cold, even though that barely helped.

I don't want to think about her like that.

I don't know why, but she doesn't seem like the

type of woman you sleep with and forget about. For a one night stand, I could just text the bartender, have some fun, and go to bed.

I got out of the shower, threw on joggers, checked a few emails, and told myself to be productive. The Hayes board wanted updates on the transition timeline. Max had sent over a polite, "When you're ready, I'd like to introduce you to a few key folks in Paris. No rush."

No rush. Right.

I tossed the phone on the nightstand, stared at the ceiling for a while, and finally let sleep win.

It was barely 6 a.m., and I was wide awake.

I rarely slept past six anyway, and this bed, while wrapped in overpriced sheets and comfy pillows, wasn't mine.

I laced up my sneakers and headed downstairs to the gym. No music. Just the hum of treadmills, the clink of weights, and my own thoughts looping on a track of their own. I picked up my pace and ran faster than usual.

I needed this.

By the time I got back to the room, I was still dripping in sweat, but my mind was clearer.

When I stepped out of the shower, my phone was

lighting up with emails and missed alerts. Mostly junk, one flagged as High Priority, from Harper. I pressed call instead of replying. "Good morning, Theodore." She picked up after the first ring.

"Good morning, what's going on?"

"Wanted to run through your day," I sat on the edge of the bed, rubbing a towel through my hair. "Okay, hit me."

"You've got lunch at Maison with Max Hayes and one of the senior VPs. He wants it to be casual, a small table, outdoor seating, no pitch deck."

"No pitch deck, yeah, right." I echoed.

Harper laughed softly. "He's easing you in. This is about optics. Getting the 'new guy' visible without being threatening."

"Great."

"You also got your contract approved. I'm officially back on your payroll as of today." A small grin tugged at my mouth. "Would've walked away if they said no."

"I know, and they knew it too," she replied.

Harper had been with me since year two of my previous company. She can manage three calendars, negotiate with half of my board, and tell when I haven't slept, all in a single call. "Anything else?"

She paused. "Just that Paris restaurants late at night looked good on your schedule," I smirked. "Are you spying on my location?"

"I'm managing your life. It's part of the job

description." We hung up after a few more logistics were discussed.

I threw on a tee and dark jeans, grabbed my blazer just in case the weather got colder later on.

I decided to skip the hotel breakfast. I need air and distractions before my lunch meeting.

But while I crave all of that, my mind wandered on the possibility of running into her again. I haven't even left the lobby yet, and I was already trying to lurk into the hotel across the street.

I found a café tucked just off Rue des Archives, the sun catching in the windows, the scent of espresso already cutting through the morning air.

I liked places like this, places with chipped mugs and waiters who didn't try too hard. I had just placed my order, black coffee, a pain au chocolat, and a bottle of sparkling water, when a familiar voice cut through the hum.

"Do I need to file a restraining order?" I turned with a smile already on my face.

She was in jeans and a cropped sweater, her hair up in a loose bun, sunglasses pushed up on her head. Rose was beside her, carrying enough energy for both of them.

She grinned as she stepped closer. "Twice in twelve hours, 1A?" she teased.

"I was here first," I said, holding up my hands. "I've got receipts." Rose leaned in, peering at my table. "We'll try not to ruin your brooding breakfast."

"You're welcome to join," I said, gesturing to the empty chairs.

Rose lit up. "I'll grab us some coffee." Sam glanced at her, then sat across from me without hesitation. She crossed one leg over the other and stared at me. "Big plans for the day?"

"Lunch meeting with my new bosses," I said, "After that, the day's all mine. And you two?" Something in her face shifted. I couldn't tell what it was, or why. But I did notice.

"Rose and I are doing some light shopping. Maybe hit the museum later. It's a lazy day." Her voice was lighter than her expression. But I didn't push. Rose returned just in time. Two coffees balanced precariously in her hands. "Caffeine delivery," she said, sliding one toward Sam.

"Actually, we should probably head out and enjoy the museum before it gets too crowded." Sam stood and turned to me, the playful glint from earlier softening into something else, something I'm not sure I understood yet.

Before she could walk away, I asked, "Will I see you again?"

She paused, then looked over her shoulder.

"I don't know, but I hope so." She said with a smile, and then she was gone.

Maison was in a quiet corner near the Seine, the kind of place where old money met modern plates. White tablecloths, polished silver, staff who never hovered but always appeared exactly when needed.

Max Hayes' type of place. He was already seated when I arrived, in a gray suit, no tie, and a drink in hand. His expression said Paris vacation, but his eyes said quarterly earnings. "Jones," he said, standing up and offering a firm handshake. "Glad you made it."

"Wouldn't miss it."

"Have a seat. Louis is running a few minutes behind. Typical." I slid into the chair across from him, adjusting my blazer as a waiter poured still water into glasses that probably cost more than my watch. "Paris treating you well?" Max asked, gesturing for me to look at the menu. "It's been good," I said. "Got some rest, caught up on emails. It almost feels like a real vacation." He laughed lightly.

"You haven't been CEO long enough to forget what rest feels like. That'll change."

"Looking forward to it." I joke as he leaned back.

This lunch is unofficial, but I want you to meet Louis Dubois. He is our main point of contact here in

France. He's old-school and worked under my father, so he's seen more mergers and restructurings than I can count. He will manage our accounts across Europe, but obviously following directly what happens at Hayes HQ back in NYC. He is not a bad guy to have in your corner."

"Understood."

"Also," he said, taking a slow sip of his drink, "we'll need you back in New York early next week. I've scheduled a formal announcement for the press, internal teams, and the board. You'll be officially introduced as CEO. Nothing major, just a few hundred people and a dozen reporters."

"Nothing I haven't done before," I said calmly, though my mind was already sketching logistics. Flights. Prep. Talking points. "Harper's your assistant, right?"

"Yes, sir. She is."

"Good. We'll get her squared away." Louis arrived just then, all warmth and crisp cologne, shaking my hand with a grip that tested something unspoken.

"Bienvenue à bord," he said, smiling. "Welcome aboard."

"Merci," I replied, matching his ease. We got down to business over duck confit and truffle risotto. They talked numbers, subsidiaries, brand reputation in Europe versus North America, our supply chain partners in Hong Kong, and upcoming ESG commitments. I kept pace easily. I'd run three companies by thirty-five. This wasn't new.

But the stakes felt different. This wasn't mine, not entirely. Not yet. Max leaned in after the waiter cleared our plates. "We'll give you a few weeks in transition, then it's go-time. I want this to be seamless."

"It will be." Louis nodded. "Hayes International is ready for new blood. Just don't bleed us dry, hm?" I smiled.

"Only if you deserve it." They laughed.

Deals like this were always made in places like Maison, under the glow of gold chandeliers, with the clink of wine glasses to soften the blow of what was really being said. You're in, but you're being watched. You're trusted, but not yet proven. You're wearing the title, but the crown's still warming.

By the end of lunch, we'd agreed on a working timeline, press talking points, and a follow-up dinner with the European directors two weeks out.

When I left, I didn't feel overwhelmed, but not entirely comfortable.

CHAPTER SEVEN

Sam

"YOU'RE BEING WEIRD," Rose said as we crossed Pont Royal, the sun glinting off the Seine like it was trying to blind us.

"No, I'm not," I replied too quickly.

"Um, yes, you are," she said, not even looking at me. "Your face is doing that weird thing. The thing where you look like you've seen a ghost and you're jumpy, and I don't know…"

I sighed, "He's having lunch with my dad. Today. Like… right now."

"Oh shit, so that means your dad is here, in Paris, and you're here." She blinked hard, like she was doing a math problem in her head or something. I know she does this when she's processing, but it's creepy.

"Exactly."

She let out a low whistle and started walking again. "You don't do boring. I'll give you that."

"I don't do family dynasties either," I muttered.

We turned onto the museum steps, the grand stone façade of the Musée d'Orsay towering above us. The tourists clustered near the entrance, and somewhere inside were the quiet hallways I'd been looking forward to, my kind of sanctuary. Stillness, beauty, and rooms full of people who didn't know or care who Samantha Hayes used to be.

We made it through security and headed toward the Impressionists wing, dodging slow walkers and kids on school tours. "I just hate that everything is always tied back to Hayes," I said as we climbed the stairs. "Even when I've built my own life, my own career, my own world… it circles back. Like I can't outrun it."

"You're not running," Rose said gently. "You're flying, remember?" I cracked a smile despite myself.

We walked in silence for a moment, letting the colors and strokes of Monet and Degas pull us into their stillness. Then Rose leaned in. "So… do you think you're going to see him again?"

I shrugged. "He asked."

"And…what did you say?"

"I didn't say yes. I didn't say no." Rose let out a low hum.

"Well. That's progress." I glanced at her, "What about you? You and the pilot? I didn't notice if you came last night." Now it was her turn to blush.

"Oh my God," I gasped. "You *came*…"

"Samantha!"

She yelled at me, and I just laughed, looking at

her so she could continue spilling the tea. "We got drunk last night, and we spent the night together at his hotel room," she said, suddenly fascinated by a Renoir. "But he is a jerk, and while he fucked me amazingly good, whatever happened is not happening again."

"Rose, you are allowed to have fun."

"Yes, I know, but not with Captain Flirt. He is an asshole, and he is like twenty years older than me. It was a mistake."

"A mistake, twenty years older that fucked you amazingly good. Got it," I cackled, loudly enough that everyone looked at me.

"Oops," I whispered.

"Art makes her emotional. I'm so sorry," she said loudly, making an excuse for me. We were standing in the museum gift shop, Rose flipping through a stack of postcards with vintage aviation prints, when my phone buzzed.

Naomi Hayes: We need to talk.

Call when you can.

My stomach dropped.

Naomi never texted first. Hell, Naomi barely texted at all unless there was a birthday, a funeral, or a scheduling conflict at the Christmas table. I quickly typed back.

Me: I'll call soon.

Naomi Hayes: What time zone are you even in?

Me: I'm just a few hours ahead of you.

She didn't reply.

By the time we stepped out of the museum and into the chill afternoon air, the weight of her message had settled deep in my chest. Rose flagged down a passing vendor for a Nutella crepe, and I walked a few feet away, phone pressed to my ear.

She picked up on the first ring. "Hey, Samantha." Her voice was tight, clipped. "Thanks for calling."

"Hi. You're scaring me."

"Sorry, I didn't mean to," she said, then paused. "It's just that—, I talked to Susan this morning." The name alone made me roll my eyes. "And?"

"And apparently, Dad's sick." The words landed like a drop of ink in a glass of water. Sinking, spreading, staining everything around it. "Sick? Sick how?" What the hell is happening?

"They're not saying everything yet, but… Susan told me it's something with his liver." Her voice dropped. "He's stepping down because he has to, not because he wants to. The board's already preparing to announce the transition, but they're keeping the health issues private."

I leaned against a stone wall near the museum gates, watching tourists take selfies and pretending my stomach wasn't suddenly in knots. "Why would Susan tell you this if he doesn't want anyone to know it?"

"I don't know Samathan, maybe because I actually have a relationship with them."

"Of course you do." Naomi sighed.

"Look, I know you and Dad have… whatever it is you have going on. But I figured you should know before you see it in the press." I didn't respond right away. Max Hayes had always been more of a boss than a father. He gave me my last name and a spreadsheet full of expectations. The man was made of ambition and obligation. Love was never part of the contract. Yes, I was the 'favorite daughter' up until they realized I didn't care about anything Hayes-related.

"Thanks for telling me," I said finally.

"I didn't know if you would care, but you're still his daughter, Sam."

"Technically." I rolled my eyes.

"You still matter to him." We stayed on the line for a few more seconds. The kind of silence that comes from two people related by blood and not much else.

"I have to go," I said. "Thanks for the call."

"Of course. Take care," Naomi said softly.

I hung up just as Rose came over, with a warm crepe in hand. Her eyes were curious, but cautious. I didn't say anything. I didn't have to. She handed me the first bite without asking, and we kept walking.

We cut across a quiet street lined with pâtisseries and designer storefronts, the crisp afternoon air pressing against our coats as we walked toward

Galeries Lafayette. Rose was unusually quiet, letting me process in the lull between bites of crepe and cobblestones.

Finally, I said, "Naomi just told me my Dad's sick." She stopped mid-step. "What?" I nodded, barely looking up. "Something with his liver, apparently. That's why he's stepping down." Her expression softened immediately, the playful glint from earlier gone. "Damn."

"Yeah." We kept walking, the sound of traffic and distant church bells threading through the quiet. Paris was moving on, like nothing had shifted in my orbit. "I know he's here," I added after a beat. "Somewhere. Having lunch. In a restaurant where the bill will probably be higher than our rent."

Rose glanced over. "Do you want to see him?" I didn't answer right away. We passed a florist, the scent of fresh lavender and eucalyptus wafting out in waves. "I don't know. I don't know if I should call. Or wait until I'm back in New York. Or... not do anything at all."

Rose tilted her head. "Okay. So, what's the real question?"

I frowned. "What do you mean?"

"You're not asking if you should call him," she said gently. "You're asking if calling him makes you care." My chest tightened. Because she was right. I didn't want to care. I'd built an entire life to prove I didn't. I'd taken a job that flew me thousands of miles away from boardrooms and quarterly earnings and all things Hayes.

But now my father, distant, driven, and difficult, was *here*. In the same city. Possibly dying, and I didn't know what to do with that. "I just don't want to regret not doing it," I murmured. "But I also don't want to play the daughter card only when it matters, like now that he's sick."

Rose linked her arm through mine. "Then don't do it for him. Do it for you. Call him, or don't. But whatever you decide, just make sure it's by choice, not out of obligation."

We reached the edge of the shopping plaza, glass walls gleaming in the late afternoon light. Tourists milled around the entrance, their bags swinging with the promise of retail therapy and distraction.

"I could really use a new pair of sunglasses," I said, my voice lighter but still far off. "And maybe a nice coat,"

"For when you accidentally bump into your father's new CEO," Rose said, and I laughed, the tension loosening just a little.

"Let's go spend money we don't have," I said.

"Now that's the Sam I know. Although you do have it, you just don't use it." I rolled my eyes at her.

CHAPTER EIGHT

theo

THE CLINK of ice in lowball glasses and the hum of jazz from a Bluetooth speaker filled the hotel bar with a lazy kind of charm.

I'd claimed a seat at the bar, nursing a whiskey, half-watching a French rugby match I didn't quite understand. The commentary was way too fast for me to get a hold of any French I actually know.

It was impossible to keep up with.

After my corporate lunch, I needed the quiet. I needed to unwind and just get a drink, and probably a late-night snack. But then I saw her *again*. She was across the room with her friend Rose, one guy that seems like the kind of person who laughed too loudly and probably flirted with flight attendants for sport, and an older man I recognized from the other night.

She looked relaxed, animated, radiant in the dim light. For a second, I let myself watch her.

Just a second too long. There's nothing weird about it.

I think.

That was until she saw me. She crossed the room with that effortless confidence that could silence a crowd. "1A, twice in one day," she said, voice laced with amusement. "Hey, Sam."

"We're having more fun than you are," she teased, tilting her chin toward her table. "Come join us." I raised a brow.

"Are you allowed to hang out with your passengers? Or are we still talking around technicalities?"

"We're not, and you're not my passenger anymore. Besides, you're being invited." I followed her back, more curious than I wanted to admit. Rose greeted me with a knowing smile, and Sam introduced both pilots, Alexander and Ryan. She looked at me with a spark in her eyes that told me she already knew I was watching her.

We drank, talked, and laughed. The game faded into the background noise. "What are they even saying?" Ryan asked, squinting at the screen. Sam leaned in with a grin. "They just said the guy with the ball looks like a goat wearing cleats." I blinked. "Seriously?"

She laughed. "No. But you believed me for a second, and that's concerning."

"Dangerous combination," I said, smirking. "Looks and lies." Rose raised her glass. "To looks and lies." Alexander chimed in, "To wine and whatever this sport is, Ryan doesn't seem to get."

"To not working for twelve hours, until next week," Sam added. Our glasses clinked. It was easy. Too easy. The kind of effortlessness that makes you forget time.

Every brush of her hand against mine felt intentional, every glance charged. The air between us carried its own current, low and steady like the jazz in the background.

Eventually, the night slowed down. The bartender yawned, Alexander stood to settle their tab, and Rose started gathering her things. "We should call it," she said, slipping on her coat. I started to stand up too. "I'm actually staying here." Sam arched a brow. "Oh, so you are fancy like that."

I shrugged. "I like good room service and short elevator rides." Then, I leaned in, whispering in her ear, "Can I repeat yesterday's invitation?"

Her smile curved slowly. "If it includes a bottle of wine, I'll think about it." I turned to the bartender. "Bottle of your best red, two glasses. Room 1103."

As he nodded, I saw how Rose smirked and whispered something to her that sounded close to 'have fun'. She smiled at me and then walked away with the guys.

Sam picked up her things and then followed me to the elevator. Neither of us said a single word on the entire ride up.

Inside the suite, I flicked on the lamp. Warm light

spread across the room. And the Paris view stretched out in gold beyond the windows. The wine was already there. I poured two glasses and handed her one. She didn't sit. She just watched me, studying, maybe still deciding. "Did you change your rule about not sleeping with passengers," I asked, "or why did you accept my invitation tonight?"

She sipped on the wine, eyes steady on mine. "Well, I accepted the invitation to your room tonight," she said, "but sleeping with you? I'm still debating on that one." I laughed. "Okay, that's fair."

"You said you're not my passenger anymore, which is technically true," she added. "Also, the wine might help."

"Always happy to support informed decision-making." She finally sat on the edge of the chaise lounge, legs crossing in that effortless way she had. "So," she teased. "Are you always this good at luring women to fancy hotel rooms with vintage Bordeaux and Eiffel Tower views?"

"Only on Thursdays." She laughed, soft, more genuine this time. "You give off serious 'experienced' vibes."

"Experienced, huh?" I leaned back in my chair.

"Well, let's be honest here. You're twelve years older than me," she said with a shrug. "I just assume you've… studied abroad, so to speak."

I chuckled. "Well, if you put it that way. Yeah. I have studied abroad, practiced, and even mentored."

"Oh, mentored," she echoed, smirking. "That sounds very… educational."

"I believe in lifelong learning." Her grin widened. "Any kinks I should know about before we end up making poor life choices?" She is teasing and testing me.

"Define poor choices."

"I mean questionable. Fun? Memorable? Something that requires a safe word, perhaps?" Now we're talking.

"I'm not much for theatrics," I said, sipping my wine. "I like enthusiasm, mutual curiosity. The occasional lack of impulse control." She looked at me for a long moment while she took a sip of her wine. "You know what's funny?"

"What?" What could she possibly find funny about this conversation? "You're very composed. You seem very controlled, and you give businessman vibes. But underneath…" She tilted her head like she was examining me. "I think you like being undone."

I met her gaze. "And you think you can undo me?" Her grin was quick, sharp. "I don't know yet, but you're the one who invited me here."

"Touché."

We fell into silence. She is still walking around. Like, she is still thinking about what this might entail. "I haven't decided what could happen tonight, *yet*," she said softly, setting her glass down. "But so far? So far, I'm glad I came up."

"Wanna check the balcony?"

She nodded. “Sure. Impress me, 1A.” We stepped outside. Paris glowed beneath us. The Eiffel Tower glimmered like it had been lit just for her. The air was cool enough to raise goosebumps. She didn’t seem to notice.

I refilled her glass and handed it to her, “What do you like in bed?”

She laughed. “This escalated quickly.”

“I’m just asking the important questions,” I said. “You look like a woman of taste. I like being prepared.”

“Prepared for what? A Yelp review?”

“I take pride in my five stars.” Her smile softened into something more adventurous. “I like confidence. Attention to detail. A little dominance if it’s earned. And not too much talking unless it’s worth hearing.”

“So dirty talk is allowed?”

“If it’s dirty, yes, if it’s nonsense, nope.” She was really laughing now, which was refreshing to see.

“Got it. Nothing like ‘yeah baby.’”

She mock-cringed. “Immediate blacklist.” I grinned. “Good to know.”

She tilted her head. “What about you?”

“In bed?”

“No, in chess,” she said dryly.

I stepped closer. “I like control, I like surrender. I like it when someone knows exactly what they want and asks for it.”

“That sounds dangerously close to a fantasy.”

“Only if you’re the one fulfilling it.” Her breath

hitched, barely, but I caught it. I set my glass down. She did the same.

I reached for her, my hand sliding around her waist, the other threading through her hair, tilting her head back just enough.

She inhaled with her eyes locked on mine.

I kissed her.

She moved against me, fingers gripping my shirt, pulling me closer. Her gasp against my lips sent heat straight through me. I bit softly on her lower lip, then kissed her harder.

It wasn't rushed. But it wasn't gentle either.

CHAPTER NINE

Sam

WE BROKE THE KISS, breath uneven, his hands still framing my waist like he hadn't quite decided to let go.

I hadn't either.

"So about your invitation," I whispered, pulse drumming in my ears. "Yes."

He let out a soft laugh, the kind that vibrated down my spine. It was dangerous, the way he smiled, like he knew exactly what he was doing and exactly how I liked it.

We grabbed our wine glasses again, mine now barely half full, and walked back inside. The room was warm compared to the balcony's chill, but I still felt flushed. Whether it was the wine, the kiss, or the way his eyes tracked me like I was the only thing in the room, I couldn't be sure.

I took a seat on the edge of the bed while he

adjusted the lights, dimming them to a soft amber glow.

"I should warn you," I said, swirling my wine. "I don't do this with everybody. I like to have fun, but I'm careful with whom I do it with."

He joined me, not too close but not far either. "I'm the same way." I gave him a look.

"What?" he said, mock offense in his voice. "I'm serious. I'm not the reckless type."

"No, you're the contractually bound, wine-seducing, corner-office type," I teased.

He smirked. "And you're the rule-breaking, cheeky flight attendant with a mysterious past type." That made me laugh, because he wasn't wrong. And he didn't even know how right he was. There it was again, the secret humming beneath my skin. The weight of my last name, the invisible tether pulling me toward a life I'd spent years avoiding. He didn't know. Not yet, and I wasn't planning on telling him. Not tonight, at least. Maybe not ever. What use could that do?

But it sat there, quietly between us, like a loaded suitcase I hadn't unpacked.

He looked at me, then, *really* looked. No flirting, no smirking. Just that stillness, that quiet steadiness that made me feel like he was trying to read the fine print on my soul. "You good?" he asked.

I nodded. "I'm great," And in that moment, with Paris glittering behind us and his wine-dark gaze holding mine, I almost believed it.

His hand brushed my knee first, fingertips slow and testing, then slid higher, under the hem of my skirt, dragging heat with it. I didn't stop him.

He kissed me again, deeper this time, less teasing, more need. My glass hit the nightstand with a soft clink. His glass was forgotten somewhere near the window. He pulled me into his lap like it was muscle memory for him, like I'd been there before. My legs were on each side of him. I could feel just how much he wanted me, and God, it made something curl low and hot in my stomach.

He kissed me like he negotiated deals. Intentional, dominant, and *very* precise. His hands gripped my waist, grounded and greedy, like he couldn't decide if he wanted to memorize me or ruin me.

"You're bad news, Sam," he murmured against my skin as he kissed down my throat.

"Thanks," I whispered, dragging my fingers through his hair, tugging just enough to make him growl a little.

Clothes came off in a slow blur, pulled, tugged, peeled away. His hands were everywhere: my thighs, my back, my ass. My body reacted before my mind caught up, arching into him, needing more, needing it now. "You're so soft, you—" he muttered, mouth tracing the line of my collarbone. I cut him off with another kiss, biting his bottom lip, hard enough to make him gasp.

"Oh, she bites," he said, voice dark and amused.

"You are a big boy, you can take it," I shot back.

He flipped us, me flat on the bed, his body covering mine, hips pressing down just enough to tease, to make my breath hitch. His mouth found my chest, he teased my nipples with his mouth, with his tongue, his teeth, my stomach, all while his hands pinned my wrists above my head.

I bucked under him, but he held me steady, his control only making me want to undo it more. I moaned and breathed heavily. "I like this view," he said, breathless.

"Are you going to do something with it or just look at it?" And oh, he did.

His fingers traced along the edge of my underwear, slow and purposeful, a light touch that sent heat surging between my thighs. He didn't rush. He just watched me, his lips parted slightly, like he was savoring the way I squirmed under him.

Then, with one finger, he hooked and slid my panties to the side, exposing me to the cool air and his hungry eyes.

"You're so wet already," he murmured, voice thick, rough, like gravel laced with silk. I arched my hips just slightly, chasing his touch. "Do you want a taste?"

That made something flicker in his eyes. They turned dark, wild, and barely restrained. He didn't answer with words. Instead, he kissed down my stomach, his hands anchoring my hips as he moved lower. When he reached the crease of my thigh, he paused.

Eyes locking with mine one last time as if giving me the chance to change my mind. I didn't.

He dipped his head and licked me. My breath hitched. Then he did it again, and again, and again, with the kind of patience that made me ache. His tongue explored every inch of me, tasting me like he'd been starving. When I gasped his name, one of his hands slid under my thigh, lifting it over his shoulder, giving him better access, deeper angles.

He moaned into me, *moaned*, like the taste of me did something to him.

And it did something to me, too.

My hands fisted the sheets. My body bucked. And I stopped caring about how loud I was, how shameless it was, how much I wanted more. Because this man, this stranger in 1A, was devouring me like it was the first meal he'd had in weeks. To be honest, I was starving too.

He kissed his way back up my body, lips gliding across my stomach, the curve of my breast, my collarbone, until we were face to face again, both of us flushed and breathless. "I should grab a condom," he whispered, starting to rise.

I reached for him, fingers sliding around his wrist. "I have an IUD," I murmured, voice soft but certain. "And I'm clean. If you don't mind, I don't—"

His eyes searched mine, then he nodded. "I'm clean too. I can show you my latest tests if you want. I have them in my email." I smiled, pulling him back down toward me. "Of course, you have your STD test results in your email." That made him laugh, well, we both did. But he didn't question me further. He just leaned in and kissed me.

His body pressed against mine, hot and heavy and perfect. I could feel him, hard, thick, teasing against my thigh, and God, I wanted him. All of him.

I slid my hand down between us, wrapping around him. Oh my god. He was hard and really *big*.

He let out a sharp breath, his jaw tightening as my hand moved. "Sam, what are you—"

"I want to taste you," I whispered, sitting up, pushing him gently back against the bed. "To touch you… to feel all of you."

His hands gripped the sheets when I took him in my mouth, slow at first, teasing him, watching how he unraveled. The way his hips flexed. The way his head fell back. The way he said my name felt like a prayer.

When I looked up at him, his eyes were gone.

"Come here," he demanded. I moved, straddling him, and his hands gripped my hips. "No more teasing," I said, guiding him to me. He pushed inside, slowly, stretching me, filling me, claiming me, and I gasped. My nails were digging into his shoulders. He hissed but didn't stop. He just smiled at me.

He was big, thick, and stretching me in a way that bordered on pain but settled deliciously into pleasure.

"Fuck," he breathed. "You feel so fucking good, Sam…"

I moaned, loud and unashamed, my thighs wrapping around him tighter as he moved into me. The sound of skin on skin echoed off the suite walls, a rhythm that was all that was needed, with no hesitation. His pace was ruthless, fucking me like he had something to prove.

"You can take me, sweetheart?" he growled into my neck, his breath hot against my skin. "I can," I moaned, head falling back, body trembling. "And I want more."

He pulled out suddenly, and I whimpered at the loss, my body clenching around nothing, already aching to have him again."Shh," he said, kissing my thigh. "I'm not done with you."

He dropped to his knees at the edge of the bed, dragged me down with a firm grip on my hips, and buried his face between my legs. "Oh fuck—" I cried out, hands tangling in his hair as he licked, sucked, and devoured me. He held my thighs apart with both hands, his tongue moving in tight, devastating circles that had my entire body quaking.

I was already on the edge when he slipped two fingers inside me, curling them, and that was it, my release tore through me. It was wild and had me shaking. His name was leaving my mouth like a plea. A plea for more, honestly. When he finally looked up at me, his mouth was slick, his eyes dark and burning with heat. He wiped his mouth with the back of his hand and smiled.

"You're addictive," he murmured. "I don't think I want to be done with you yet."

That's when I knew I was in trouble.

I was still catching my breath when I pushed up onto my elbows and looked at him, his body sprawled across the sheets, skin flushed, chest rising and falling in heavy pulls. He looked wrecked and perfect. I straddled him in one slow motion, fingers tracing a line down his chest. His hands instinctively found my thighs. "Round two already?"

"Unless you're tapping out," I smirked, leaning down to press my mouth to his jaw, dragging my lips to his ear. "I figured a man like you wouldn't need recovery time." He groaned. "Not with you." I reached between us, lined him up, and sank down onto him in one slow slide.

His head dropped back with a hiss. "Fuck, Sam —" I didn't move, not yet. Just watched him squirm, felt him twitch inside me, let the tension coil tighter between us. I liked this power. I liked the way he looked up at me like I was the only thing in the world that mattered. Then he grinned. "Do I need a safe word now?" I laughed, rolling my hips just once, deep and slow. "You think you're in danger?"

"I think I'm about to be ruined," he breathed.

"Good," I said, my voice dropping. "Then hold on."

I started riding him, slow at first, savoring the stretch, the drag, the way he filled me so perfectly. My hands braced against his chest, nails dragging across his skin as I picked up the pace. His hands gripped my hips tight, guiding, encouraging me, until the rhythm turned punishing. He thrust up to meet me, over and over, the bed creaking beneath us, our moans tangled together like music.

My name was a curse on his lips, and his was a prayer on mine.

The friction, the heat, the control, it was overwhelming in the best possible way. And when I came again, it was with a cry, shaking on top of him, every nerve ending lit up. I was still pulsing around him when he gripped my hips, slowing my movement just slightly, his eyes locked on mine.

"Sam—" he panted, voice rough, desperate. "Wait. I'm about to come, and I need to know if I can do it inside you?"

I nodded, breathless. "Yes. I want you to." That was all he needed. He groaned, deep, and thrust up into me one last time, holding me down as he spilled inside, his body tensing beneath mine, chest rising hard against mine like a wave crashing.

We stayed like that, tangled, breathless, pulsing with an afterglow. My head dropped to his shoulder, our skin slick and hearts pounding in sync. "Okay," he whispered after a beat, lips brushing my temple. "If that's what happens when you're in charge… I surrender."

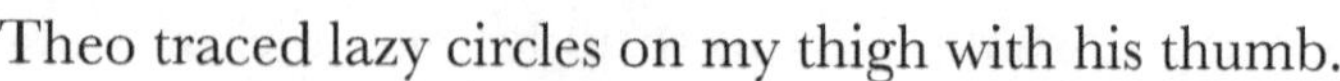

Theo traced lazy circles on my thigh with his thumb.

"So… what's the plan for your last few hours in Paris?" I let out a breath. "Rose and I were thinking of heading to Montmartre later, maybe one more round of pastries and overpriced souvenirs."

"Sounds… fun," he said, eyes soft. "What about you?" I said, adjusting myself enough to grab our wine glasses from the nightstand.

"I've got a few meetings on my calendar I'm thinking of ignoring."

I raised a brow. "Very professional of you." He chuckled. "I'm already ahead of schedule. I can afford a few stolen hours." I took a sip of wine, watching him over the rim of my glass. "Stolen hours, huh?" He didn't answer, just leaned over and kissed me, slow and deep, like he was imprinting the taste of me on his memory.

After a few minutes, I stretched and slid off the bed. "I'm going to take a quick shower." He sat up, his gaze tracking me as I walked toward the bathroom.

"Mind if I join?" I paused at the doorway, turned slightly, and gave him a small, teasing smile. "Only if you promise me shower sex."

The steam filled the shower quickly. The second I stepped under the water, he was behind me, hands on my hips, lips at my shoulder, he was already hard again. "You're driving me insane," he muttered against my skin.

"Good," I whispered, pressing back into him.

He didn't waste time. He spun me around, lifted

me easily against the wall, and took me again with a force that made the water pressure irrelevant. This time, there was no teasing. No gentle build. Just raw, hungry need.

He fucked me like he owned me.

The slap of wet skin, the steam fogging the glass, the way his hands gripped my ass as I wrapped my legs around him and bit down on his shoulder to muffle my moans. It was chaos, and I loved every second of it.

When I came, it was explosive. His name on my lips. My nails are dragging down his back. He followed right after, groaning into my neck, pressing deep one last time. We stayed like that for a moment, under the spray, our bodies still pressed together, hearts hammering. Eventually, I stepped out, wrapped myself in a towel, and began to gather my things.

"I'm not staying by the way," I said gently, slipping back into my clothes. "I texted Rose that I'd come back."

Theo sat on the edge of the bed, towel around his waist, watching me like I was slipping through his fingers. "You could text her again. Say you got caught up in something… important."

I laughed softly, zipping up my dress. "Hmm, tempting."

He stood and came to me, hands resting lightly on my waist. "Stay. Please. Just… stay."

His voice was cocky and demanding, but in a soft way that made me ache, and wet at the same time. I looked up at him, eyes searching his. “Fine. I’ll stay, on two conditions.”

“Give them to me,” He grinned.

“You make me come again, and you don’t snore.” That made him laugh. “The first one, I promise, the second, I’ll risk it.”

I took off my dress and crawled back into bed with him, tangled up once more, this time under the covers, his arm slung over my waist, our breathing syncing as sleep found us.

CHAPTER TEN

theo

WE CLEARLY FORGOT to close the curtains last night.

Because the morning sunshine slipped right through the windows.

I shifted in bed, and I could feel her warmth near me. She was lying on her side, her hair a mess against my pillow, one leg tossed over the sheet like she owned the bed. The curve of her back, the slow rise and fall of her breath, it was unfair how beautiful she looked doing absolutely nothing.

"Are you staring at me?" she murmured without opening her eyes. I smiled. "Maybe." She stretched like a cat. Her arms over her head, her legs stretching to opposite sides. "I slept like a baby. It was a really good sleep."

"It was the best night of sleep I've had in months. So, thank you." I admitted. She rolled toward me, resting her chin on my chest. "That's cute, 1A. But, I gotta run if I want a full Parisian breakfast before I'm back in the air tonight." I brushed her hair back from her face.

"What time are you flying?"

"Late. It's an overnight flight again. But check-in is in a few hours, and I have to meet Rose before she shops her entire suitcase weight limit." I laughed. "Sounds serious."

"You've never seen her around a European Zara. It is serious." She yawned and pushed herself up, grabbing her clothes and slipping them on with ease that made it somehow sexier. I leaned back against the headboard, watching her move. "Are you going to ghost me now? Because I don't have any information on you, but you can easily find all of mine."

She looked over her shoulder, raising an eyebrow. "Well, that's true. But, you're not exactly ghostable, 1A."

I tilted my head. "So, what happens now?"

Sam smiled faintly as she pulled on her coat. "Now? I find coffee, you go become a CEO. And if fate wants us to bump into each other again, then who are we to argue?" That made me smile a little. She walked to the door, then paused. "Thanks for the wine, the invite, and the orgasms."

"It was *my* pleasure." She smirked, and I watched the door click shut behind her, the room suddenly so quiet in her absence.

By the time I was on my second espresso in the hotel lounge, Harper called. "Morning," she said, voice crisp as ever. "I figured you'd be up and working already."

"I never really stopped working," I replied, staring out at the street below. "Just changed the location."

"I got confirmation in the boardroom for the Monday meeting in New York. 10:00 a.m. Max Hayes will be there to officially introduce you as CEO. Full company rollout starts the following week."

I nodded, even though she couldn't see me. "Let's lock it in. Push the strategy meeting with Ops to Tuesday. I want a buffer after the board intro."

"Got it. Also, heads up, there's a press lunch scheduled in two weeks. I'll send over the potential outlets. Do you want to do a one-on-one sit-down with Forbes or keep it group style?"

"Group," I said without hesitation. "Keep it clean. I don't want any personal angles." She hesitated. "And if they ask?"

"They'll ask," I muttered, glancing at my reflection in the window. "Just make sure the story stays on Hayes and the future of tech."

"Copy that." We went through the rest of the calendar, stakeholder intros, internal department reviews, and onboarding meetings. I confirmed, declined, and rescheduled. It felt mechanical, clean. Safe. And yet, every time there was a pause, my mind drifted. To the woman with sunlight in her hair and the kind of laugh that made my chest tighten. To last night, and to the mess she left in my bed, and apparently on my mind too.

Harper's voice brought me back. "Your car to the airport is set for noon. The flight is at 2:15. I sent the boarding pass to your email."

"Perfect."

"And Theo?" she added.

"Congratulations. You're officially *the guy*." I gave a dry laugh. "We'll see if that's a good thing." After we hung up, I sat for a moment longer. Watching the street. Letting the city live around me.

Then I opened my phone and scrolled to my camera roll. There, faintly blurry, completely candid, was a picture I'd taken last night of her laughing across the table, wine glass in hand, cheeks flushed with color and life. Which, by the way, I don't recall taking.

I stared at it for a long moment. Longer than I would like to admit to myself. Anyway, I closed the photo, grabbed my bags, and headed for the airport.

At the airport, the lounge was quiet, polished, and almost empty. A soft hum of conversations, the occasional clink of glass, a wall of windows looking out onto the tarmac. I slid into a leather chair with my lunch. A grilled chicken sandwich and a Jack and Ginger, because I kind of enjoy being haunted by my choices.

One sip and I smirked.

I leaned back, the glass was cool in my hand, and let my eyes drift across the lounge. But all I could see was her, Sam. The way she smiled at me over the rim of her wine glass. The way she moved like she wasn't trying, but knew you were watching. Her body. Her laugh. The balcony. The bed. The way she sighed into my mouth like it was the only place she wanted to be.

I shook my head, trying to snap out of it.

It was a fling, I reminded myself. A fun layover. A wild, sexy chapter in a city I hadn't visited in a decade. Nothing more. Just a stunning flight attendant with a quick wit, a ridiculous body, and maybe the best sex I've ever had.

But nothing more.

My phone buzzed.

Nico: ✈️ You land yet, CEO Daddy?

I laughed into my drink and texted back.

Me: Still in lounge life mode. Flight boards in 45.

Nico: And how's our empire builder feeling?

Me: Like I traded freedom for a billion-dollar to-do list.

Nico: So… exactly like you?

Me: Shut up.

He sent a GIF of someone dramatically weeping into a suitcase full of money.

Nico: Tell Paris I said thanks for softening you up before Max Hayes chews you out.

Me: Paris was actually pretty good. Can't complain.

Nico: Uh oh. You found great croissants and great sex?

Me: Something like that.

Nico: Just don't bring a Parisian back with you unless she codes or does brand strategy.

Me: I don't think she can code, but she can pour a perfect Jack and Ginger.

Nico: Close enough.

Put her on payroll.

I shook my head, smiling as I finished the last bite

of my sandwich. The comfort of Nico's banter grounded me and reminded me of who I've been before all this Hayes nonsense.

I opened my laptop, answered a couple of emails, flagged a few reports, and reviewed tomorrow's calendar. Then the boarding call echoed through the lounge. It was time to go. I packed up, left the last sip of my drink, and headed for Gate 11.

Back to New York, back to responsibility, and back to being the man who doesn't get distracted.

But as I stepped onto the plane, I couldn't help it — I glanced toward first class.

She wasn't there.

CHAPTER ELEVEN

Sam

New York always felt different after a long trip.

It's like the city had shifted slightly in my absence. It has the same skyline, the same noise, but not quite the same version of me returning to it.

And to be honest, that's something I really like and enjoy.

After I got home, I slept for ten hours straight. No alarm, no Rose banging around in the kitchen, just me and the silence of our overpriced, over-loved Upper East Side apartment.

When I finally opened my eyes, everything felt… heavier. Not in a jetlag kind of way, also yes, but it was more like an emotional whiplash. I stared at the ceiling for a while before reaching for my phone.

'*Max Hayes*', just a name on the screen, but my thumb hesitated. Against my better judgment, I called him. He picked up after two rings. His voice sounded softer than I remembered. He sounded kinda tired.

We talked for about three minutes, enough time for him to tell me that he wanted to see me. He was planning a family dinner so he could tell us more about what's going on. Naomi, Susan, him, and of course, me.

"Okay," I said. "I'll come."

I wasn't sure why I agreed to this. Maybe it was guilt, maybe. Or maybe it was more curiosity. Or maybe, just maybe, I wanted to see if this man who shaped so much of my life without ever really knowing me at all, had finally started to shrink in the shadow he always cast.

Walking into my childhood home always made me straighten my spine and hold my head high. Maybe it was muscle memory, maybe it was childhood trauma.

What the hell do I know? I'll talk to my therapist about this later.

This wasn't a house to raise some kids and build a family. This was a house built for power. It has marble floors, white walls, and an oil painting of my father looming in the hallway like a corporate god.

Who the fuck does that in their home? Well, a narcissist.

Susan greeted me at the door like she didn't resent every decision I'd ever made. "You're late, but I'm glad you're here," she said, her lips curving into what I assumed was her version of a smile. Fuck her. "Traffic was bad," I said, brushing past her perfume cloud. It smelled like wealth and disapproval.

Naomi was already in the living room, with a glass of red in hand. Her posture was straight, and her bun was tighter than the tension in the air. I gave her a quick hug; the kind you give coworkers at awkward holiday parties.

"Glad you made it," she said, not sounding particularly glad, but not as cold as I expected. She sounded warmer, like she did over the phone. "Wouldn't miss a family gathering," I replied, my tone edged just enough to sting if you knew me well. Naomi did. She arched an eyebrow, took a deep breath, but said nothing.

"Shall we sit?" Dad's voice came from behind us, slightly raspy, slightly slower than I'm used to. He looked... older. More fragile than I remembered. Still sharp in a navy blazer and slacks, but softer if that makes sense.

We gathered around the long mahogany dining table. The food was plated. There was steak, roasted potatoes, and sautéed greens. Probably catered by someone with no idea this family hadn't eaten together in months.

The clink of silverware filled the silence until Dad cleared his throat. "I'll just get to it," he said, looking at Naomi, then at me. "I have liver cancer. It's treatable, not terminal. But it's going to take some time and energy to manage." I didn't speak. Naomi nodded once. "Stage?" she asked.

"Two," he replied. "Caught relatively early given my lifestyle." Susan reached over and placed a hand on him. Her diamond bracelet glittered. "We thank God for it," she said. "We're optimistic." I bit into my steak and chewed, as if it were the only thing keeping me from talking. "As you may know, I'm stepping back from the company," Dad continued. "Effective immediately. It's what my doctors are advising. I need to rest and focus on treatment."

I already knew that part. What I didn't know was how he'd spin it. "I've asked the board to transition Naomi into Head of Legal," he said, turning to her. "It's time." Oh, there it is. The *spin*.

"I'm ready," Naomi said without hesitation. "I've been ready." Of course, she has. "And Samantha," he added, and I knew this was coming. I could feel the weight of it pressing down like a storm front.

"There's an opportunity for you, too. We'd like to bring you on as an International Business Strategist." I almost laughed. *Strategist.*

That's what they called it when they wanted to lure the black sheep of the family back into the pen. "Because I speak four languages and have a passport with more stamps than diamonds on Susan's jewelry box? No offense," I asked, forcing a smile.

Dad sighed. "Because you understand global movement. The culture, the trends we're living in.

You've seen how people work, how they think. We could use that."

"Right," I said, leaning back in my chair. "Because nothing says *family* like roping your daughter into a corporate empire she's spent her adult life avoiding."

"You'd be paid well," Susan chimed in, as if that mattered to me. "Seven figures. You'll have travel perks, full autonomy of your work, and your own office." She talks like she still works at the company, but in truth, she's just the mistress-turned-wife now. "I already have travel perks and full autonomy."

"I think that if you really care about your father, you might think about it," she replied sharply. That one landed. I looked at Dad again. He looked tired, but hopeful. And for once, not in a manipulative way, more like in a real 'I want you there' way.

Like maybe he really meant it.

"I just want to offer you the choice," he said, softer this time. "You don't have to say yes tonight. But I hope you'll consider it." Naomi leaned forward. "You can still keep flying or doing whatever it is you do, Samantha. But this? This is our legacy. One day it won't be a choice, it'll be an obligation."

"Good to know the guilt hasn't aged a day," I said, standing.

"Samantha," Dad warned.

"I'll think about it," I replied, grabbing my coat. "I will. But please don't expect me to pretend like this isn't complicated for me." Naomi stood too, ever the collected one.

"It's family. It's always complicated." I turned to her. "Maybe for you it's a legacy, but for me, it's something I had to escape just to breathe." Susan opened her mouth, but Dad raised a hand. "Let her go. Let her think." I nodded once. "Thanks for dinner."

And with that, I walked out, into the cold air, into the night, into the city that still felt more like home than that house ever did.

I get to my apartment, but hesitate at the entrance.

I need a walk.

New York was quiet tonight. The steam rising from subway grates, the occasional honk, the rhythm of footsteps that weren't mine. I walked aimlessly, past boutiques I couldn't afford or didn't want to. Cafés where I once dreamt about becoming a writer, galleries that felt like therapy. All these little places I'd built a life outside the shadow of my last name. And yet tonight, that shadow had followed me home.

When I finally stepped back into the apartment, it was like being wrapped in a version of myself I still liked. Warm lights, the smell of Rose's overpriced candles. The distant hum of our shared playlist in the background. Rose was curled up on the couch, wearing a hoodie and holding two glasses of wine.

"You're late," she said, but her eyes were soft, curious. She already knew. "I needed a walk," I murmured, kicking off my boots with more force than necessary.

"I know. I've been following your location for the past hour or so," I laughed and flopped onto the couch beside her and accepted the wine. She waited. She always did.

"Talk to me," she said. Just that. No pressure, no judgment. Just an open door and a key already in my hand. So, I did. I told her everything. I told her about the dinner and the infamous oil painting of my father that is still hanging there like a warning. Naomi's too-easy yes, like she'd been rehearsing it since birth. The job offer. International Business Strategist, what a laugh. As if putting a pretty title on it would make it feel less like a trap.

But mostly, I told her about my father. Even though I always felt neglected by him, by my mom, by all of it, he looked softer tonight, more human, and that shook me more than the word cancer ever could.

Rose didn't interrupt me. She just nodded in all the right moments and sipped her wine while I talked. Her eyes were doing that thing they always did, wide and understanding, reflecting everything I didn't want to say out loud.

"I just…" I exhaled slowly.

"I don't want to owe them anything, Rose. Not my

time, not my mind, not even my fucking language skills. I worked so hard to be something outside of Hayes, outside of him, and now he's dangling a seven-figure role like a consolation prize."

Rose didn't speak. She just reached out and tucked a piece of hair behind my ear like she used to do when I was sick or heartbroken or halfway through a breakdown. And then, softly, "You don't owe them, Sam. But maybe, just maybe, you owe yourself the chance to do something *big*. Something that uses every part of you. And this could be that. On your terms, obviously."

I looked at her, the lump in my throat rising like a wave. "So… take the job?" She shrugged. "Try it. Take the money. Run the game. Make it yours. And if it sucks? Walk away. But don't say no just because it's them. Don't let spite make your choices."

I swallowed hard. God, I hated when she made sense. "I just don't know if I can go back to that world without losing myself."

"You won't," she said, no hesitation. "Because you've already fought too hard to become this version of you. The Sam who lives here. Who drinks green juice and flies to Tokyo for forty-eight hours and knows herself better than anyone else ever did. You're not the scared kid who left home anymore."

I blinked, trying not to cry. My throat felt tight. "And if I say yes, and I fail?"

She leaned forward and touched her glass to

mine. "Then you fail fabulously in red bottom heels and collect your severance like a queen."

I laughed. I didn't mean to, but it burst out of me. "God, I love you." She smiled, leaning back into the couch. "I know."

Two days, that's how long it took me to open the email.

Not because I forgot.

Oh no, I saw it every time I checked my inbox. Sitting right there with its overly formal subject line like a smug little ghost.

Hayes International, Official Offer to Samantha Hayes.

Very on-brand.

There was no warmth in that email. It was filled with just cold fonts and calculated benefits. But this morning, after Pilates kicked my ass and my matcha set me straight, I decided it was time.

I padded barefoot across our apartment. My hair was still damp form the shower. I was in leggings and one of Rose's old, oversized tees that I'd permanently borrowed. The Upper East Side was buzzing outside, muted by thick windows and somewhat soon to be *rich girl privilege*.

I needed silence to do this. I opened the email, clicked on the PDF and scrolled.

Position: International Business Strategist
Salary: Eye-watering.
Benefits: Generous enough to make capitalism blush.
Start Date: Negotiable
Reporting To: CEO, Mr. Theodore Jones

I stared at that line for a full ten seconds, Mr. Theodore Jones. I could still hear the low rasp of *'You can take me, sweetheart?'* in the back of my mind like it was carved into the damn neurons. I could still feel his hands on my hips. His fingers tracing my body, even his co—. *Fuck.*

Focus, you little slut.

I read the whole thing twice. This wasn't an easy decision for a lot of reasons. But especially because I was going to be working with *him*. He doesn't know who I am. I wasn't planning on telling him because it didn't matter. It wasn't supposed to. As much as he might wish to see me again, he doesn't expect to. And now? Now I have to walk into his office and shake hands with this man.

My pulse was racing as if I were running a marathon. I took a sip of my matcha, and after a long, slow breath, I clicked *Accept*.

Just like that, I was in.

I logged in to my airline portal and filed for a leave of absence for the maximum time allowed. This wasn't goodbye, it was just a see-you-later. Or maybe never. I don't know yet. The screen flashed Submission confirmed, and I shut the laptop with a soft click that echoed louder in my chest.

I was officially part of the Hayes empire. Just like I swore I never would be.

I sat there for a moment, legs curled under me, staring out the window at a slice of New York skyline that had always made me feel untouchable and independent. Like I'd chosen this life. Now, that skyline looked like it was laughing at me.

What the hell are you doing, Samantha?

I let out a breath somewhere between a laugh and a groan and buried my face in my hands. I pulled my phone out of the couch cushion and texted Rose.

Me: Hey, so I did a thing.

Rose: Which thing? A sexy thing or a scary thing?

Me: Both? Because I just hit accept on my family's scary career offer, that means 1A is my boss.

Three dots blinked for a very long time.

Rose: OH FUCK, sexy and scary it is...

Me: Yup.

I tossed the phone on the couch and flopped backward like the drama queen I am.

The ceiling didn't offer any answers, but at least it didn't expect me to have a plan. This was real now. I was no longer a flight attendant, Sam. I was now corporate Samantha. Ew.

"I can't wear this," I groaned, standing in front of my closet in nothing but a lace bra and matching underwear, holding up a silver satin mini dress like it personally offended me.

Rose didn't even look up from the bed where she was sprawled with her third glass of wine and a face mask that made her look like a dewy alien. "Why not?"

"Because I'm about to start a corporate job at the company I swore I'd never touch, working for the man I definitely touched." I paused. "Extensively." She peeled a cucumber slice off her eyelid and stared at me. "And this is relevant to how you dress because…?" I threw it onto the bed dramatically.

"Because I need to look powerful. Unbothered. Like I didn't just accept a high-level position while completely compromised by sex hair and childhood trauma."

"You're getting dressed for a night out," she said

slowly, "not your first board meeting. Also, if you don't wear that, I will, and I swear I'll make out with someone who can't pronounce 'Pinot.'" I sighed, grabbing the skirt again and holding it in front of me.

"It's short."

Rose grinned. "So are you." We both cracked up. God, I needed this night. Not the tequila shots and body glitter part, though I was fully ready for that, too, but the part where I remembered who I was outside of the Hayes orbit.

"I'm going to be in a boardroom with a man who's seen me naked," I said, slipping into the dress anyway.

"Cheers to feminism," Rose muttered, standing and shimmying into her jumpsuit. It was black, backless, and illegal in at least three states. She looked like trouble. The best kind.

"Are you gonna tell him?" she asked casually, blending highlighter. "Tell him what?"

I tried to play dumb. Rose just raised an eyebrow. "That I'm a Hayes?" I muttered. "I mean, I'll have to. What's the etiquette on disclosing a secret billionaire lineage to a man who's now your boss but also maybe remembers how loud you moaned his name?"

Rose blinked at me in the mirror. "I don't know, but you're doing amazing, sweetie."

Lipstick. Perfume. Anxiety. Check, check, check.

We called an Uber and headed downtown. This night was like a bachelorette party, minus the bride, plus a bunch of our favorite hot messes, including

Marcus, our mutual friend and professional instigator, and Josh, my ex-situationship, who was somehow still in our group chat and still impossibly hot in a chaotic, DJ-with-an-MBA kind of way.

We walked into the bar like a slow-mo scene in a movie. Stilettos, laughter, city lights, and dangerous nostalgia. Josh whistled.

"Damn, rich girl, you look good." I smiled sweetly. "And unemployment still looks good on you, babe." He winked. "Still mad I ghosted you?"

Rose slipped between us. "Still mad she never slept with you again?" We claimed a booth, ordered a round of espresso martinis, and for a second, just a second, I forgot that my life was on the verge of imploding. Theo didn't exist here. Hayes didn't either. Just music, friends, and Rose's foot tapping mine under the table, saying 'breathe, babe'.

I got this.

I looked around at the people I'd chosen to build my life with. I looked at the chaos, the glitter, the city that had always made me feel like anything was possible. And I let myself smile.

Tomorrow, I'd deal with corporate realities and office politics and pretend I hadn't seen my new boss naked.

Tonight? Tonight, I was just Sam again.

And that was enough.

CHAPTER TWELVE

theo

WHATEVER I THOUGHT Hayes International Headquarters was, this is way more.

Floor-to-ceiling windows with more coffee rooms than I can count. There are people here for everything and anything. It looks like everyone has an office and assistants. I can tell by the desks outside each office.

Which I'm not sure is necessary, but we can work on that later.

As soon as I got to my office, I was mesmerized by the view. You can see the whole city from here. And this is at least 1,000 sq. ft. bigger than my first apartment. I have a fully stocked bar cart, an espresso machine, two couches, two chairs, and my desk occupies the whole corner.

Maybe this won't be as bad as I thought.

I was halfway through my espresso when the door opened. "Good morning, you are here early," Harper said, barging in with coffee in one hand and a stack of papers in the other. "I've been here since six, just wanted to get comfortable before everyone arrived."

"That's smart. It will make you look like you know the place," She says and winks at me. "I sent you a floor map with all the boardrooms you'll be using, the immediate offices, so you know who you'll have around, and I synced your calendar to mine, so I can see and change whatever needs to be changed."

"Thanks, Harper," She just smiled and walked out. I could hear how the office buzz kicked up a notch. I can hear the heels clicking, greetings exchanged, whispers.

When I opened my computer, I saw that my calendar looked like a murder scene. *Thanks, Harper.* I was buried in back-to-back meetings, board briefings, and PR run-throughs.

And then I heard the chattering. "Mr. Hayes brought both his daughters today. The tall one's the lawyer, I think." My head didn't even try to argue the curiosity. I just snapped toward the glass doors in time to catch Max Hayes entering with two women in tailored suits flanking him like royalty. And there she was.

Sam. What the fuck?

There was no flirty smile this time, no curious eyes wandering around the room.

She was wearing a wine-colored silk blouse and white trousers that fit her as if they were custom-made for her. They probably were. Her hair was up in a high ponytail, but I could still see the curve of her neck, and I still remembered kissing it. She was coldly laughing at something Max said, confident, poised. That's not her real laugh.

She is a *fucking Hayes*.

The second woman had to be her sister, same cheekbones, but a completely different vibe. If I had to guess, I'd say that's the lawyer. But Sam was also his daughter. Fuck. I felt like the room tilted, just enough to make me nauseous.

"Meeting in ten, Theo," Harper said, handing me the agenda. "They'll be joining us for the strategy review." I nodded, more mechanical than I intended.

She lied to me. No, she didn't lie. She just didn't say anything. Who am I kidding? It's the same shit. She lied, period. What the fuck was that night then? A distraction? A game? Did she think I'd never find out? Did she want to screw the CEO before she had to work under him?

Was I just— a power move to her?

I remembered the wine, her laugh. The way she curled into me when she fell asleep. The sound she made when she came around my co— stop stop stop.

I clenched my jaw and took a deep breath. I need to be professional. She doesn't get to make me nervous.

I'm thirty-eight, I'm a grown ass man. A CEO. I'd built companies from a single code in my garage. I negotiated billion-dollar deals before breakfast. And I let myself fall for the lies of a twenty-something flight attendant just because she was flirty, funny, and let me fuck her how I wanted? Goddamn it.

I took a breath, straightened my jacket, and headed for the conference room. I don't care that she is a Hayes.

This is *my* company now.

It's time to play boss, even when it feels like she has played me.

The boardroom was too warm.

Or maybe it was just me.

Max stood at the head of the table, beaming with that kind of legacy pride that couldn't be faked. "Thank you, everyone, for being here. I won't waste your time. I never have," he said, drawing a few chuckles from the board. "As many of you know, I've made the decision to step down as CEO to focus on my health, and more importantly, to spend time on the things I used to put off. Starting with living."

He looked at me, eyes steady. "I spent a lot of time choosing the right person to lead Hayes into the next era. And I trust him to do it better than I ever could. Please welcome our new CEO, Theodore Jones."

There was polite applause, some murmurs, as expected, and of course, all eyes turned to me. I stood, straightened my jacket, and stepped forward. I'm focused, I'm controlled, I'm okay.

"Thank you, Max," I began. My voice sounded confident, too confident for the war going on in my chest. "It's an honor to step into this role. Hayes International has a legacy of innovation and global leadership, and I plan to honor that while pushing it into new frontiers."

I let my gaze drift around the room and settle on her. She sat still, her expression unreadable, but her eyes—those damn blue eyes—darted at me. Her lips were pressed together like she was holding back more than a smile. I didn't let that distract me. I kept going. "This won't be a one-man job. It'll take all of us, working together, challenging each other, growing as one unit. I look forward to getting to know all of you."

I sat back down. Felt the weight of the room shift. The tension between us was a wire stretched too tight. Max picked up again. "And that brings me to the rest of our leadership updates. You've met Cameron, our new Head of PR." Cameron, tall and smug, gave a nod. Typical PR.

"And of course, my eldest daughter, Naomi Hayes, who will be stepping up as Head of Legal." There was more applause. Naomi smiled in a polished, sharp, confident way. Lawyer through and through.

"And last but not least," Max continued, "my youngest daughter, Samantha Hayes, who will be joining us as our new International Business Strategist." I didn't clap. Not because I didn't want to, but because I couldn't. Not without my hands shaking.

Samantha.

She offered a perfect little wave, cheeks flushed, eyes flicking toward mine for half a second. Max cleared his throat. "I'll still be involved, of course. Just not in the day-to-day. I'll serve as a consultant, as needed, while Jones and the team take the lead."

The room erupted into casual chatter, ideas being tossed around about strategy, expansion, and branding. Harper sat beside me, typing furiously, highlighting notes in real time. But all I could think about was her.

The way she crossed her legs. The way she bit her lip once when Naomi spoke about international litigation strategy. The way her blouse dipped just enough to remind me of last week. Of how her bra cupped her breasts perfectly, and how well they fit into my mouth. Theodore, stop before you get hard.

At the break, I stood. "I'll be back," I told Harper. Coffee. I needed coffee. Or cold water. Or ice down my pants.

In the hallway, I was halfway to the coffee table when I heard heels. Light, crisp. A rhythm I already knew by heart. She stepped beside me, reaching for a bottle of water."Congratulations on your new job, Samantha," I said in a cold, precise tone. "We'll have a meeting at 1:45. Harper will put it in your calendar. I want to get to know my new International Business Strategist better."

She cracked open the water, didn't even look at me as she took a sip. Then she turned, lips curling into that same wicked smile I'd seen in my bed.

"Of course," she said, smooth as silk. "It's not like you haven't seen me naked, been inside me, or know exactly how I sound when I come with your name on my lips. But sure, let's get to know each other."

My jaw locked, and I nearly dropped the coffee cup. I couldn't even speak.

She winked. "See you at 1:45, Mr. Jones." And then she walked away, hips swaying, leaving me painfully hard, emotionally confused, and in desperate need of something stronger than coffee.

1:45 PM.

Harper's knock was a polite double-tap. "Samantha Hayes for you." I didn't even look up. "Send her in. And close the door behind her." The click of heels echoed before she appeared in the doorway, her smile already loaded with something, smugness? Nerve? Whatever it was, it crawled under my skin.

"Hi, boss man," she said, stepping inside like she owned the damn building. And, in a way, she did. I stood, walked over to the panel beside my desk, and pressed the dim button. The glass walls around us went opaque in an instant. I don't need eyes on me right now.

Besides, this was standard protocol. Every exec

used it. I've done it three times today already. But this time, it was personal. "Take a seat," I said.

She did, crossing her legs slowly. My blood pressure was already up. "I'm impressed," she said, leaning back, surveying the space. "Big corner office, nice view, a fully stocked bar cart. Very alpha male of you."

"Cut the shit, Samantha," I said, sharper than I meant to. Her eyebrows lifted, just a bit. "Did you know?" I asked. She tilted her head, playing coy. "Know what, exactly?" I just stared at her. Her smirk dropped. "Yes," she said.

My jaw clenched. "So, the whole time, you knew who I was? You knew exactly what you were doing when you got into my bed?" She sighed and glanced at the frosted glass wall before turning back to me. "When *you* invite *me* to your bed."

"Same shit, Samantha. Explain," I said, voice low and tight. "Because from where I'm standing, it looks a hell of a lot like a game." That stung her. Good. That's what I wanted.

She sat forward, resting her arms on the chair. "I knew your name. I knew who you were. And I knew the role you'd have, but I didn't know I was going to be here, working under you, after well… being under you." She smiled, hiding what was really going on in her head.

"At what point did you decide not to tell me?" I asked, cold now. "Before or after you moaned my name loud enough to wake the entire floor?" She didn't flinch.

"I almost told you before all of that. I wanted to tell you the first time we ran into each other, but I wanted you to get to know me as *me*, as Sam, not as part of *this*," she said, signaling around the place.

"Look, I didn't know you'd be my boss. I didn't know I'd have to give you this explanation. I thought we'd have our fun in Paris, and that was going to be it. Besides, you wouldn't fuck me if you knew me as the daughter of Max Hayes," she said that with a smile on her face now. I stared at her, arms crossed, breathing through my nose.

She looked down at her hands. "You were the first thing in a long time that felt… not planned. So yeah, I didn't say anything. I held on to that moment like a secret. I wasn't trying to hurt you. I was trying to protect something for myself. For once." A long beat of silence passed.

"I should've told you," She added. "But I didn't. And now we're here. I'm sorry, Theo. Really sorry." I let the silence stretch. God, I wanted to kiss her again. And throw her out. And pull her back in.

Instead, I said, "This is our workplace now. You and I, we're nothing more than colleagues."

She lifted a brow, but nodded. "Of course, Mr. Jones. As you wish." My jaw twitched again. "We're done here." She stood, adjusted her blazer, and walked to the door.

Then she turned, a smile curling onto her lips like

it was wired into her DNA. "You know," she said, "it's kind of hot when you're mad."

And she was gone. Leaving me pacing behind frosted glass, trying not to lose my goddamn mind.

I pressed the dime button as my calendar buzzed sharply at 2:00: Meeting with Naomi Hayes — Head of Legal. Harper gave me a thumbs-up through the glass. Naomi stepped in exactly one minute later. No smile, no hesitation. "Mr. Jones," she said, offering a firm handshake. "Thank you for making time."

"Of course, Naomi. Please, have a seat, and call me Theodore, or Theo." She nodded and sat, her posture immaculate, her folder organized with color-coded tabs that would make a litigator weep with joy.

"I want to keep this brief and clear," she said, flipping it open. "I've reviewed the current corporate litigation backlog and pending international filings. There are a few landmines in the Southeast Asia division I'd like to get your sign-off on, but overall, I'm confident we can bring the average close-out timeline down by twenty percent by Q4." I nodded, flipping through the printout she handed me.

Naomi was brilliant, controlled, and strategic. Every word is carefully measured. Every move is calculated. "We'll need a formal sit-down with the external counsel team by next week," she added, "and I'd prefer to personally manage all litigation involving regulatory affairs. I've done it since I was an associate, and I know where the bodies are buried."

I glanced up from the page. "You're impressive,

Naomi." She didn't smile at the compliment, just nodded once, as if saying, 'I know'.

"The family name carries weight," she said. "It's my job to make sure it also carries protection." She leaned back, fixing me with a cool, intelligent stare. "I trust you'll let me know if I ever fall short."

"I will," I said. "And I trust you'll do the same." We shook on it. She stood, collected her folder, and smoothed a wrinkle from her blazer. "And Theodore"

"Yes?"

"My sister's smart. Don't underestimate her because she doesn't lead like us." I raised an eyebrow. "She's different," Naomi said, matter-of-factly. "Always has been. That doesn't mean she's not capable. It just means she's not built for these rooms."

I sat back, tapping the corner of her report against the desk. Not built for these rooms. Not interested in power plays or posturing. Not following the dynasty plan laid out for her.

Sam had chosen the sky. The freedom, instead of quarterly earnings and boardroom battles. She'd made a life out of escaping this place.

And maybe I… I'd just become the anchor that pulled her back in.

Fuck, now I feel like shit.

CHAPTER THIRTEEN

Sam

It's been a week of working under Theo.

But God, what I really want is for him to be under me again. Or on top of me. Or behind me. Or anywhere, really. Just close to me.

I miss it.

Which is insane, because it was just sex. Maybe the best sex I've ever had, but still. Why am I missing *him*?

We've kept it civil and professional. If you don't count the loaded glances across meeting rooms, the accidental brushes of fingers when passing documents, or the very intentional innuendos we toss at each other like darts during our 1:1 check-ins.

Twice this week, we were left alone in a glass conference room and talked about budget projections like we weren't remembering what we looked like naked. He hasn't touched me, not once. He hasn't tried to kiss me or to get me alone more than needed. He hasn't even dimmed the glass during our meetings. But the restraint in his jaw? The way his eyes paused just a beat too long on my mouth. It made me want to scream. Or to beg him to touch me again.

But today? Today broke me. Because my office is finally ready. After a week of squatting in Naomi's overly beige workspace, someone from facilities walked me down the hall and opened a door directly across from Theo's office. "You've got a nice view," the guy joked, motioning toward the skyline. But the view wasn't glass and buildings.

The view was Theodore Jones, framed by steel and ambition, barely ten feet away.

He had to be the one who planned this. It had to be him. That smug, calculating bastard wanted me within his line of sight. And you know what, maybe I wanted to be seen. By him, anyway.

I didn't even have time to unpack. Because twenty minutes later, I was sitting in a meeting with Harper and Theo, pretending to care about merger memos. And when he walked past me, fingers grazing the small of my back like a whisper of ownership, I almost choked on my breath.

I don't remember what I said in the meeting. Just that I felt high off the heat between us. Afterward, I returned to my office to breathe and maybe steal a second to think. The space was sleek, modern. All white, with chrome details and minimalist furniture. It was elegant, like me, I guess. Like they wanted me to be anyway.

I was walking toward my desk when the door clicked shut behind me. I already knew who it was. He didn't say anything, he just pressed the dimmer on the glass wall until it turned opaque, swallowing the office in a soft, hazy privacy. His voice was low and controlled. "Pull up your skirt, sit on the desk, and open your legs."

I didn't move. I *should've*. I *could've*. Instead, I turned and raised one brow. "Excuse me?"

He stepped forward, slowly, like a lion in a tailored navy suit. "You heard me, Samantha," he said, eyes burning into mine. "Skirt up. On the desk. Legs open."

I paused and let the silence thicken. Let him wonder if I'd obey. But I wanted this. God, I needed this. *Him*. Us. Whatever the hell this chemistry was, addictive and dangerous, I wanted to overdose on it.

I reached behind and slowly unzipped the pencil skirt. Tugged it up to my waist and boosted myself onto the desk. He exhaled, sharp and low, as I leaned back on my palms and spread my legs. I had lace panties on. A bold choice I made this morning and now, *clearly*, the right one.

Theo stepped between my legs and pulled me closer by my thighs. "I've been thinking about it since I saw you walk into this place."

"Just about this?" I teased.

His mouth crashed onto mine, rough, hungry,

tasting like control lost in an instant. I moaned against him as his hand slid under my blouse, fingers brushing my ribs, then my bra, then gone again. Teasing. Always fucking teasing me. His lips moved to my jaw, my neck.

"Tell me you want this, or I stop." I gasped, arching into him. "I want this."

He kissed down my chest, his lips grazing the swell of my breasts through the silk of my blouse. His hands were steady as they slid down my waist, fingertips trailing along the edge of my skirt, igniting every nerve beneath my skin. Then he dropped to his knees in front of me, and everything in me stilled, except my heart, which was pounding like it was trying to climb out of my chest. My breath hitched. The room shrank. The air thickened.

He looked up at me from between my thighs, his hands firm on the backs of my calves, holding me open. His fingers hooked the lace of my panties and pulled them to the side with a patience that only made it worse, maybe better? And then his mouth was on me.

His tongue moved like he remembered every shudder from Paris and wanted to relearn them all again. My hips jerked instinctively, searching for more friction, more of him, and he didn't stop. He just groaned low in his throat like my reaction turned him on, and I swear I could feel it vibrating through my entire body.

My hands flew to the edge of the desk, the wood

creaked under me, the only other sound besides my broken breaths and the obscene wet rhythm of his tongue. He flattened his hands on my thighs, holding me there as I gasped and rolled my hips against his mouth, chasing that edge, spiraling into it.

And I shattered, biting my lip to keep from crying out, fingers threading through his hair as I came against his mouth. When he stood, his lips were slick and his eyes dark. I was already breathless. He didn't speak. He just looked at me, as if trying to save this exact version of me into his memory. Flushed. Unraveled. Still trembling from his mouth. Then his hands went to his belt. The sound of the buckle unfastening made my breath catch all over again.

"I need to be inside you," he said, voice low and hoarse. "Now."

I leaned back slightly on my elbows, legs still parted, skirt still bunched around my waist, silently daring him to take what he already owned. *Me.*

His gaze burned across my body as he unbuttoned his pants, shoving them down just enough, and then he stepped between my thighs like he couldn't stand another second without us being connected. One hand slid around the back of my neck, pulling me up to kiss him, and I tasted myself on his tongue. Then he pressed into me in one long, slow, but hard thrust. My head fell back as I moaned.

His grip tightened on my waist, the desk scraping slightly beneath me with each sharp movement. He moved roughly, hungry, as every second in this office had led to this. His rhythm was fast, deep, claiming me all over again.

He was fucking me like he was mad at me. And, now I know, he still was.

"Fuck, Samantha," he groaned, lips at my ear. "You feel— Fuck, you feel so good." I smiled through a gasp. "I know, you're welcome."

He let out a broken laugh and thrust harder, deeper, until my reply disappeared into another moan. His hand slid between us, fingers finding just the right spot, and I shattered for the second time, with his hand on my mouth trying to muffle the sound. He pulled back just enough to look at me, brushing the hair from my face with a gentleness that did not match what had just happened on that desk.

"I'm still mad at you," he whispered, his voice all low and gravelly like that was supposed to scare me. I smirked. "You seemed a lot less mad two minutes ago." He narrowed his eyes, but the corner of his mouth twitched. "I'm serious." I dragged a finger down his chest. "Serious looks good on you."

He groaned. "You're impossible."

"And yet… wildly irresistible," I said, tilting my head. "It's a curse, really." He shook his head, biting back a smile. "You're going to be the death of me, Samantha Hayes."

"Please," I said, breathless and smug. Clothes half-on, hair disheveled, skin flushed and sticky in the most delicious ways. My blouse was still unbuttoned, his tie hanging loose like we'd just survived a hurricane. Honestly, we had.

Theo reached for a tissue box on the corner of my desk, of my pristine, still-smells-like-paint office, and handed me one like it was the most casual thing in the world. "Classy," I said, swiping at my inner thigh. "Very CEO of you." He tucked himself back into his slacks and smirked. "I have range."

I rolled my eyes, buttoning my blouse. "Remind me to have this desk burned." He grinned, straightening his shirt. "Don't. I plan on using it again." I gave him a look. "You're still mad at me, remember?" He paused, like he had to recalibrate. Then he stepped closer, smoothing a wrinkle from my skirt, letting his fingers drag just a beat too long. "I am mad," he murmured. "But that doesn't mean I want to stop."

"Dangerous words, 1A." He arched his brow.

"You made me dangerous, now you'll have to face the consequences." I swallowed, suddenly aware of how quiet the office hallway must be, how glass, even dimmed, still had ears. Thankfully, it was lunch hour, and at this time, the office was practically empty.

"We have a meeting in ten," he said, back to business. "Fix your lipstick, Samantha."

I smirked. "Yes, sir."

When he opened the door, Harper was sitting on her desk. She didn't say a word, just looked up from her laptop, arched one perfectly sculpted brow, and gave the kind of smirk that said 'I know exactly what you've been doing', and I'm choosing silence. Theo paused. Adjusted his tie like it hadn't just been used to pull my mouth against his. She typed something on her screen without looking up again.

"Meeting in eight, Theodore."

He nodded and walked off. His shoulders squared, and his head held high, as if nothing had happened. I stared at the door for a long second, then whispered under my breath, "Great. Now she knows too."

The walls of Hayes International were officially full of secrets. And I had lipstick to reapply. I walked over to the small mirror by my bookshelf, caught my reflection, and actually laughed. "Corporate goddess," I muttered. "With freshly fucked hair."

There was a heat still buzzing under my skin, part leftover arousal, part adrenaline, and all of it screaming one thing: What the hell are we doing? I fixed my lipstick. Reapplied some concealer. Smoothed out my blouse the best I could, tucked it back in, and found the strength to stuff everything that had just happened behind a mask of perfectly poised professionalism.

Hayes' rule #3: Never let them see you sweat.

By the time I grabbed my notebook and walked out of the office, I was every bit the International Business Strategist they'd hired. Straight back. A calm smile. Lip gloss. But when I walked into that boardroom and saw Theo already seated at the head of the table, tie fixed, jaw set, and his eyes flicking up just long enough to meet mine, I felt it all over again.

Every look. Every touch. Every secret under this roof.

I slid into my seat across from him, keeping my expression neutral, even as the memory of his mouth between my thighs pulsed through me like a live wire.

"Good afternoon," Max said as he entered, shuffling a stack of papers. "Let's get started, shall we?"

Yes. Let's. Before I lose my shit.

CHAPTER FOURTEEN

theo

I WAS HALFWAY through my second espresso when Harper knocked once and stepped into my office without waiting for an answer.

That's never a good sign.

She closed the door behind her like she was sealing a vault. In one hand, she held her tablet. In the other, a folder with my name on it. "Good morning to you, too," I said, eyeing the folder like it might detonate. Harper didn't smile.

"We need to talk about yesterday." Right. That. I leaned back in my chair, trying to look unfazed. "If this is about the stock briefing—"

"No. This is about the way you dimmed the glass in Samantha Hayes' office for twenty-two minutes and forty-seven seconds."

I blinked. "Wait, you timed it?"

"I am your assistant. It's literally my job to know what you're doing when you forget you have eyes on you." I rubbed a hand down my face. "So… are you here to scold me?"

"No," she said. "I'm here to cover your ass. Once again." She set the folder down with the precision of someone placing a trap. Inside was an HR disclosure form. The kind that allowed relationships between peers. Providing evidence that they were declared and disclosed, and all proper chains of command were respected.

"In short," Harper said, "if you want to continue hooking up with Samantha, she needs to be reassigned to another direct report. She can't work under you." I stared at the form. I didn't touch it.

"And you think I'm ready to be in a relationship with her?" I asked, voice lower than I meant it to be. Harper's expression softened, but only a little.

"I honestly don't care if you want to be in a relationship with her, but if you're going to be hooking up with her during office hours and within the office building, you need to do something about it. It doesn't matter that this is your company now. She is the daughter of the literal owner of this place, and you need to be careful." I let out a breath, long and slow. "Fine, I'll think about it."

"No, Theodore, you need to do something about it." She let out a frustrated breath. "Are you talking to me as my assistant or as my friend?"

She looked me dead in the eyes. "Do you want the friendly version?" She asked, and I nodded.

"You can't be fucking around with Samantha

Hayes, pun very much intended, without expecting to get fucked over. So you need to take care of yourself."

She left without saying another word. That was Harper's way, never overstaying her welcome, just dropping truth grenades and disappearing like smoke.

The truth was, I didn't know what the hell I was doing. It had started out as fun, electric, unexpected. I promised myself a long time ago that I didn't want to be involved in another relationship where I get to the point of thinking about engagement, marriage, and all that shit that already didn't work out for me.

But now, every time I looked at her, I wanted to ruin her lipstick and offer her the world at the same time. Which terrified me because I don't usually do this.

A calendar notification pinged on my screen, another meeting. I minimized it and opened my email. There was an invitation to a Gala that Hayes apparently hosts every year. And now it was part of my job. So, I did the best thing I could. I invited the only two people I know will be there, with no excuses.

I opened my messages and sent Nico a text.

Me: So, there's a work gala. Wanna come?

I'll need the support.

Nico: I'm honored to be your plus one.

Should I wear a tiara?

Me: I don't think that would be appropriate, but whatever you see fit.

Nico: jk, of course, I'll be there.

Can't wait to meet your new coworkers.

Are they all as fun as your office "strategist"? 👀

Me: 🖕

I rolled my eyes, then tapped through to my contacts and hit the dial button on one I hadn't used in a few weeks. "Hey stranger," Elena answered, her soft voice lilting with curiosity. "El, I need a favor, which is in your email."

"Already saw it, black tie, charity, soulless billionaires, and tiny hors d'oeuvres?"

"That's a way to put it, yes." She laughed. "Of course I'll come. Do you want emotional support or someone to mock the 1% with you?"

"Can it be both, please?"

"Done. I'll fly in tomorrow, but pay for my ticket, yes?" I laugh. "My treat." I hung up and stared at the ceiling for a moment, wondering how this was my life now.

I'm the CEO of one of the largest companies in the country, and I'm out here dodging HR landmines. For fucks sakes, I just invited my flirty best friend and my artistic baby sister to the Hayes Gala, just because I need emotional support.

Support to deal with the man who owns this place, which also happens to be the father of the woman that's been driving me crazy.

My life is a shit-show.

The conference room was all glass and steel and sharp angles, just like the conversation that unfolded inside it. Max sat at the head of the table, flanked by Naomi and Cameron. Sam was on the opposite side from me, thank God. But it did nothing to help my concentration.

"We've confirmed the venue," Cameron said, flipping through his tablet with the crisp efficiency of someone who didn't miss details or power plays. "The invite list includes our major partners, press, political donors, and some longstanding Hayes family supporters. No surprises."

"Are we doing speeches?" Naomi asked, already sounding tired.

"One from Max, one from Theo," Cameron replied. "Brief. Five minutes each. We'll prepare a teleprompter just in case." Max nodded. "I want the tone to be hopeful. This is the passing of a torch, not a funeral." Sam stiffened a little beside Naomi, her face unreadable except for the slight clench in her jaw. "And press access?" I asked, mostly to keep my eyes off Sam's lips.

"Limited," Harper answered from the far end of the table, typing as she spoke. "A ten-minute photo op at the entrance, then only one crew inside to cover the speeches. We've vetted them." Max turned to me. "Are you good with that?"

"Of course," I said smoothly. "I'll keep it polished." And polite. And professional. Even if one of the attendees knew what I sounded like, fucking and whispering her name against a desk. Sam glanced up at that moment, almost like she could hear the thought.

Our eyes met, Naomi leaned over to whisper something to her, and Sam nodded quickly, breaking eye contact. I could still feel it like static under my skin. Cameron ran through logistics, menu options, seating charts, and security.

Harper chimed in with a rundown of the show, every transition timed to the second. She'd already color-coded the schedule, of course. Sam asked two smart questions and made an offhand comment that had the table laughing, and I hated how much I wanted to touch the side of her neck again, just to see if her skin flushed like it did when I had her pinned to the glass.

The meeting wrapped up with Max standing. "This isn't just a gala, it's a statement. We're not just changing faces. We're building the future. Thank you all." Chairs scraped. Laptops closed. Polite murmurs filled the room.

Harper gave me a pointed glance on the way out, her look saying, 'keep it zipped, figuratively and literally'. As the room emptied, Sam walked past me without a word, but her perfume lingered in the space between us.

I got a text from Elena, which took my mind off Sam for a second.

Elena: Actually, I got the flight for today.

See you later, I'll text you the deets.

That made me smile. I've missed her.

I spotted Elena before she spotted me, curled up in an airport lounge chair with a book in one hand and a cold brew in the other, wearing paint-splattered sneakers and an oversized hoodie that probably belonged to some ex-boyfriend she never mentioned. She looked up, blinked twice, then grinned.

"Oh my God," she said, standing. "You actually came in person?"

I held my arms open. "Disappointed?"

"A little. I was hoping for a guy in a suit holding a sign with my name in cursive. Or at least a town car."

"Well, the driver's outside," I said, giving her a

quick hug. "But I figured you'd appreciate the personal touch." She pulled back and studied me.

"You've got the CEO-face on already. You always squint when you're stressed."

"I do not squint."

"Whatever helps you sleep at night." We made our way to the car, her backpack slung over one shoulder like she was still in art school, not working in galleries and freelancing illustrations for magazines that paid in exposure and bad wine.

"You look good," I said once we were on the road. "I look tired."

"You always say that." She said, rolling her eyes at me. She turned in the seat to face me. "Okay, so give me the non-press release version. How's it really going?" I exhaled through my nose, eyes on the Manhattan skyline blurring closer.

"Well, the job's intense. Max is still hanging around like a ghost in the walls. His daughters are… involved." Elena raised a brow. "That tone means that's complicated."

"It's a corporate family business. Trust me, everything about it is complicated."

When we got to my apartment, she whistled low.

"Wow, you're really leaning into this powerful CEO lifestyle."

"I worked for it," I said, not defensively, just stating a fact. She followed me through the front door, eyes taking in the tall windows, the clean lines, the art on the walls that she'd helped pick out years ago.

"I still can't believe you bought that ridiculous bronze piece," she muttered, gesturing at the sculpture by the entryway. "It's not ridiculous. It's industrial elegance."

"It's a sad, melting toaster." I laughed. "Your room's on the left. The one with the view." She stepped inside, dropped her bag, and spun in a slow circle. "Okay, fine. It's very grown-up. And extremely you." I leaned on the doorframe. "Are you hungry?"

"I could eat. But you better feed me wine too."

"Done." She looked at me again, this time more seriously. "You okay, really?" I hesitated. "Yeah. Just adjusting. There's a lot of… legacy in this place." She nodded slowly. "Don't let it swallow you."

"I'm trying not to." She smiled softly and disappeared into her room. For all our differences—her ink-stained fingers and chaotic light, my structured days and scheduled nights—Elena was the one person who saw through everything. The only one who ever really had.

The wine was already breathing by the time Elena wandered into the kitchen, barefoot, hair in a messy bun, one of my oversized t-shirts replacing the hoodie. "You're the only person I know who has wine that needs to 'breathe,'" she said, sliding onto a stool at the island.

"Trust me on that one," I replied, pouring her a glass of Bordeaux. "And don't let the aesthetic fool you. I also have instant mac-n-cheese in the pantry." She laughed, took a sip, and let out a satisfied hum. "Okay, this does not suck." I poured my own and leaned on the counter, facing her. "So, tell me things."

"Elena Jones, current status report?" she asked, then sighed. "Okay. Let's see. I'm still paying more in rent than I make in art, which is fine, really. My landlord installed a new fire alarm that goes off every time I toast a bagel, I swear, every single time. My last commission was for a 'tastefully erotic' book cover, don't ask me about that because the plot was weird. Oh, and I may or may not be in love with my barista." I raised an eyebrow. "Again?"

"Well, she is just the nicest person ever. And, she remembers my order rotation. Which changes every 4 days. That's practically marriage material." I snorted. "Your life is a cliché."

"I like to see my life as a 2000s rom-com." She shrugged. "It does sound cliché, doesn't it?" We both laugh at that. There was a beat of silence before she looked at me, her tone softening. "I know it's different for you. You're all... Forbes lists and gold pens now. But I like my mess."

"I know you do," I said. "That's why I've stopped trying to fix it."

"Growth," she teased.

"But really," I said, watching her more closely, "Are you okay?" Elena looked down at her wine.

"Yeah. I mean, not 'perfectly stable,' okay. But, like... still-showing-up kind of okay." I nodded, understanding more than I let on. "You know me. If life doesn't make me cry or question capitalism, what's the point?" I reached across the counter and tapped my glass against hers. "To messy art and overpriced apartments."

"To control-freak big brothers that want to pay for your life, but you don't let them because they keep weird bronze sculptures." We laughed, drank, and for a moment, everything felt still.

No boardrooms. No headlines. No power dynamics or secrets.

Just me and my little sister, drinking wine in a kitchen way too big, finding that rare kind of comfort you can only get from someone who knew you before the world expected anything from you.

The city was unusually quiet for a Saturday, probably because most of Manhattan was still nursing hangovers or stuck in overpriced yoga classes.

I pulled the car into the arrivals lane at JFK, glancing in the rearview mirror as Elena applied makeup as if she were meeting with someone important. "It's just Nico," I said.

"Exactly. He'll make jokes about how I look like I haven't slept, probably crying over a barista I barely know again." That made me burst into laughter. "To be fair… you have," I say, teasing her.

"That was a long time ago, shut up." Before I could fire back, my phone buzzed.

Nico: Touchdown.

Look for the hottest guy in arrivals with a chef's kiss luggage.

Moments later, there he was. He had aviators, a leather weekender bag slung over one shoulder, and that same smug grin he'd had since forever. "There he is," I said, putting the car in park. He spotted us immediately, waving dramatically like a washed-up pop star.

"Why does he look like he's about to sign autographs?" Elena deadpanned. "Because he totally would. If someone asked him." He climbed into the backseat, throwing his bag onto the empty seat next to him. "My favorite power siblings," he declared, leaning forward between us. "You two look disgustingly well-rested. Gross."

"You look like you bribed a flight attendant for extra drinks and then gave her your number," Elena said, twisting in her seat. "I did both of those things.

But she upgraded me to first class." I shook my head and pulled into traffic. "Brunch?"

"Please. I'm starving. And slightly hungover. But mostly starving."

We ended up at a French café in the West Village. It was Elena's choice, which meant overpriced pastries and coffee strong enough to wake the dead. We found a corner table on the patio, and by the time the waiter brought our drinks, Nico had already launched into a story about his latest failed situationship with a ceramicist in LA. "She said I didn't 'respect her creative boundaries.' I said her creative boundary was ghosting me mid-work days."

Elena snorted into her cappuccino. "I swear," Nico continued, "I'm going to marry someone boring. A dentist. A dog groomer. Someone who thinks foreplay is paying the bill early."

"I don't think that's your destiny," I said. "No?" He raised an eyebrow. "And what's yours? Because rumor has it, Monsieur CEO has been busy playing sexy boss with the heiress of Hayes International."

Elena blinked. "Wait—what?" I didn't answer fast enough. "You fucked Samantha Hayes?" she asked, sitting up so fast she nearly knocked over her drink. "That's Sam?"

"I didn't know who she was the first few times, and let's avoid the word fucked, we are adults. But yeah, we spent the night together in Paris." I muttered.

Nico nodded dramatically. "A classic romance

movie. She was hot, smart, and flirty. He was emotionally avoidant, but charming. Sparks flew."

"You have got to be kidding me," Elena said, eyes wide with a strange mix of awe and horror. "Theo, you realize this is your actual life, right? Not a bad t.v. series drama?"

"Trust me, I'm well aware."

"And you're working on top of her now?" Elena asked with a smirk. "And under her," Nico whispered, and I swear they started laughing like it was the most hilarious joke ever. "She works for the company," I corrected. "Technically not under or *for* me."

"She's literally across the hall," Nico added helpfully. "And according to Harper, the sexual tension is so thick it qualifies as a fire hazard."

"Jesus. Harper needs to shut up," I muttered, finishing my espresso. Elena leaned forward, lowering her voice. "Okay. But… are you okay with having her there after you… Well, fucked her?"

"Elena Jones! And yes, I'm okay with having her around. I'm just trying not to fuck everything up."

Nico raised his glass. "To not fucking everything up, just Hayes' daughter." I rolled my eyes as we clinked. Elena almost choked laughing.

"Also," Nico added, "I want to meet her properly. The whole 'I fu— slept with her, but now I don't know what to do' energy is killing my vibe."

"You'll meet her," I muttered. "Tonight. At the gala."

"Ooh," Elena said, eyes lighting up. "This is going to be so much fun."

"No, it is not."

"Yes," she and Nico said in unison. I sighed, finishing my coffee. It was too early for whiskey.

Elena starts to get in full glam mode when we get back, a makeup bag explodes across the bathroom counter, hair tools scattered like weapons. "Don't even think about using this bathroom," she called from behind the bathroom door. "I wouldn't dare," I called back, heading toward my room.

Nico tossed his weekend bag onto the guest bed and flopped down like he'd lived here for years. "Nice place," he said, glancing around. "Modern minimalism with a side of repressed emotion." I chuckled, pulling my shirt off. "It's quiet. I like it."

"It's lonely," he countered, but not unkindly.

We got dressed in a comfortable silence until Nico broke it again, more seriously this time. "So, Samantha Hayes." I paused mid-button. "What about her?" I ask without making eye contact. "Are you into her, like more than sex into her, or what?" I sighed. "Yes." Nico nodded slowly, thoughtful. "And?"

"And Harper handed me a 'just-in-case' HR

document that allows a relationship between us if she reports to someone else."

"That's… thorough."

"Well, it is Harper. She's thorough." I tugged on my jacket. "But that's not the point."

"Then what is?"

"She's twenty-six. I've lived a whole life, with baggage included. She's just stepping into the empire she never wanted. I'm the new CEO of said empire. We are not on the same page. We're not in the same book."

"Maybe," Nico said, adjusting his cufflinks. "Or maybe you're both just reading ahead in different chapters." I raised an eyebrow. "Look, what I'm saying is," he continued, "how do you know if she's not interested in more if you don't ask her? She slept with you again. Even after you guys argued and tried to act professionally about your work situation. I'd say she wants you too." I didn't answer, mostly because I didn't know how to.

The doorbell buzzed. It was Harper. I opened the door and immediately blinked. She was in floor-length navy silk, hair in a sleek bun, red lips the only pop of color. Classic Harper, stunning, polished, and already twenty minutes early.

"Wow," Nico said under his breath. "You're terrifying in the best way." Harper smiled, then she looked me up and down and nodded. "Acceptable."

Elena emerged a few minutes later, all bronzed

cheekbones and old-Hollywood curls. "I'm ready. Should we drink champagne now or pretend to be classy and wait until we arrive?"

"Pretend," Harper said. "Damn, okay," Elena muttered.

"Harper, a word," I said a bit rougher than I intended. Elena and Nico kept walking. "Yes?" She looked surprised. "Can you please quit gossiping with Nico about… Sam." That's when she relaxed her expression. "Sure, when you stop fucking her during business hours and ask for my friendly opinion."

"Har—" She put her hand up, shutting me down.

"Theodore, I absolutely love you, as my boss, as a friend. You know you're like an older brother to me. I can keep the business side of things quiet and professional, but we are all friends here, and we know you. And well, it's kinda great to gossip about your sex adventures when I'm the only one seeing them." She tapped my chest with a grin on her face and walked away.

I hate these people, but she is right. We are all friends, and I should take her advice more seriously than 'the office Harper's advice'.

We headed downstairs, into the waiting car, four pieces of very different energy buzzing in the same space, me with nerves I wouldn't name, Nico with too much charm, Harper with invisible spreadsheets in her brain, and Elena already halfway into character for whatever role she decided to play tonight.

The city rolled past the windows like a film reel. The gala was waiting.

And so was she.

CHAPTER FIFTEEN

Sam

"You look like a sexy Bond villain," Rose said, dramatically placing a hand on her heart as I slipped on my earrings.

"I'm pretty sure that's not a real compliment."

"Oh, it is. You're giving danger, mystery, and just enough cleavage to ruin someone's life. Probably the CEO's life." I turned to face the mirror, smoothing down the black silk dress that clung to me like it had been designed for this exact moment. Floor length and backless.

A soft drape at the front that revealed just a hint of cleavage. My lipstick was the exact shade of classic red he liked, with a little bite. My hair was down, the blowout still fresh.

"Tell me again why I'm going to this?" I asked, mostly to hear someone else say it out loud. "Because your dad asked. Because Naomi will be there. Because it's the Hayes Gala and you're a Hayes, and you work there now." Rose said, sitting cross-legged on my bed with a glass of wine like we weren't about to head into a ballroom full of legacy, expectations, and people who probably thought I still lived in Europe.

"And because I look really good in this dress," I added, twirling once, just to feel the fabric float around my ankles. "There it is," she smirked. But then I caught my reflection again, and the butterflies were back. Because somewhere across that ballroom would be Theo. And that made things... complicated.

It has been a couple of days since he came to my office, and *in* my office. But since then, I don't know. Something has shifted between us, and I don't know what it is. We've been working together for almost a month now, and seeing him every day makes me feel things that I don't know if I want to feel.

Then there's the teasing, the flirting. "He's distant," I said suddenly, walking over to grab my heels. "Like really distant." Rose cocked her head. "Cold-distant, or… scared-distant?" I sat on the edge of the bed and buckled one strap.

"Professional-distant. Which he should be, I guess. We're at work. He's the CEO. I'm technically his employee. But... I don't know. It's like it meant nothing to him. The sex, the moments we've shared. It's like he forgot the way he looked at me that night in Paris, and the way he begged me to stay."

"You don't believe that, Sam," she said softly.

"I don't want to. He said some things that I now don't know whether he was just caught up in the moment or meant more. " I admitted. "But every time he avoids eye contact or keeps things surface-level, I feel like I'm the idiot who caught feelings after one too many orgasms." Rose laughed. "Babe. You caught feelings before the second glass of wine. I was there, remember?"

I groaned and flopped back on the bed, careful not to mess my hair. "He's bossy, smart, and mysterious. And hot in a 'take-me-on-the-desk' kind of way. He's emotionally repressed and probably allergic to intimacy, and yet I want to peel him apart like he's a damn clementine."

"You're not falling for him," Rose said, moving beside me. "You're just falling for the idea of someone wanting you back in the way you showed yourself back in Paris." I looked at her. "You're terrifying when you're insightful."

"I know," she grinned. "But listen. Whatever this thing is? Fling, crush, slow-burn power play? It doesn't define you as a woman. And if he's dumb enough not to want more with you, that's on him." I sat up and looked at her. "You think I want more?"

"I think you want someone who sees you. All of you. And maybe Theo does. He's just too stubborn or scared to admit it." We stood together, and she helped zip the last bit of my dress.

The Hayes Foundation Gala was the kind of event where every smile was rehearsed, and every champagne glass knew the weight of silent judgment.

"Okay," Rose whispered under her breath. "This is giving Succession meets the Met Gala." I grinned. "Welcome to my childhood."

Susan found us first, of course. "Darling," she said with that kind of smile that never quite touched her eyes. "You look stunning. So classic."

Translation: at least I hadn't embarrassed the family name yet.

"Thank you, Susan. This is my friend, Rose Vell." Susan blinked, processed, and offered a hand. "Lovely to meet you." Rose shook it, then stepped back as Naomi appeared beside us in an emerald dress that was practically designed to say I make partner before thirty.

"You brought a friend," Naomi said to me, giving Rose a polite nod. "Are you a flight attendant too?"

"She's Rose, and yes, she is," I said smoothly. Naomi's brows rose. "Well, we're lucky to have you on the ground. I'm sure all that travel makes you both great with people." It wasn't malicious—not exactly. But it had the crisp tone of someone who never had to hand out peanuts at 30,000 feet. Rose caught my eye, and I knew she caught it too.

"We are great with people," I said. "Way better than most." Naomi turned her attention to someone more useful, an investor, maybe, and Susan was already drifting off to work the room. Max stepped in with a scotch and a tired smile. "Glad you're here, kid."

"Someone had to hold the good name," I said. He chuckled. "Always the sharp one."

"I brought my friend Rose Vell," I added, gesturing. "She's basically family for me." He offered his hand. "Thanks for keeping this one in line."

"She makes it a full-time job," Rose said with a grin.

After some polite chatter and another round of introductions, Rose and I wandered to the edge of the room, claiming two glasses of champagne from a passing tray. "You weren't kidding about this crowd," she said, sipping. "I meant it when I said you're the only person I have around that I feel good with," I said.

"This place is cold without backup. I could use someone like you." Rose raised an eyebrow. "Are you offering me a job?"

"Maybe," I said, smiling into my glass. "You've got skills. And you studied PR." She bumped my shoulder. "Throw in business class travel, and I'll consider it."

"I'll talk to HR."

"Maybe 1A could pull some strings," she teased, her smirk wicked. I groaned. "Shh, do not call him that here."

She winked. "Then stop giving your CEO fuck buddy code names."

"He's not—ugh. He's barely speaking to me anyway."

"Probably because you make silk blouses look like foreplay."

"Stop," I whispered through my teeth, laughing. "You're not helping." She linked her arm through mine. "I'm always helping." We sipped our champagne and scanned the room. "Let's make some power moves," Rose said, eyes sparkling. "And pretend I run this place." I took one more sip and lifted my chin. "Who says you don't?"

We were mid-way through politely sipping champagne and dodging small talk when Rose stiffened beside me. "Don't look now," she said, gripping my arm like a scandalized Victorian woman. "But your sexy fuck buddy boss man just walked in." Naturally, I looked immediately.

There he was, Theodore Jones, storm cloud in a tux. The man wore formality like a second skin: clean lines, crisp posture, the quiet authority of someone who didn't need to speak to command a room. But it wasn't just him who made my stomach do that traitorous flutter. He was with three other people, two of whom I didn't recognize.

Rose let out a low whistle. "Who is that with him?"

"That's Harper," I said, nodding toward the woman on his left. "His assistant. She basically keeps his world spinning. And probably tells him when to eat, go to the bathroom, and all of that." Rose tilted her head. "She looks like she eats billionaires for breakfast."

"Oh, she does," I murmured. "And him?" she asked, eyes landing on the man beside Theo, the one with tousled brown curls, designer stubble, and the kind of cocky smile that said, I flirt with grandmothers and win. He wore a deep green velvet jacket over a black shirt, no tie, like he got the gala memo and said I'll do you one better. "I don't know," I said slowly. "I mean, I've heard Theo talk about his best friend, but we've never met. Maybe that's him."

"Well, if that's the best friend," she whispered, "then I need to make some bad decisions tonight."

"And the girl with them? She is absolutely stunning." Younger, with big, curious eyes, messy curls, and a floaty dress that made her look like she'd wandered in from an art gallery. She stuck close to Theo's side, but not in a romantic way, I think. She looks protective of him, almost. "No clue," I said.

"She looks like his sister," Rose said, squinting. "They have the same eyes and same cheekbones." I nodded. "True. I guess we'll find out soon enough."

"Are you nervous?" Rose asked. I took a long sip of my champagne and smiled through it. "Only about everything." She grinned. "You'll be fine. You look devastating. That's all that matters."

Theo made his way across the ballroom like he owned the damn floor, which, technically, he kind of did tonight. He greeted donors, smiled for photos, and shook hands with a curated balance of power and charm.

When he finally reached us, I was mid-laugh at something Rose had whispered, and his eyes landed on me like he'd been holding his breath since the moment I walked in.

He smiled, lingering a little too long. "Samantha."

"Mr. Jones," I said, like it was a toast and a warning. "Allow me to introduce a few people," he said. "This is Nico." Nico gave a lopsided grin and tipped an imaginary hat. "Pleasure. I've been told I'm the fun one."

"By whom?" Elena murmured with a teasing smile. "Because that sounds made up." Theo cleared his throat, a little amused, a little exasperated. "And this is my little sister, Elena."

"Hi," Elena said warmly, extending her hand to me. "You're the legendary Samantha."

"Oh god," I muttered, shaking it. "What did he say?"

"Only good things," she promised, her voice playful. "And maybe one thing about desks." My cheeks flushed as Rose choked on her champagne. "This is Rose, my best friend." I offered quickly, trying to change the subject. "We are here for the gala and some sibling time."

"Sibling time," Nico echoed, smirking at Elena. "That's what we're calling it now?"

"Better than 'gossip hour and trauma unpacking,'" Elena replied. Everyone chuckled, the tension easing. Theo stayed long enough to offer pleasantries, then Harper appeared at his side, whispering something with that no-nonsense tone that only assistants and older sisters could perfect.

"I'll be back," he told us, giving me one last glance before following Harper into the crowd. "Is it always like this?" Elena asked me once he disappeared. "What, the tux, the charm, the slow smolder?" I said.

"No," she laughed. "The tension."

"Oh," I said, faking innocence. "That? That's just unresolved power dynamics and sexual history in formalwear." She cackled, clinking her glass to mine. "I like you already."

We started chatting, falling into an easy rhythm. Turns out Elena was an artist—illustration and mixed media—who'd spent the last few years bouncing between Lisbon, Florence, and Copenhagen. Her vibe was chaotic-neutral with a soul-deep kindness I hadn't expected. Meanwhile, Rose and Nico were in their own orbit. Flirting.

Full-on, no-subtlety, laughing way too loud, eyes sparkling, lean-in flirting. I watched them for a moment, smirking. "They're going to hook up," I whispered to Elena.

"Oh, 100 percent," she whispered back. "He's already picked out his best boxers." I nearly spit out my drink. I could see how she was Theo's sister, clever, quick, and quietly disarming. But unlike Theo, she didn't carry that edge of calculation. She was open, breezy. If he was the storm, she was the sea. The clink of glasses and soft hush of the crowd around us signaled a shift in the room.

"Looks like the gala's officially starting," Elena said, checking the time on her phone. "I should go mingle with my family," I said, straightening the fabric of my dress and reaching for my clutch. "Keep Rose safe from your best friend."

"No promises," Elena grinned. "She looks like she bites."

"She does," I said, winking. "But only if he asks nicely." We both laughed as I stepped away from our corner of comfort and glided into the storm.

The moment I reached the main cluster—Max, Naomi, Cameron, and Theo—I could feel the air change. It was thicker, heavier. Like all the unspoken things between Theo and me had walked in with me.

Naomi barely glanced up, deep in conversation with Cameron about the silent auction list. Max gave me a once-over with a rare soft smile. "You look beautiful, Samantha," he said, voice warm and low. "Thanks, Max."

Theo didn't say a word. But his eyes dragged over

me for just a second too long. And that was more than enough. My father stood beneath the grand chandelier, a glass raised, his voice calm and commanding as ever. "Thank you all for being here tonight. The Hayes Foundation was built not just on business, but on belief, belief in change, in legacy, and in the future. Tonight is about that future."

He continued on, gracious, proud, practiced, mentioning the foundation's work, the family company's evolution, and how honored he was to be surrounded by those helping to shape its next chapter. Naomi gave a perfectly polished follow-up. Cameron charmed the crowd. And somewhere in there, I smiled and nodded and let flashes of cameras wash over me. We were the picture of power, composure, and carefully chosen designer outfits.

And then there was Theo. He stood with that calm intensity only he could pull off, his hand briefly brushing the small of my back as we took a group photo. I didn't dare move, not when I could still feel the imprint of his fingers, the heat of that touch in the hollow of my spine.

"Smile," Harper whispered from behind the camera, and I did.

But I felt him step closer. "You look amazing in that dress," he murmured, low enough that only I could hear. I turned my head slightly, lips still fixed in a smile. "Careful, someone might hear you flirting with your strategist." His lips were right at my ear now. "It's my company, no one can tell me what to do or say," I swallowed. Hard.

"I can't wait to take it off," he added. My blush was immediate. I laughed, soft and controlled for the cameras, and whispered back, "No need. It's got easy access." His breath caught, just a little, and I felt that tiny, delicious shift in the air between us.

"You are a dangerous woman, Samantha," he said under his breath.

"A strategic woman," I corrected, still smiling. "Who knows how to pick her battles… and her underwear, which is nonexistent today." Theo straightened just as the cameras clicked again. Naomi gave me a suspicious side glance but didn't say anything.

I stayed perfectly composed, the picture of corporate daughter charm, while my pulse raced like I'd just sprinted through midtown.

The night blurred into a parade of perfectly polite conversations and backhanded compliments wrapped in satin and ego. I sipped my champagne like it was armor, smiling on cue, listening to industry types tell me how proud my father must be, while silently wondering if any of them would recognize me outside of this silk dress and borrowed legacy.

Theo and I moved through the crowd like magnets repelling, always circling, always aware. At some point, Harper whispered something to Theo, and I took the opportunity to slip away past executives, socialites, and people who liked to call themselves 'old family friends', but couldn't name a birthday. I found my way back to the one place that didn't feel like a performance, our little corner of chaos. Elena, Rose, and Nico posted up near the bar like it was their private island.

"There she is!" Nico announced, raising a flute like I'd just walked into my own party. "We were about to send a search party." I rolled my eyes. "I was being corporate." Rose handed me a tequila shot. "Now be feral." We clinked glasses and downed them, laughing as we scrunched our faces through the burn. Elena topped off our flutes while Nico reached for another round.

Theo reappeared, with a smile on his face that was enough to make me forget how to blink. He didn't say anything, just grabbed a shot and joined the circle like he belonged there, like he always had. We did another round, and there was more laughter and more glances that lingered.

And then, of course, Naomi. She materialized like a thundercloud in Louboutin heels, lips pursed tighter than her updo. "Samantha," she said in that voice she used when she was pretending not to judge me. "It's not great optics, taking shots with the CEO and… whoever these people are."

I blinked at her. Then turned around and shouted over the music, "Cameron! Come take a shot with us!" He looked surprised, then amused, and shrugged before making his way over. Naomi sighed so hard I could feel the air shift. Rose leaned over and whispered, "Is she always like this?"

"Only when she's breathing," I muttered. Nico watched Naomi retreat into the crowd, as if she had somewhere important to be. "Who was that?" he asked, brows raised. "Because she just gave me a very specific urge to behave badly." I pointed at him with my half-empty glass. "Nope. Don't think about it."

"But—"

"Nope," I said again. He grinned, completely unbothered. "I love a woman with an attitude." We all laughed again, and for a moment, it didn't feel like legacy or pressure or corporate optics. It just felt like life. Chaotic, tipsy, and weirdly… good.

Theo caught my eye from across the circle, and even with the noise and the music and the people, I felt it, but I looked away. Harper's hand was barely on my arm when she leaned in, voice low against the hum of the gala. "Right stairs. Don't use the elevator. Room 389." She slipped a key into my palm like it was an invitation and a warning all at once. I turned to ask, but she was gone.

I blinked once, twice, heart thudding as I scanned the room again. He wasn't with Max. Not with Elena. Not even pretending to listen to Cameron wax poetics about next quarter's projections. Just… vanished. Like smoke. My fingers closed around the key. Cool metal, warm pulse.

Shit.

"Cover for me," I said to Rose, who immediately narrowed her eyes. "Oh, okay." I slipped away before I could change my mind.

The stairs were quieter than I expected, carpeted in rich navy and lined with antique sconces. Room 389 was three flights up and to the left, tucked just out of sight, just like him. The key turned smoothly. My heart did not.

The door clicked open to low lights, soft music, and something that looked suspiciously like romance. A bottle of Dom chilled in a bucket of ice. Two long-stemmed glasses. French doors open to a small garden terrace where a fire pit crackles softly. And there, back to me, hands in his pockets like he wasn't deliberately unraveling my entire life, was Theodore Jones.

He turned at the sound of the door, his expression unreadable in the flickering firelight. But those eyes, they knew exactly why I was here. "Took you long enough," he said, voice low and steady. I stepped inside and shut the door behind me. "You didn't even say please."

"I didn't think I had to." He paused.

I kicked off my heels by the door, letting them fall with soft thuds against the carpet. "Would've been polite. But then again, you're not exactly known for playing fair." He moved then, slowly, crossing the room until we were toe-to-toe. He took the key from my hand without breaking eye contact, then set it on the table beside the Dom.

"I didn't ask you up here to be polite." My breath caught. I should say something witty. Tease him or something, but his hand was already grazing the small of my back, and I melted like I'd been waiting for that touch all night.

"You really had Harper do your dirty work?" I asked, barely above a whisper. He smiled, close now. "She believes in efficiency." I snorted.

"And what do you believe in, Samantha Hayes?" I met his gaze. "Right now? Letting my boss fuck me in a beautiful hotel room." He took my hand, brought it to his lips.

"Then you're exactly where you belong."

CHAPTER SIXTEEN

theo

SHE TASTED like champagne and bad intentions.

Her lips found mine the second I closed the space between us, soft at first, testing, teasing, then hungry. Desperate, even. Like we'd both been holding our breath all night, and this kiss was oxygen. Her hands found the sides of my jacket, tugging me closer until I could feel every curve of her pressed against me, silk on silk, heat under skin.

"God, you're bad for me," I muttered, mouth brushing her jaw as my fingers slipped the pin from her hair. Dark brown waves tumbled down, wild and soft, and I fisted a handful as she gasped.

"And you're terrible at pretending you don't want this," she whispered, tugging my tie loose with a practiced flick of her wrist. She pushed the jacket from my shoulders. I let it fall. The tie followed. She unbuttoned my shirt like she had a plane to catch, fast, focused, not even pretending to be delicate. I loved that about her. I hated how much I loved that about her.

"You wore this dress on purpose," I growled, lips skimming her collarbone, hands sliding down the open back, fingers brushing bare skin. "Knew exactly what it would do to me." She laughed, breathless and cocky. "I wore it because it makes my ass look great."

"Accurate," I said, gripping said ass and lifting her onto the edge of the table beside the champagne. Her legs wrapped around me instantly, instinctively, like we'd done this a hundred times. My hand slid up her thigh, pushing the silk higher, until I found exactly where she should have panties.

"You weren't joking about not wearing panties?" I asked, my voice hoarse. She tilted her head, smug. "Would've ruined the line of the dress."

"Jesus Christ, Samantha." I kissed her again, rougher now, teeth grazing her bottom lip as she tugged my shirt open. Her hands were everywhere, chest, shoulders, neck, like she couldn't get enough. Neither could I.

She pulled back just enough to breathe. "Take off your pants." I stepped back and did as I was told, dropping them to the floor. She watched, chest rising, lips parted, looking at me like she was hungry for me. She got down from the table, took her dress off, as I served the champagne without looking away from her. She wasn't wearing anything.

Her breasts bounced slowly as she sat at the edge of the bed. She opened her legs, "Come here, Mr.

Jones." Her voice was low, teasing, almost dangerous. "Show me how you take control."

"Bossy," I murmured, stepping between her knees, giving her the glass. She took a sip of the Dom, eyes focused on mine, and set the glass on the floor next to her. I step between her legs and push her back onto the bed, slow but firm, watching the way her eyes flicker with heat. She let me. Her legs stayed open, inviting, daring me to do something about it.

So, I did. I dropped just a little bit of champagne on her body. It splashed onto her breasts, her stomach, and just a bit under her belly button. She gasped at the cold. I set my glass on the table and went to kiss her. Her mouth opened beneath mine, soft and sweet, until I deepened my tongue, teasing her lower lip with my teeth. She moaned into my mouth.

I moved lower, my lips trailing down the elegant line of her throat, licking the drops of champagne there, stopping to feel the flutter of her pulse under my tongue.

Then further, down the curve of her collarbone, and lower. She gasped when I sucked lightly on the soft swell of her breast, her back arching, her fingers tightening in the sheets now. I took my time licking the rest of the Dom off her.

My tongue flicked over her nipple, drawing another breathless sound from her lips. I circled it, teased it, feeling it harden under the attention. Her body shifted beneath me, hips pressing up as if every nerve ending in her body was bound to my mouth.

Then I bit, just enough to make her cry out. Her hand fisted the sheets, head thrown back, lips parted in something between a moan and a curse.

"Fuck, Theo…" That sound, my name, raw in her throat, sent heat straight through my spine. I moved to her other breast, kissing a trail across her chest before repeating the same slow torture. My tongue teased, my teeth grazed, and her hands never stopped moving—my hair, my shoulders, the space between us, she couldn't get enough.

"Are you trying to kill me?" she breathed, voice wrecked. I looked up at her, lips wet, jaw tight with restraint. "Not yet." I dragged my mouth lower, across her stomach, pausing just above where she was already pulsing with heat. Her breath hitched, hands fisting the sheets again as I looked up at her, watching her squirm beneath me, completely undone.

I kissed the inside of her thigh, slow and open-mouthed, letting my tongue graze her skin. She shivered, legs falling open further like a silent invitation. I did the same to the other thigh, nipping gently this time, just enough to make her whimper and try to shift her hips closer.

"Patience, sweetheart," I murmured, even though I had none myself. She moaned my name, a plea and a curse in one, and when I finally dipped my head between her thighs, I didn't hesitate.

One long stroke of my tongue, finding her clit on the first try, and she gasped like the air had been punched out of her lungs. "Oh, fuck—" Her hips lifted off the bed. I wrapped an arm under her thigh, locking her in place, and did it again, slower, firmer. Her fingers tangled in my hair, tugging hard as I devoured her, tracing her rhythm, matching her breath.

She was sweet, warm, soaked, already on the edge, and I wasn't going to stop until she fell apart completely. Her thighs trembled. Her voice was wrecked. And when I sucked her clit into my mouth just once, she shattered, hips jerking, mouth open in a silent cry, eyes squeezed shut as the waves took her.

I didn't stop. Not until she begged. Not until her hands tugged me up, pulling me to her mouth like she couldn't stand one more second without kissing me. She tasted herself on my mouth, and I felt her unravel, right there in my arms. Her fingers wrapped around me with a grip that made my jaw clench. My breath hitched, every muscle going taut as she stroked me slowly.

I tried to say something, maybe her name, maybe a warning, but then she sank down, lips parting around the tip, and my thoughts scattered. "Fuck, Samantha," I groaned, one hand gripping the edge of the bed, the other buried in her hair, not guiding, just there.

Her mouth was warm, soft, and so goddamn confident. She moved like she knew exactly what I liked, exactly how far to push. Her tongue slid along my length in slow strokes, her fingers curled around what she couldn't take. Every sound she made, every glance up through those lashes, was wrecking me. I looked down at her, flushed and focused, and I swear I'd never seen anything more dangerous. Or more beautiful.

"You're going to ruin me," I said, breathless. She smirked around me, wicked and knowing, and that was it. She already had. I pulled her up, her breath still shaky from the way she'd just unraveled for me. Her lips were swollen, pupils wide, skin flushed. Beautiful didn't cover it; she looked wrecked and radiant all at once.

"On your knees," I murmured, voice low.

She didn't hesitate. She slid off the bed and onto the plush rug, kneeling for me, eyes burning into mine. My hand slid through her hair as I guided her mouth back to my cock, watching her take me with praise and hunger all at once.

I groaned. God, she was perfect like this. I pulled her up roughly, my mouth claiming hers again as I walked her backward until the back of her knees hit the mattress. She turned around and climbed on, crawling across the bed like a goddamn vision, and I followed. The only sound was our breathing, too loud, too desperate.

"Face down," I growled. "Now." She did without question, arching her back just enough to tempt me further. Her ass was perfect, begging for my hands. I slid my palm down her spine before gripping her hip in one hand and guiding myself with the other.

"Do you want this?" I rasped, because even now,

even with her bare and open and shaking for me, I needed to hear her say it. "I want this, and I want *you*," she whispered.

I didn't wait another second. I thrust into her with one hard, deep stroke, and she gasped, high and sharp. I did it again, rougher this time, until her hands fisted in the sheets and her moans filled the room. My fingers dug into her hips as I set the rhythm, unforgiving, hungry.

"You feel so fucking good," I groaned. "So tight around me. Like you were made for me." She moaned in response, incoherent, pushing back to meet me each time. Her body shook beneath my hands, and the sounds she made, desperate, unfiltered, only made me harder. I leaned forward, my chest against her back, my mouth by her ear.

"Say it again," I whispered. "Say you want me."

"I want you," she breathed, trembling. "Don't stop, Theo." And I didn't.

Her voice cracked as she said my name again, broken and pleading, and that was all it took for something primal to snap in me. I grabbed her wrists, pinned them to the small of her back with one hand, and drove into her harder. She cried out, half-moan, half-sob, and it made me want to own every sound she gave me. I didn't just want her body. I wanted her wrecked by my name, ruined by the way I moved inside her.

"Look at you," I growled into her ear. "Bent over, begging, and falling apart for me." She arched deeper into the bed, her hair a wild mess over the sheets, her body trembling beneath me. I held her still and kept thrusting, each movement a claim on her body.

She tightened around me, and I felt her body reaching that edge again. I fucking loved it. "You close?" I asked, my voice rough with need.

"Yes," she gasped. "God, yes…don't stop…" I didn't. I shifted, hit her deeper, harder, and she cried out again, louder this time. Her knees slipped slightly on the sheets, but I gripped her tighter, held her in place. She was losing it. So I slowed, just enough to make her whimper.

She writhed beneath me, greedy for friction, desperate for more. I leaned forward, kept her wrists pinned, and licked her shoulder, then bit her, just enough not to leave a mark.

"You want to come?" I asked, voice low and commanding. "Yes. Please."

"Then you do it when I say," I growled. "Not before. She groaned in frustration, and God, I loved the sound of her surrender. I released her wrists and flipped her over in one quick motion. Her chest rose and fell in a frantic rhythm, her lips parted, eyes heavy with lust and fire. I reached down, grabbed her thighs, and pulled her to the edge of the bed, never breaking eye contact.

Then I thrust into her again, deep, rough, raw. "Wrap your legs around me," I said. She obeyed instantly, and I slammed into her over and over, every thrust matched with her moan, her nails clawing down my back as if she needed something to anchor her. "Come for me, Samantha."

Her orgasm hit her hard, loud, shattering, and I wasn't far behind. I followed her over the edge with a low, guttural growl, my hands tightening on her hips as I spilled inside her, breathing her name against her neck. For a second, all I could hear was our heartbeats, wild, overlapping, synced. Then I pressed a kiss to her collarbone. Still inside her. Still wanting more.

Her body was still trembling beneath mine, legs falling open, breath catching as I finally pulled back. I exhaled hard, brushing a kiss against her shoulder before rolling to the side. My chest still heaved, sweat cooling fast on my skin. She lay there for a second, stunned and quiet. Then—

"Holy shit."

I smirked, dragging a hand through my hair. "That's the review I was hoping for."

Her laugh was soft, wrecked around the edges. "No, not that. We're supposed to be at a gala." That sobered me. I glanced over at the vintage clock on the fireplace mantel.

"Oh shit." We'd been gone too long. Too noticeable. Too obvious. Sam sat up, wrapping the sheet around her. Her dress was somewhere on the floor like a silk crime scene. She reached for her glass of Dom, took a sip, then looked at me with that wrecked, post-storm glow that made it impossible to think straight.

"I can't go back down there looking like I've been completely railed," she said, blinking wide-eyed. "You were," I muttered, grabbing a towel and handing it to her. "Multiple times in fact." She laughed again, flushed and exasperated and somehow even more beautiful.

I threw on my shirt, backward the first time, then fixed it with shaking hands while she slipped back into that black silk dress, skin still glowing, hair wild in the best way. I found her clutch and passed it over. She dug out a lipstick and touched herself up in the mirror while I buttoned my cuffs. Every movement she made felt like a temptation I didn't have time to indulge in.

We needed to move.

She pulled her hair back into a clean twist, glanced in the mirror, and exhaled. "How do I look?"

"Ruined. And perfect."

"Mr. Jones!" I grinned. "You'll pass. Come on." She slipped her heels on and grabbed the keycard from the table. As we opened the door, the muted sounds of the gala filtered back in, glasses clinking, music swelling, conversations echoing against marble. Sam looked at me, lips parted. "If Harper says anything…"

"She won't," she snorted.

CHAPTER SEVENTEEN

Sam

I REAPPLIED my lipstick in the hotel bathroom like I hadn't just been ruined by the CEO of Hayes International.

Again.

I fluffed my hair, smoothed my dress, and checked for any signs of well… misbehavior. There were a few, reddened lips, flushed cheeks, a barely-there wobble in my knees, but nothing a confident stride and a glass of champagne couldn't mask.

By the time I walked back into the gala, Theo was already on the floor, speaking to a senior board member and a man I vaguely recognized from a European subsidiary. He looked cool, composed, and untouched. Of course he did.

Meanwhile, I felt like my skin was still vibrating from the feel of his mouth on me. From the way he'd taken control, how he whispered filthy things with that deliciously calm voice of his. From the way he'd made me come so hard, I forgot what planet we were on.

I spotted Rose before I spotted a drink, which said a lot about my priorities. "You're glowing," she whispered, barely hiding her smirk. "And not from a highlighter."

"Shut up," I hissed, grabbing a flute of champagne from a passing tray. "I'll debrief you later," I said, giving her a wink. We rejoined Elena and Nico near the stage, and Harper gave me a small nod from across the room. Cool, polished, as always. If she thought anything of my brief disappearance with Theo, she didn't show it.

He caught my eye a moment later, and for a second, the world faded. The way his mouth twitched in the slightest smirk. The way his gaze dropped to my lips, then back up. The way he looked at me was like he was still undressing me with his eyes. God help me.

I turned away first. Not because I didn't want to look. Because if I didn't, I'd melt into the carpet and start round three in front of the press. The rest of the night was a balancing act full of small talk, toasts, and strategically timed smiles.

Naomi looked pleased with herself, no doubt thinking her little optics lecture earlier had actually sunk in. Little did she know I had just had the most unprofessional, utterly inappropriate, absolutely mind-blowing sex of my life, and walked back into the ballroom like nothing had happened.

The car ride was quiet. Not the kind of awkward silence, but the kind that only comes when the adrenaline fades, and your body finally remembers it's tired. Rose pulled her heels off and sighed dramatically. "Remind me why people throw these things?"

"To be photographed looking richer than everyone else," I muttered. "And so, Harper can prove herself by executing an event flawlessly without blinking," I added.

"Okay, she's terrifying. In a sexy, Olivia-Pope-on-steroids way." I smirked, letting my head rest against the window. "Yeah. And she knows everything." There was a pause before Rose said, "Including what happened in a hotel room a couple of hours ago?" My eyes slid shut. "God, is it written on my face?"

"No, but I can smell Dom Pérignon and guilt from a mile away." I turned to face her. "It's not guilt. Not really. It's more…" I searched for the word, "It's more like whiplash. He's so good at making me feel like I'm the only person in the room, and then in the next moment, he's all boardroom and brass tacks. Like he didn't just—"

Rose nodded, understanding too well. "I don't know what this is," I admitted. "It's not nothing. But it's not exactly something. And I can't afford to be stupid about this."

"Do you want it to be something?" I hesitated. "I think… I want him to want it to be something."

"Well, you're not stupid. You're just a woman who got tangled up with a very complicated man in a very complicated job situation." The car pulled up outside our building. I didn't move right away. "I think I just need to sleep," I said. "And not think about Theo or Hayes or optics or power plays."

"Done," Rose said. "Tomorrow, we'll have brunch. We'll wear sunglasses, order too many mimosas, and pretend to be women with far less baggage." I laughed softly, grabbing her hand. "Thanks for being there tonight."

"For you? Always."

We walked inside together. Two tired women in heels, holding secrets we weren't ready to unpack just yet. I was already in bed, makeup wiped off, hair tossed in a bun that still smelled faintly of champagne and expensive perfume, when my screen lit up.

> Theodore Jones: You looked stunning tonight. Hope you made it home safe.
>
> Goodnight, Samantha.

It was the first time he'd texted me. The first time he used my full name outside of a moan or a meeting. I stared at it for longer than I should have, rereading the words, letting them settle under my skin like warmth from the inside out. It wasn't a novel. It wasn't even a paragraph. But it was him. And it was real. I tapped a reply.

Me: Got home safe. Thanks for the champagne. And the… rest of it.

Goodnight, Mr. Jones.

I hit send before I could overthink it.

I turned my phone face down and let myself smile into the dark.

The clink of coffee cups and the low hum of Sunday chatter filled the tiny café near our apartment.

My gear was simple. Oversized sunglasses, a vintage tee, a light coat, and jeans that had seen better days. Rose looked unfairly flawless in a sundress, a cardigan, and lip gloss, sipping her mimosa like she hadn't taken tequila shots with the whole Hayes International team twelve hours earlier.

She looked at me over the rim of her glass. "You're being suspiciously quiet."

"I'm hungover."

"Still, you're glowing. Which is weird."

"I'm sweating the alcohol." Rose narrowed her

eyes. "You got a morning text, didn't you?" I raised a brow. "What makes you think that?"

"Because you haven't stopped checking your phone, you look like your head is a mess, and you are barely touching your food, which means you're nervous." I sighed, then slid my phone across the table like it was Exhibit A in my emotional trial. She read the text and gasped.

"Oh, a goodnight text? Oh my God. That's even better than a morning text." I nodded, sipping my iced coffee to avoid smiling. "First time he texted me."

"And he used your government name?" Her eyes widened. "Sam, that's… something? I mean, it's CEO-appropriate but also, like, low-key swoony." I shrugged, but the blush was creeping up my neck. Rose leaned in. "Okay, but do we think it's just post-coital etiquette, or are we entering the land of feelings?"

I stared at the bubbles in my mimosa. "That's the million-dollar question." She reached over and squeezed my hand. "You don't have to answer it today. But I'm here for every chapter of this love story, bestie." I laughed, finally relaxing for the first time since slipping out of Theo's hotel room. "Thanks," I said. "Also, next time I even consider sleeping with someone I technically report to, slap me."

"Oh, I will," she said sweetly. "But I'll also bring wine and ask for every single detail." I smiled, knowing she meant it. And knowing, deep down, I'd already decided to keep writing this story, mess and all.

I kicked off my sneakers by the door, my apartment still smelled faintly of dry shampoo, last night's perfume, and the citrus candle I forgot to blow out. My phone buzzed. I reached for it without thinking, thumb already swiping the screen.

Theodore Jones: Good morning.

Did you sleep well? How are you feeling today?

I blinked at the words. Good morning? Sleep well? How was I feeling? Was this him being cute? I grinned, sinking deeper into the couch and stretching my legs out.

Me: Are we texting now? Is this a thing?

His response came almost instantly.

Theodore Jones: We are.

Is that a problem?

Me: Not at all. Just want to make sure this is part of our... updated terms and conditions.

A little late-night sin, followed by polite morning follow-up?

Theodore Jones: You forgot something.

Also includes: ongoing anticipation, occasional professional tension, and the promise of more.

I laughed softly. God, he was good at this.

Me: Is that in the fine print?

Theodore Jones: No.

That's in bold. Underlined. Red ink.

I could picture him as I read it, smirking, composed, leaning back somewhere with that damn confident look he wore like a second suit.

Me: Then I guess I'll read the full document next time. Thoroughly. Line by line.

Three dots blinked for a long moment.

Theodore Jones: Careful, Samantha. I might hold you to that.

I set my phone down for a second, staring at the ceiling with a stupid grin on my face.

What were we doing? Whatever this thing we had was, it was getting addictive.

CHAPTER EIGHTEEN

theo

MONDAY HIT LIKE A TRUCK.

By 9 a.m., I was two coffees deep and seated across from three investors, running point on Q3 projections and international partnerships. By 11 a.m., Nico had found his way to my office, sunglasses still on, coffee in hand like he belonged here, which, soon, he might, if he says yes.

"I still don't get how you talked me into this," he said, plopping into the chair across from me. "Because you like money, status, and expensive coffee," I said, flipping through files. "And because I need someone I trust leading the Tech strategy team. Hayes International is behind the curve in that area."

He shrugged. "You're not wrong. But it's going to cost you. I like first-class accommodations, a good salary, and benefits that signal you work for a multi-billion-dollar company.

I glanced at him. "You'll have all of that." He

grinned like he'd won something. "Pleasure doing business with you then."

After a quick sync with Max, who was surprisingly on board, we brought Naomi into the conversation. She walked into the conference room like she was running the place, polished, sharp, unreadable. Nico stood and offered a hand. "Naomi Hayes, you are the hottest and scariest woman I've ever met."

She didn't even blink. "And you are insufferable and underqualified to be here." I cleared my throat before the tension caught fire. "He's coming in as a consultant for the Tech division." Naomi crossed her arms. "Consultant, huh? Fine. But if he crashes our internal systems, it's on you."

"Noted," I said. We called Cameron and Sam into the boardroom to finalize the vote. "All in favor?" I asked. Everyone's hand went up, even Sam's, though her eyes flicked to mine, unreadable. When the room cleared out, I asked Harper to come in. She handed me a folder. "Still thinking about the HR policy?"

"Just weighing my options." She didn't say anything. She didn't have to. Harper had seen me through three startups, one marriage, and a nervous breakdown at thirty-two. She knew what I meant. Once she was gone, I opened Sam's calendar, found a slot, and typed:

> Me: Dinner Date tonight at 7:00 p.m. — Tulips. I'll send you a car if you want.

Also, wear that red lipstick, please.

Sent.

Later that day, the apartment felt too quiet.

Elena's bag was by the door. "You sure you don't want the car to take you?" I asked.

"I'll survive a cab, Theo," she said, smirking. "Text me when you land." She nodded, then pulled back, her gaze softening. "Try not to screw this one up." My mouth twitched. "I won't." She just winked, grabbed her bag, and was gone.

I stood at the window for a minute, watching the cab disappear into the stream of city traffic, then turned to find Nico already halfway through a protein bar and scrolling something on his phone. "She's cool," he said, still chewing. "She's better than both of us combined."

"The bar is very low." We sat in the living room for a while, with him pretending to work while I actually did. We reviewed some onboarding plans for his new consulting role, drafted a few notes on the tech integration strategy, and traded barbs like we were still in college.

Then, around 5:45, Nico looked at me over the rim of his glass. "So. Date tonight?"

I glanced up from my laptop. "Yeah." I kept typing. "Are you nervous?" He set the drink down and really focused on our conversation now. "No."

"You are." I rolled my eyes at him, "I'm really not." He grinned. "Did you shave your balls?"

"Get out of here."

"Just saying. The first 'official' date is in a different territory. You need a clean shave." That was the cue I needed. I stood to walk toward the bedroom. "I'm taking a shower. Don't burn the place down."

As the hot water hit my skin, I let myself think about her. Samantha Hayes. Smart-mouthed, sharp-eyed, frustrating as hell. Inherited charm and danger from her father. And I was walking straight into the fire tonight.

By the time I stepped out, the bathroom mirror was fogged. I wiped it clean and stared at myself, at the man who hadn't cared this much in a long time. About how I looked. About how she might look at me.

I buttoned a charcoal-gray shirt with rolled sleeves, the collar open, and reached for the cologne she had complimented in Paris. A final check in the mirror. My pulse is steady. My mind is less so.

I texted Harper.

> Me: Out for the evening. Forward anything urgent.

And then, I picked up my phone and checked my calendar. 7:00 p.m. — Tulips.

She didn't text me back, but she still hasn't declined.

Game on.

The back of Tulips was quiet and intimate, without trying too hard. This is exactly what I wanted for tonight. I was already seated and waiting for her. I keep moving the bottle around, reading the label, but at this point, I'm just trying not to let the nervousness show.

When she walked in, my hands started shaking.

The hostess barely had time to gesture toward our table before Sam was making her way to me. She wore a deep green dress, short enough to grab my attention, but long enough to leave the rest to the imagination. Her hair was loose, long waves falling around her shoulders, and her eyes caught the light in a way that I swear, it made my heart skip a beat. But no red lipstick.

I stood to help her sit down, "No red lipstick, huh." I said as she reached the table. She smiled, that sharp, infuriating, captivating smile. "Didn't feel like following orders today." I laughed softly, pulling out her chair. "And here I thought you liked a little structure."

"I do," she said, slipping into the seat with grace. "But I also like pushing boundaries. You seem to know that already." She glanced at the bottle. "Already ordered?" I nodded. "A cab you'll pretend not to like but end up finishing."

"You're bold." I poured. "I've just gotten to know you." She took the glass and raised an eyebrow. "That's cute." The waiter came and went, invisible and efficient. We sipped, we settled in, and suddenly it was like Paris again, playful, light, as if the last few weeks of boardrooms and glass offices had been a shared hallucination.

"So," she said, crossing one leg over the other, deliberately, I was sure. "Is this a date… or a very fancy 1:1?" I set my glass down and tilted my head. "Do you want it to be a date?" She leaned in, chin slightly raised, fearless. "Yes."

That one word, so sure, so unfiltered, made something sharp and warm twist in my chest. I smiled. "Then it's a date." Her eyes flicked toward the wine, then back to me. "Does it come with dessert?"

"Only if you've been very good." She rolled her eyes and laughed, and for a moment, nothing else existed. "Define 'very good,'" she said finally, her tone casual, but her eyes were not. I leaned forward, elbows on the table, smirking. "You wore that dress. That gets you halfway there." She pretended to be scandalized. "So, I'm being judged by how I look now?"

"You're being admired," I corrected. "Wow, you're being really charming tonight," she said, taking another sip. "Is that a bad thing?" I asked. "The total opposite," she replied with a smile. "You're charming in an intense way. You walk into a room and make people feel as if gravity has shifted slightly. It's… disorienting."

"I think I'll take that as a compliment."

"You should," she said. "It's annoying how much I like it, how much I like *you*." There was a quiet beat between us, but I couldn't help but smile. "I didn't think we'd be here," I admitted. "After we saw each other that last time in Paris, I never thought I would see you again."

She traced the rim of her glass. "Me neither. I thought Paris would be it. I didn't expect what's been happening between us; I wasn't even sure I wanted it to happen. I don't mean it in a bad way, I just—"

"You just?" I looked at her. "You just wanted to say yes to a free dinner?"

"I did." Her voice was quirky, and her laugh was something else, but then she got softer. "All jokes aside, I said yes because I'm trying to figure this out, to figure *you* out. And I know we can't do that in the office with all those eyes on us, the pressure, and everything. And, I've been enjoying all the… well, let's say the experiences we've been having so far. But, I don't know what this is." I nodded.

"I get it, and honestly, neither do I." She met my eyes. "I didn't allow myself to feel anything for anybody, not after my divorce. I wanted to focus on my career, on myself. I didn't want a distraction, least of all to find someone who makes me question everything I've been avoiding for the past eight years."

The waiter reappeared, interrupting us to ask if we were ready to order. We murmured a few choices, laughing over the fact that we accidentally ordered the same entrée. When he walked away, she tilted her head. "You were saved by the waiter, but keep going, tell me something real," she said. "Something outside Paris, outside the office, the sex, the hotel rooms. Tell me how you really feel about this, about me." I blinked. "Right now?"

"Yes, Theodore, right now."

I paused, looking at her, and, pushing my sanity, my control, and everything in between aside, I said, "I like you, Sam. More than I should." I could see how her brain was trying to process what I just said. Her brows lifted just slightly, she opened her mouth, but she didn't speak. "I know it's fast," I continued, voice lower now, rougher. "I know we haven't exactly done things the *conventional* way." Her lips parted, but I wasn't done.

"But, you're in my thoughts all damn day. You drive me crazy, Samantha. In the best and worst ways. I can't concentrate when you're near me, and I can't breathe when you're not. And I think—" I ran a hand through my hair, suddenly unsure to tell her all of this. I feel like I'm seventeen again. What the fuck is wrong with me? "I think I'm falling for you."

She stared at me, and this time, I didn't fill the silence. I let it hang. She leaned back in her chair, studying me like she couldn't decide if I was being brave or foolish. "Okay," she said softly. Like she's still processing. "Okay?"

"I don't know what this is either. I don't know what it can be." Her voice was careful now. "You're my boss. This is my family's company. And we're… complicated to say the least."

"But," she added, slowly, like the words might shatter her, "I haven't stopped thinking about you since the first time you made me laugh in that airplane. And I sure as hell didn't fall into your bed, or on your desk, or the hotel room at the gala just because I wanted a fling."

"So you're saying…" She nodded. "I'm saying I might be falling too." That did something to my chest I wasn't prepared for. "I don't want you to say something you are not ready to say just because—"

"Theo, stop. I know what I'm feeling, I'm sure about it. I'm scared, but I'm willing to give this a chance, because you also drive me insane, in the best way." We both laugh at that, at us, at everything. I don't know how I allowed myself to fall for her, but I'm so fucking glad she feels the same way.

We walked out into the cool night air, the city buzzing around us, and I reached for her hand without thinking. She looked down, then up at me with a crooked grin. "You're a hand holder?"

I smiled, fingers lacing through hers. "Only with women who drink red wine and steal all the bread from the basket." She laughed, and the sound did something stupid to my heart. "Well," she said, squeezing my hand, "I guess you're stuck with me now." She was relaxed, glowing, actually, and I realized I'd never seen her like this in New York. She'd always had her guard up. A joke ready, a comeback for everything. But right now… she was soft.

"Do you always take your employees on dates?" she asked suddenly, and I exhaled a laugh. "No. But I've been known to break protocol for women who know four languages and look dangerously good in silk dresses."

She smirked. "So, you're a rebel. Wow."

"A controlled one." We turned down a quieter street, the hum of traffic fading behind us. Her thumb brushed over my knuckles. "Thank you," she said. "For what?"

"For seeing me. Like really seeing me." We stopped at the corner, the kind of moment that usually ends in a cab ride or a kiss, at least in the movies. I didn't want to rush her, or this. "I don't want to mess this up," I said quietly.

"Then don't." Her answer was simple. No fear, no conditions. I leaned down, brushing my lips against her temple. "Let me walk you home." She paused, just for a breath, then looked up at me with a small, wicked smile. "Actually…" Her fingers tightened around mine. "Can we go to your place instead?" I pulled back just enough to see her eyes.

"Are you sure?" She nodded, a little too confidently. We kept walking towards my building, with the city humming quietly below us. The lights flickered as the elevator climbed to my floor. Sam leaned against the glass, her reflection merging with the skyline.

As soon as the elevator opened, I could hear her mocking me, "Still too fancy," she said, toeing off her heels at the door, and taking her coat off. I loosened my tie. "Still too judgmental." Her laugh echoed off the walls. "You love that about me." But she was wrong.

I loved a lot more about her than that.

She wandered toward the window, hair cascading over her shoulders, silhouetted against the city glow. I tossed my jacket in the chair next to the desk and walked towards her. I pulled her against my chest and wrapped my arms around her waist. She turned in my arms, hands resting on my shirt collar. "Thank you for tonight."

"Oh, the night is far from over." I brushed her lower lip with my thumb, and her lips parted in reaction. I bent down, kissed her slowly and deeply. Without breaking the kiss, I start undoing the bow on the back of her dress, making the straps fall off her shoulders. She gasped a little at the sensation, and I took the opportunity to start kissing her neck. Her head fell back, giving me more space.

My mouth traced her collarbone, her shoulder, and I pulled her dress down, exposing her breasts. She lifted my chin, guiding my mouth to her nipple. And as soon as my tongue flicked over her nipple, she grabbed my face and kissed me.

There wasn't any softness left in her. She kissed me like she needed me, like she was waiting for this moment, and to be honest, so was I. Because it doesn't matter how romantic I wanted to be, I couldn't stop thinking about having her in my bed this whole night.

Her dress fell to the floor, and she stepped out of it without breaking eye contact with me. I started taking off my shirt, but she stopped me. "Let me." She undressed me from head to toe. It was rough and fast, but still sweet. We made our way to the bedroom, and I swear we both lost the last thread of self-control we had.

I lay her down on the bed, and she looked up at me like I was exactly what she wanted. Her hands gripped the back of my neck, pulling me down, closer to her. Her legs slid around my waist, locking me in.

There was no more teasing, no more waiting. I grabbed her, pulling her to the top of the bed, and slid down her body, landing exactly in between her legs. I grabbed her panties, and she moved up just enough for me to take them down her legs. As soon as I did, she opened her legs, inviting me in.

When she felt my mouth on her, she gasped and squirmed. I held her thighs open and licked her again. This time, she moaned. "I preferred this as a dessert rather than anything on the restaurant menu." She laughed and pulled my head closer to her. She was soaked, already on the edge.

When I sucked her clit, she lost it. Her hips were jerking a bit, her mouth was open, but she didn't scream or say anything. She just let me *enjoy* her.

I could feel her trembling. I knew she was close, so I didn't stop. Her hands were grabbing my hair, the sheets, everything she could find. Her hips were moving, closer to me, seeking the friction, and I held her down until she shattered.

I pulled up, kissing my way to her lips, licking and biting her nipples, until I reached her mouth and kissed her. Without warning, I entered her. It was slow, but deep. She gasped, her nails digging lightly into my shoulders. Her breath stuttered.

The world stilled around us. I wasn't thinking about work, or the company, or what the hell this meant. I was only thinking about the way she held me like she'd been waiting for me her whole life. We moved together in sync, our bodies instinctively aligned.

Her hips rolled, rising to meet me with every thrust. My name left her lips in a whisper, then a plea. My mouth found hers, desperate and searching, as if I couldn't just kiss her deep enough. She moaned into my mouth, and I felt that sharp, searing crack inside my chest. The one that made everything before her feel irrelevant.

I hadn't meant for this to mean anything. But with her beneath me, clutching me like I was hers, I knew I was already in too deep. This wasn't casual anymore. This wasn't a mistake. This wasn't a fling. It was something that felt a lot like falling in love with the right person.

And for the first time in years, I didn't want to stop it.

"Theo fuck, I'm close—" I thrust harder, deeper, and I could feel her clenching around me. We kept moving around the bed, and I honestly lost track of time and how many times I made her come. It was like, for a moment, sex wasn't the priority. It was her and our time together.

At some point, we fell into bed, and for a while neither of us said anything. "You okay over there?" she asked, her voice soft, teasing, but laced with curiosity, maybe even a little nervous. I glanced down and found her eyes on me. "Yeah," I said, brushing a loose wave of hair from her cheek. "Actually, more than okay."

She smiled, just barely. "You look like you've been thinking hard about something that's making you second-guess what we just did." I laughed under my breath. "You're not wrong about the thinking, but I would never second-guess any moment with you."

"Wanna share with the class, Mr. Jones?"

I hesitated. Then, "I don't know how to do this." She tilted her head. "Do what? Because let me tell you something. You absolutely know how to fuck me and how to make me come." We both laugh at her joke, but I know that's part of her defense mechanism, which means she is feeling exactly like I am.

"I meant this." I gestured between us. "You. Me. Us. I can't stop thinking about how much I want you, even when I'm having you. Literally speaking. And I keep trying to figure out if this is the smartest decision I've ever made."

She propped herself up on her elbow, staring at me like she was reading a book she didn't want to put down. "We don't have to figure it all out tonight," she said.

I reached for her hand.

"You've changed my life, Samantha."

Her fingers curled into mine.

"Then stop overthinking it and just let it happen."

CHAPTER NINETEEN

Sam

He said he was falling for me.

Not in passing. Not with his hands on me, his lips at my neck, or in the middle of sex. But across a candlelit table, wine in our glasses and laughter still on our lips. It felt real. Maybe it was the calm with which he said it, or how certain he sounded.

And I didn't run. God, I didn't even flinch. Which is something big coming from me. I used to pride myself on my ability to detach. The jet lag made it easy, and the uniforms helped. I'm used to the polite, practiced smile of someone always passing through. But there was none of that here.

Just *him*.

I could still feel the weight of his gaze when he said it. Like it wasn't a risk for him, but it was for me. Because what do you do when the man you've been pretending not to fall for confesses that he's already halfway down? You just hold your breath, but now? Now I was exhaling for the first time in a while.

I should've panicked, maybe felt cornered. But all I felt was… full.

Full of something I wasn't used to. Something that scared the shit out of me. *Hope.* That's it, that's what I felt. The risk of feeling it is that you can't unfeel it. And maybe I'm not ready to name this. Maybe I don't know if this will last. But I know what it isn't. It isn't casual anymore. It isn't forgettable. It isn't a fling.

I blinked up at the ceiling, disoriented by sunlight and softness and the arm draped across my bare waist. Theo stirred behind me, his voice groggy. "What time is it?" I turned, stealing a glance at the phone on the nightstand. "6:47," I whispered.

"Shit." He groaned and buried his face in the pillow. "No."

"Yes." I rolled out of bed in one chaotic movement, pulling the sheets with me. "We have a meeting at nine, and I need to look like I slept in my bed, not my boss's," Theo smirked. "But you did sleep in your boss's bed, actually, you did way more than that."

Before I could throw a pillow at him, a familiar voice echoed through the apartment. "Theo," Harper called from the living room. "I brought emergency supplies. You're welcome." I froze mid-sprint toward the bathroom. "You gave her a key?" I hissed.

"She gave herself one," he said, sitting up and rubbing his face. I peeked around the corner of the bedroom door. Harper stood there, impeccably dressed at seven in the morning, holding a garment bag in one hand and two coffees in the other like some kind of goddess in stilettos.

"Morning," she said without even blinking. "Sam, I guessed your size. There's a black jumpsuit and a wrap dress. Both professional. Coffees are on the counter." I stood there, speechless. "I… I love you," I finally said, grabbing the coffee and backing toward the bathroom. "Truly. Deeply."

She gave me a wink. I'd barely made it to the bathroom when I heard the rustle of paper, followed by Harper's signature I-mean-business tone. "Theodore," she said, voice sharp and clean like a scalpel. "The HR documents. Sign them. Today." My hand froze on the zipper of the jumpsuit. HR documents?

I opened the bathroom door. "What HR documents?" I asked, staring at both of them.

Harper didn't flinch. Theo, however, looked like he'd just been caught doing something bad. He cleared his throat and ran a hand through his hair. "Just… some HR formality stuff." I raised an eyebrow.

"That doesn't sound vague at all." Harper held up the envelope. "A consensual workplace relationship disclosure. You know. In case two people working together are…" she looked at both of us pointedly, "engaged in extracurricular activities that could lead to a conflict of interest or, God forbid, a lawsuit."

"You've had that ready?" She didn't miss a beat.

"I had them ready three weeks ago." Theo looked down, muttering something that sounded dangerously close to "I was going to sign it." Harper raised a single, perfectly arched brow. "Before or after your next unscheduled boardroom sex session?" I nearly choked on my coffee. Theo groaned. "Harper."

I bit back a laugh and looked between them. "So… what happens if he doesn't sign it?"

"Then you still report to him directly," Harper said simply. "Which, let's be honest, is a PR nightmare waiting to happen. If you keep doing whatever it is you're doing. It could lead to issues. On the other hand, if he signs it, you'll get reassigned to Cameron's oversight. No direct conflict there, and fewer reasons for me to have a potential aneurysm."

I blinked. "So… wait. I'd work under Cameron instead of Theo, and that's it?" Harper sipped her coffee. "Yeah, that's it." Theo rubbed his temples. "I'm going to sign it."

"Good," Harper replied, cool as ever. "Because if you don't, I'm going to text your mother." I blinked at Theo. "You're scared of your mom?" Harper answered for him. "He should be." I stepped closer, gently plucking the envelope from Harper's hand.

"Then I guess it's official," I said, smirking at Theo. "I'll be working under PR at the office, and under the CEO in bed." His mouth twitched. "Don't make that sound so nasty."

I smiled, turning back toward the bathroom. "Then stop giving me material."

By the time we pulled up to the Hayes International building, Harper had fully transitioned into her operations-overlord mode.

"Sam, you go first," she instructed, already tapping something into her phone. "Elevator bank C, use service one. Theo, you follow in 2 minutes. You'll take the main entrance." Theo raised a brow. "You've timed our entrances?"

She didn't even blink. "Down to the second. We're not running a rom-com, we're running a billion-dollar company." I hid my grin behind the rim of the coffee she'd handed me earlier. "Got it," I said, stepping out into the chaos of the Manhattan sidewalk. "Right elevator, and no eye contact."

"Exactly." Harper gave me a once-over. "And for what it's worth, you look like power today." I turned back with a wink. "That's because I slept with it." She snorted, but didn't disagree.

I walked into the sleek marble and glass oasis that was the executive floor, just in time to receive a calendar notification from Harper.

9:45 – Meeting with Cameron (PR + IB Strategy Oversight Transition) 11:30 – HR: Relationship Disclosure Documentation Review

Oh, good, my sex life has an itinerary now.

As I turned toward the hallway that led to Cameron's office, I passed Naomi by the espresso machine. She glanced up from her cup, gave me a look, then raised her brow. "You look... refreshed."

"Must be the new salary that's making me feel fancier," I quipped. She didn't respond, but the knowing smirk was all the commentary I needed. I slipped into the meeting room just as Cameron walked in, clean-cut, sharp, and already mid-sentence with someone on his AirPods. He waved, finished his call, then looked at me with a warm smile. "Samantha," he said, gesturing for me to sit. "Excited to finally work more closely."

"Same here," I said, settling in. "Though I have to admit, I wasn't expecting to be reassigned so early into the game." Cameron chuckled. "It's not personal. HR just likes a clear structure. And Harper likes preventing lawsuits."

"Both valid priorities." We exchanged a few updates about the role, his expectations, how I'd be looped into international partnerships and media relations from a strategic lens, and I realized something strange. I didn't hate it. The job, I mean. The responsibility. The sense of purpose. Maybe Rose was right. Maybe I did owe myself this. As the meeting wrapped, Harper appeared in the doorway with a new folder. "HR is ready for you."

Cameron shot me a look. "Good luck, time to make things legal."

I stood. "Wait, legal? As in paperwork? With the legal department?" I turned and, of course, Naomi was standing just outside the glass wall. Shit. Shit. Shit. "Naomi," I said, voice light. "Fancy seeing you here."

She raised an eyebrow. "You're formalizing a relationship with the CEO of Hayes International?" I shrugged one shoulder, trying to play it off. "There's a form. Harper insisted." Naomi stepped closer. "Samantha, I'm Head of Legal. And not once did this come across my desk."

"Well, maybe because it wasn't a legal, *legal* thing yet," I said quickly. "More like… HR technicalities. Like a boundary form. Or a 'please don't fire each other mid-orgasm' kind of agreement." Cameron covered a cough that sounded suspiciously like a laugh. Naomi's eyes narrowed. "This is what happens when you let inexperienced rich girls into boardrooms."

My mouth dropped open. "Excuse me?" She sighed, already annoyed that she let that one slip. "I didn't mean it like that."

"Then how did you mean it?" Harper appeared again, folder in hand like a rescue mission in four-inch heels.

"Oh, good, everyone's here. Naomi, I looped you into the doc for final review an hour ago. Check your email. And let's not derail this with sibling drama. I have actual fires to put out." Naomi didn't move, just sipped her espresso and stared at me as if it was my fault she hated me. "See you at the next family dinner," I said with a too-sweet smile, brushing past her and taking the folder from Harper like it was a shield.

Harper handed me a pen. "Sign here. Here. And here." I glanced back at Naomi, who was now muttering something to Cameron. Then I looked down at the dotted lines. What's one more scandal in a house built on them? I signed.

My phone buzzed as I stepped into the elevator. I sighed and rolled my eyes. "Yes, Max?"

"Good morning to you, too, Samantha," my dad said, his voice smooth but clipped. "Do you have a moment to talk privately?" The elevator doors closed. "I'm literally in an elevator, so sure, why not?"

"You've signed an HR agreement?" Of course, he knew. Nothing stayed quiet in this building for more than ten seconds. "I did," I said. "Because Harper handed it to me this morning, and because it's apparently a condition of sleeping with someone in this place." There was a pause.

"So you are sleeping with him, then." I squeezed my eyes shut. "Are you seriously calling me to ask about my sex life?"

"I'm calling to ask if your choices are going to jeopardize the company I built. The legacy I'm trusting you to help lead. Because sleeping around with the new CEO while being new in the company isn't exactly a way of showing respect, Samantha Nicole Hayes."

"Okay, wow." I shifted my weight, voice flat. "This is wildly inappropriate, even for you."

"Samantha—"

"No, Max. I'm not having this conversation. You don't get to have an opinion or judge me for what I do outside working hours, especially when you're the one who hired him. And, might I add, failed to mention that detail until I was already in too deep."

"This isn't about judgment—"

"Oh, really? Because it sounds a lot like judgment from the man who has had more affairs than you can count, and who, by the way, *married* one of his mistresses, who was his PR director at the time." Silence.

I exhaled slowly. "I'm doing the job you asked me to do. I'm keeping it professional where it counts. If you have a problem with that, you can talk to HR. Since apparently that's where we air out our dirty laundry now."

The elevator chimed. I stepped out. "I expect discretion," he said, tone colder. "From both of you. I don't need a headline saying that the newest CEO is sleeping around with one of Hayes' heirs."

"Then stop fueling gossip by calling me before 10 a.m. to ask if I'm fucking my boss." I hung up before he could respond. My fingers were trembling, but my spine stayed straight.

Family dinners were going to be so fun moving forward.

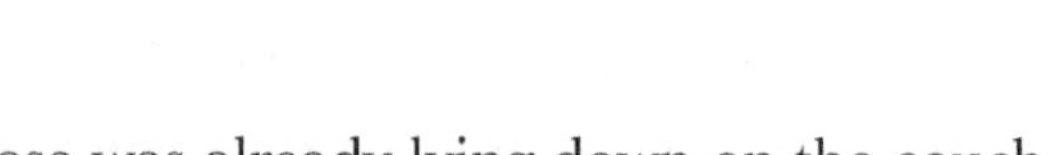

Rose was already lying down on the couch when I got home, holding a pint of overpriced matcha ice cream. I slammed the door behind me.

"My father asked if I was sleeping with *his* CEO today." She blinked. "Wow. So, we're just skipping foreplay and going straight to family trauma?" I collapsed next to her, groaning. "He called me to use the word 'jeopardize' on me, like I'm a walking HR liability."

"Well, I mean," she said in a very high pitch, "you *are* sleeping with the CEO. But he didn't need to say it."

"He said he expects discretion, that he doesn't want a headline with this information." Rose paused, then gave me the most deadpan stare imaginable. "Okay, but to be fair, you had sex with him at a work gala, Sam. And you have had office sex."

I hit her with a pillow. "You're not helping."

"I'm helping you." I took the glass and sighed. "He made me feel like I'd done something wrong. Like I was risking everything we've built for a man."

"Are you?" I hesitated.

"No. I mean, maybe, emotionally? But professionally? I'm killing it. I negotiated a logistics deal today that made Cameron fist-bump me in the hallway."

Rose smirked. "See? You can be brilliant and fuck a billionaire." We sat in silence for a moment.

"I haven't told Theo." Rose raised a brow. "About the call?" I nodded.

"Oh, he's going to be pissed."

CHAPTER TWENTY

theo

YESTERDAY WAS EASIER than I expected.

While it was one hell of a complication, I felt safer now. That was the right move. For me, for her, and for the company as a whole.

I leaned back in my chair, phone pressed to my ear, trying not to yell but fully failing at keeping my temper in check. "With all due respect, Max, you don't get to interrogate Samantha about her personal life like she's some college intern screwing around with the TA," I said, my voice was probably way sharper than I thought, but he deserves it.

"She's your daughter, not your property. And more importantly, she's a grown woman who can make her own decisions by herself without the influence of anyone, let alone yours."

A pause. Max said something smug and condescending about what was best for the company, optics, or what people were saying. I didn't care. "No," I said coldly. "This is *my* company now. You handed me the reins, remember? I'm the CEO of Hayes International, not your errand boy."

He went quiet. Good. I stood and walked toward the window, the skyline bright and smug under the morning sun. "You don't get to intimidate her, Max. Not as her father. Not as the former CEO. Not as anything."

"Careful, Theodore," he finally said. "You're getting personal." I smiled, but there was no warmth in it.

"It is personal to me." I didn't wait for him to say goodbye. I ended the call, tossed my phone on the desk, and took a slow breath, still vibrating with fury.

And then, like some perfectly timed plot twist, there was a knock. Sam. She stepped inside like she'd done it a hundred times, in wide-leg navy trousers and a silk blouse the color of my last rational thought. Her hair was down, her lips glossed, and I could only think about bending her over right here, right now.

"Bad call?" she asked softly, closing the door behind her. I ran a hand down my face. "Your father has a real talent for pushing my buttons." She exhaled, walked to my desk, and leaned against it, right where I'd had her last week, legs open, mouth full of wit and wickedness.

"Let me guess," she said. "He thinks I'm a distraction. Or a liability. Or just a girl who spread her legs for the CEO." I stared at her. "He crossed a line." She tilted her head. "Oh, he's crossed a thousand." I stepped around the desk. Closed the space between us. "Samantha," I said. "You don't have to explain anything. Not to him. Not to anyone."

"I'm not planning to," she said. But there was something in her eyes, hurt, maybe?

"I told him," I said, voice low. "That *this*, this is my company now. That he doesn't get to treat you like that, daughter or not." Something in her face softened a little. "You did?"

"I did. And I'll say it again. To anyone." She nodded slowly. "You really meant it when you signed those papers, huh?"

"Harper wouldn't let me live if I didn't. And honestly, I couldn't live with myself either." Her laugh cracked through the tension like a match. "Well. I guess we're official then."

"We are company-official," I said, stepping closer. "This still leaves room for interpretation elsewhere." She smirked, tugged at my tie. "Guess we'll have to define those terms." I leaned in and whispered in her ear, "We can start with you taking off those pants and sitting back on the desk with your legs open for me."

Her breath caught just a flicker, but I saw it. I felt it. That pulse of anticipation under the surface of her composed exterior.

She tilted her head, studying me like she was deciding how far she'd let me go. "Careful, Mr. Jones, you are being way too bossy around here." I brushed a strand of hair from her cheek and let my fingers trail down her jawline. "And you love that. Don't you?"

She didn't deny it. Instead, she stood up and started playing with her pants. The afternoon light poured in through the office windows, creating soft lines across her chest as she unbuttoned her trousers and slipped them off, folding them with care and setting them on the chair beside her.

Then she turned, hopped up onto the edge of the desk, and looked at me, daring me. "I think this is where you take over." I moved to her without hesitation, stepping between her knees, my hands sliding up her thighs as her breath hitched again.

I dropped to my knees, never breaking eye contact. Her breath caught, her thighs tensed beneath my hands, but she didn't pull away. If anything, she leaned in, inviting me closer. Her hands gripped the edge of the desk as I pressed a kiss to the inside of her thigh, then another, higher.

This wasn't just desire anymore— this was me claiming her *again*, but now on different terms.

Terms I hope she agrees on moving forward.

When my mouth finally met her, she gasped, her fingers tangling in my hair as her body responded to every stroke of my tongue. I found her rhythm fast. I knew what she wanted, and I gave it to her.

She moved against me, trying to free herself, but I held her down, firm and focused, savoring the way her body trembled under my touch. The taste of her. The feel of her losing it. This wasn't about showing off. This was about knowing her, learning every sound she made when I pushed her to the edge. And when she shattered, head thrown back, body arched, thighs trembling, I didn't stop right away.

I rose, mouth still wet with her taste, eyes locked on hers as I stood between her knees. Her breath was ragged, her chest rising and falling in sharp bursts. She looked wrecked and so beautiful. She looked like she was *mine*, and I wanted her to be.

Without a word, I undid my belt, pushed my slacks down just enough, and pulled her to the edge of the desk. She was still pulsing beneath my hands when I teased her entrance.

But it was when I pushed inside her in one deep thrust that her moan punched straight through me. I swallowed it with a kiss as I buried myself on her neck. Her body was still trembling around me from before. Her hands clutched at my shoulders, nails digging in through my shirt, and I kissed her again, hard, desperate, like I was starving for the pieces of her I didn't get last night. She broke the kiss to gasp my name, head falling back, eyes fluttering closed. And I wasn't letting go.

Not yet.

"Look at me," I said, hand at her jaw, thumb stroking her cheek. "I want you looking at me when you come again." Her eyes locked onto mine, and I swear to God, I felt her way before I even heard the sound she made.

I didn't stop. I couldn't. Not until the desk creaked under us and her body clenched around mine so tight I saw stars. I held on for one more second of madness, of us, and then I followed her over the edge with a groan that tore out of me. And as the last wave of release crashed through me, raw and consuming, I buried my face in the curve of her neck, inhaling her, anchoring myself to her.

"You are something else, Samantha," I whispered against her skin, low, wrecked, unguarded. Her fingers ran through my hair, her breath still shallow, her heart thudding loud enough I could feel it.

And then—a click.

The door opened. I forgot to lock it.

"Oh my— fuck." Harper's voice cut off like she'd walked face-first into a brick wall. Sam gasped, scrambling upright, blouse half open, her legs still tangled on my body. Harper stood in the doorway, holding a folder, looking unbothered in that terrifyingly competent way she had, but her eyes widened exactly once before narrowing.

"Sorry, I should have knocked," she said flatly. "I brought the investor brief."

"Harper—" I started, trying to reach for whatever dignity I had left. She lifted one hand. "Nope. Don't want to hear it. Just… fifteen-minute warning before your call with the Singapore team. Try not to still be inside each other when it starts."

The door clicked shut. Sam looked at me, hair

wild, cheeks flushed, her blouse completely askew. And then she started laughing, bright, breathless, incredulous. "I think I just saw Harper short-circuit," she said between laughs. I groaned and leaned forward to rest my head on her shoulder.

"We are never going to live that down." She pressed a kiss to my temple. "Better make it worth it then." I let out a half-laugh, half-sigh and looked up at her. Her smile was smug, radiant, and completely unapologetic.

She stepped down from the desk and fell to her knees in front of me. "Samantha, what are you do—"

"I told you, making it worth it", she took me into her mouth, and my head fell back. I grabbed her hair, pulling it slightly as she guided me in and out of her mouth, over and over again. I finished with a groan, pulling her hair harder and one hand on the desk.

"Well, Mr. Jones, this meeting turned into something unexpected." She said, wiping her mouth and handing me a tissue.

"I believe we're officially official now," she said, voice teasing, putting her pants back on. "I guess so."

"I can't believe Harper walked in on us mid-desk sex." We both laugh at that. "Oh, and I think I might've left a heel mark on your HR paperwork."

"Perfect," I muttered, zipping up my pants. "Exactly the kind of company culture and chaos I envisioned when I took this job."

She grinned. "Oh, admit it, you love the chaos I

bring to the table, or well, the desk." I looked at her, at the way her eyes sparkled with mischief, hair still a mess from my hands, and felt it again— that crack in my chest. The thing I hadn't planned for. The feeling I was no longer trying to deny.

"I do love the chaos," I said. "But only because it's with you."That shut her up for exactly three seconds. Then she blinked, soft and slow.

"Well, Mr. Jones, good thing I'm not going anywhere."

My phone buzzed on the corner of the desk. I glanced at it. *Singapore team, in 5 min.* Sam caught the look, groaned dramatically, and leaned back on her elbows.

"God, nothing kills a post-orgasm glow like international time zones." I stood, fixing my shirt, then leaned over to kiss her, slow, deep, with just enough bite to make her hum.

"I'll make it up to you tonight," I murmured.

Her brows lifted. "Are we talking about dinner or another HR violation?" I straightened my tie. "Why not both?" She smiled and walked away. The rest of the day was uneventful, just a bunch of meetings.

I texted Sam to come to my apartment for dinner.

Me: My place, at 7 p.m.

I'll make you dinner. How does that sound?

It was a simple invite, but my pulse didn't get the memo. I stared at the message longer than I should've before hitting send, and when she replied.

Samantha Hayes: Do you even know how to turn on an oven?

I smiled like an idiot.

Me: Guess you'll find out.

And she did.

When she knocked, I was already in the kitchen trying to make sure nothing was burning. I opened the door with probably too much confidence for a guy who had nearly set off the smoke alarm twenty minutes earlier. She stepped in, glanced around, and raised one perfectly arched brow. "You really cooked?"

"I did," I said, proud but cautious. She narrowed her eyes, taking in the scent. "Did you burn anything?"

"Not a single thing," She laughed, head back, full and unguarded, and that was worth every second of effort. The kind of laugh that made a man think of forever. Dinner wasn't elaborate. Just steak, mashed potatoes, asparagus, a bottle of wine Harper insisted I try, and a chocolate tart I'd picked up from a bakery two blocks away. "This is actually really good," she teased, cutting into the steak.

"I excel under pressure," I said, pouring her wine. "And if you finish everything, you might get dessert."

"Promise?" she grinned. "We'll see, eat up." She rolled her eyes, laughing at me.

For a moment, nothing else existed. Just her, in my space. In my orbit. Exactly where I wanted her to be. I served dessert, and after she licked chocolate off her fork and made me rethink all my life choices, I reached across the table, suddenly more serious. "Samantha." She looked up.

"Be my girlfriend." She blinked. "What is this, middle school?"

I didn't blink. "You drive me crazy, you are insanely beautiful, you look at me like I deserve you, and I want to do everything to make you keep feeling like that." Her breath hitched. "Look, I'm almost forty, I'm divorced, and I'm the CEO of a company that technically belongs to you. I'm not playing games here, not with you."

I pressed forward. "I know you are still young, with a whole lot of future ahead of you, but I want you. All of you. In my life, my days, my nights. At my dining table. In my bed. All of it."

She stood. Moved around the table. Straddled my lap with that familiar mix of power and grace that always undid me. "Took you long enough, 1A," she whispered, kissing me slowly. I curled my hand behind her neck and kissed her back. "Is that a yes?" She smiled against my mouth.

"It's a hell yes, Mr. Jones." Her '*hell yes*' was still echoing in my chest when I carried her to the couch, her laughter warm against my throat. "I thought we were aiming for soft tonight," she teased. "We are," I said, settling her down gently, "but I like soft with a view."

I lit a few candles. That, yes, Harper made me keep them stocked 'in case I ever decided to have a soul', and dimmed the lights until the room glowed golden, shadows dancing on the walls like something out of a movie. She curled into me, legs tucked beneath her, her hand pressed against my chest like she was syncing her heartbeat to mine. I wrapped an arm around her and kissed the top of her head.

"I like it here," she murmured.

"In the apartment?"

"No. Well, yeah, but in this moment, I mean." God. She didn't even know how much that wrecked me.

"You make it easy to forget everything outside of right now," I said, my voice lower than I meant. "The work. The pressure. The noise." She tilted her head up, eyes soft. "That's exactly how I feel with you." We didn't talk much after that. We didn't need to.

The playlist I'd put on shuffled into something slow and nostalgic, piano and low vocals filling the space between us.

She slid off the couch and offered her hand. "Dance with me." I stood, took her hand, and we danced. Right there in the middle of my living room, barefoot.

And I swear that was the most intimate moment we've shared so far.

CHAPTER TWENTY-ONE

Sam

We danced in his living room, and I didn't know if it was the wine, the weeks of tension, or the way he said *I want you* like it was a promise, but something cracked open in me. And when he carried me to the bed, something settled too.

He undressed me with care. There was no rush this time, no hunger. He just seemed in awe of me. As if every inch of skin revealed were a secret, I was letting him keep it. And when he kissed me, his hands framing my face, I swear the world disappeared. "Are you okay?" he whispered, already inside the moment, but waiting for my yes. I nodded, breath catching. "More than okay."

We moved together as if it were always meant to be this way. No fight for control, no game to play, just warmth, trust. Skin on skin, heart to heart. I traced the lines of his shoulders, felt his muscles shift under my touch. He looked down at me like I was something sacred.

Like I was *his*.

And that's when I felt him, pushing into me, slow, deep, almost grounding me. I gasped into his mouth. It wasn't lust that stole my breath. We weren't just having sex this time.

This was different. Something I've never felt with him until now. Now that I think about it, I haven't felt this with anyone before him.

His body moved against mine with a rhythm that felt like music, slow, sure, and steady. I wrapped my arms around his back, fingers pressing into his skin like I could anchor myself to the moment. To *him*.

He kissed me again, as I rolled my hips to meet his moves. And this time, it was less about wanting or desire. It was more about being there, present in this exact moment. His lips brushed mine, soft moans and hushed gasps escaping between us as our foreheads pressed together, our breath mingling in the space that had grown impossibly small between us.

"I don't want to stop feeling like this," I whispered, not even meaning the sex, though that was incredible, but the softness of it. The surrender. "You won't," he said, his voice rough with emotion. "I'm here. I'll always be here. If you want me."

I believed him. Not because he promised me anything, but because of the way he held me. Like I wasn't a secret anymore or a mistake. Like I was something he'd been searching for. Which says a lot about an almost forty divorced man.

I cupped his jaw as his pace slowed, more a rocking now than thrusting, every movement drawing me deeper into the safety of him. I felt the tremble in his shoulders when I whispered his name, felt the way he shuddered as I kissed his throat. "I want you." And when I came, it was quiet, trembling, overwhelmed by all the sensations. He followed seconds later, burying his face in my neck as he gasped my name like a vow.

Something like… *love*?

"Are you tired?" he asked softly, fingers trailing down my arm. "Not really," I murmured, shifting so my cheek rested against his chest. "I feel like if I fall asleep, I'll miss it."

"Miss what?"

"This," I whispered. He hummed low in his throat. "I'm yours, Samantha. I'm not going anywhere."

"I know," I said, even if a small part of me didn't. But it felt right. He felt right. Theo turned his head slightly, resting his chin against the top of mine.

"Tell me something I don't know." I smiled against his skin. "I still don't know how to fold a fitted sheet." He chuckled. "No one does."

"Your turn." He was quiet for a moment. "I'm scared to ruin this." My breath caught. "Why?"

"Because I haven't been in a serious relationship for a while, and the last one, well, it didn't end with a happily ever after." I lifted my head to look at him.

"First of all, that wasn't your fault. And you have nothing to worry about with me. You haven't ruined anything."

"I hope I don't," he said, brushing a knuckle along my jaw. "It's just that… You matter to me. Way more than I expected. And I don't want to do anything that would jeopardize it."

"You won't," I said, threading my fingers through his. "Just don't stop showing up." His eyes softened. "Deal." We lay there for a long time after that, fingers laced, hearts slower, the weight of our honesty settling gently over the bed like a second blanket.

And when I finally closed my eyes, sleep came easily, for the first time in a very long time.

Sunlight spilled in through the curtains, brushing warm gold across the white sheets and the edge of Theo's jaw. I blinked slowly, letting the moment settle before moving. His arm was draped over my waist, heavy with sleep, and his chest rose and fell in a rhythm that made me want to stay right where I was forever.

I turned onto my side carefully, watching him. His hair was a little messy, his lips parted just slightly, the kind of peace you only ever get to see when someone trusts you enough to be vulnerable in their sleep. I'd never seen him like this, soft. He stirred a little, and his eyes opened, slow and lazy. "Morning," he said, voice raspy and barely awake.

"Morning," I whispered back, smiling. He tightened his arm around me, burying his face in my neck. "What time is it?" I glanced at the clock on the nightstand. "Not even seven. We've got time."

"Mmm." He kissed the curve of my shoulder. "Stay." His thumb traced small circles against my hip under the blanket. My leg hooked over his. Every now and then, one of us would smile for no reason at all. Eventually, he whispered, "I like waking up like this."

"Like what?"

"With you here. In my bed. In my arms."

My heart fluttered. "Yeah. Me too."

"Let's make it a habit." I laughed softly. "Careful, Mr. Jones, that sounds dangerously close to you wanting a long-term commitment."

He smirked. "I'm not afraid of that. Not with you." He kissed my forehead, then my cheek, lingering for a breath longer than usual. I felt the smile still on my lips, the warmth between us undisturbed, cocooned in sheets, and something more than comfort. His voice was quiet when he said it, but steady. "Move in with me."

My smile faltered, eyes blinking open. "What?" He propped himself up on one elbow, brushing a strand of hair away from my face.

"I'm serious, Sam." I sat up slightly, heart skipping once, maybe twice.

"We just made this official like five minutes ago."

"Well, that was you. I made it official when I saw you enter the building and figured out I had feelings for you," he said so effortlessly.

"Last night wasn't just about sex. Not for me. And this, waking up to you, it's not something I want to keep doing part-time." I stared at him, searching for the catch. The edge. The control. But there wasn't any. Just honesty.

"I know it's fast," he added, softer now. "And I don't expect an answer right this second. But I meant what I said last night, I'm not playing games. I want you here. In this bed. In this life. By my side."

I reached out, fingers tangling gently in his. "I didn't take you for a romantic man, but you have surprised me." That earned a crooked grin.

"And you," I whispered, pulling him in for a kiss, "are very good at ruining my plans for emotional detachment."

He kissed me back, and we got ready for the day.

"Wait. Back up." Rose dropped the half-folded sweater she was holding and turned toward me, eyes wide.

"He said what?" I flopped dramatically onto her bed. "Move in with me."

"No. No, no, no. You don't just drop that into conversation like it's 'pass the salt.' Are you kidding me? He asked you to move in? As in… toothbrush in the same cup? Shared laundry baskets? Groceries together?"

"Okay, calm down," I said, staring up at the ceiling like it might offer answers. "It wasn't like a big, dramatic proposal. We were literally in bed, and he just kind of… said it."

"Naked in bed after amazing sex the previous night is the worst time to make real estate decisions, Sam." I laughed. "You sound like my subconscious." She grabbed a throw pillow and smacked me with it. "I'm your subconscious. So? What did you say?"

"I didn't say yes," I admitted. "But I didn't say no either." Rose stared at me for a beat, then sat beside me, folding her legs up.

"Do you want to?" I sighed, tugging the pillow under my arm. "That's the part that's freaking me out. Because… yeah. I think I do."

"Oh my god."

"I know."

"You are in love with him," she said in a teasing singsong voice. I groaned. "That's terrifying, but yeah, I think I am."

"Samantha Hayes," she said, holding up a finger. "You are in love with a man who cooks you dinner, makes you laugh, and makes you come so hard you forget your name." I gave her a look. "Thanks for the poetic recap."

"I'm just saying," she added more gently, "sometimes the best decisions don't come with a five-year plan. Sometimes it's just about the person. And if he's the kind of man who makes you feel safe when everything else is not, maybe it's worth saying yes." I blinked at her. "When did you get so wise?"

She shrugged. "Somewhere between tequila shots and dating emotionally unavailable DJs." We both laughed, and I lay my head on her shoulder.

"You will say yes," she said. "I can hear it in your voice."

On Sunday night, I didn't call or text him to ask if I could come over, because if I did, I might chicken out. If I hesitated for even a second, I'd start thinking about how insane this was. About how fast things were moving. About what it meant. So instead, I went to his apartment and knocked on his door. To my surprise, when I tried to open it, the door slid open.

Theo looked up from the kitchen island, where a half-empty glass of wine sat next to his open laptop. He froze when he saw me. Then his eyes dropped to the suitcase in my hand. To the overnight bag slung over my shoulder. To me, standing there with a heartbeat so loud I could barely hear myself speak when I finally said… "Yes."

He blinked. "What?" I set the bag down, hard.

"I also want my days with you, my mornings in your bed, and my coffee in your kitchen." For a long, quiet moment, he didn't move. He didn't speak. Then, just like that, his face cracked into that boyish smile I'd fallen for a hundred times already.

He came toward me without hesitation, wrapped his arms around my waist, and lifted me clean off the floor. "You're really doing this?" he murmured into my neck, voice almost disbelieving.

"Yeah," I whispered back. "I'm all in."

He set me down, cupped my face in both hands, and kissed me like he already knew this was forever.

CHAPTER TWENTY-TWO

theo

THE ELEVATOR DOORS slid open with a soft chime, and for the first time, I didn't step into Hayes International alone. Sam was beside me, sleek in navy, confident as ever. A vision of calm until you looked closer, then you'd see the slight twitch of her fingers, the way she flexed them at her side like she was rolling the nerves out. I brushed her knuckles with mine.

"You okay?"

"I'm walking into a boardroom where my father, sister, and my boyfriend-slash-CEO will all be sitting. What could possibly be stressful about that?" I smirked. "You forgot Harper."

"Harper doesn't scare me." She laughed, and we walked down the hall, past curious glances from staff who didn't need a memo to know something had changed. I was aware, too, how natural it felt to arrive like this, with her. How *right*.

9:30 a.m. sharp.

Harper opened the boardroom door for us. Naomi sat at the far end, arms crossed. Nico winked at Sam. Cameron gave a quick nod. Max was already sipping espresso, flanked by two VPs who looked like they'd just stepped out of a yacht catalog. HR reps were poised, folders ready. And Pascal, Sam's new assistant, was bright-eyed, borderline terrified.

Everyone looked up. "Morning," I said, settling at the head of the table with Sam to my right. "Let's get started." Chairs shuffled, the conversations finished, and the door clicked shut.

"This will be brief," I began.

"Effective last Friday, my relationship with Samantha Hayes, your International Business Strategist, was formally disclosed, cleared by HR, and reviewed by legal. There will be no gossip about our relationship, no rumors, and I expect no issues. This is our personal lives, not part of the business. We all do our jobs, and we move forward."

Max cleared his throat and leaned back in his chair. "We were briefed that HR and legal approved that you sleep with your Strategist, not that you are in a formal, or soon-to-be-married serious type of relationship? What the hell did I miss?"

A few nervous whispers. Naomi rolled her eyes so hard I was surprised they didn't get stuck.

But I didn't hesitate. I looked right at Sam and smiled at her like asking for forgiveness because I might need it later.

"Well, you didn't miss anything, because to be frank, it's none of your business, or anybody else's. But just so we are all clear. Yes. We are in a serious relationship, and marriage will come whenever she's ready for it."

Silence. Every head turned to me, then to her. Sam blinked, her mouth opening just slightly like she wanted to say something, but she had forgotten how to speak. Nico let out a slow whistle. Naomi muttered something about needing stronger HR documents. Cameron whispered, "Holy shit." And Harper, Harper just sipped her coffee and smirked like she'd known it all along.

The moment the door closed behind the last VP, I felt it, Sam's stare. It burned hotter than any boardroom spotlight. She stood slowly, not saying a word, heels clicking with purpose as she walked toward me.

"My office, now," she said under her breath, low and lethal.

I followed without protest. Once inside, she shut the door behind us. She didn't wait for me to say anything before she turned on her heel. "Are you fucking insane?"

I leaned against the edge of her desk, arms crossed. "About which part? The 'that's none of your business', or the marriage comment?"

Her eyes widened. "The marriage comment. Theodore Jones, what the fuck?"

"You didn't like it?" I asked, even though I already knew the answer. But I also knew she didn't hate it either. Sam paced once, then turned back to me, hands flying to her temples. "You dropped a future marriage proposal into a boardroom with my father, my sister, and half the executive team. Do you understand how insane that is? Even if it was a joke to shut him up."

"Samantha," I said, stepping closer, "I wasn't joking. This is no one's business but ours. I said what I meant, and I'm not trying to scare you—"

"Well, you did. You scared everyone. Naomi is probably drawing up a prenup as we speak." I smiled. "Then let her. I'd sign it. Gladly."

That stopped her. Just long enough for the blush to creep into her cheeks, and her fingers to falter at her sides. "This is serious to me," I added, voice softer now. "You, us. This is not a power play. This is not some PR stunt. I'm fucking in love with you, Samantha, and I want to be honest about that, even when it's inconvenient for some."

She stared at me, chest rising and falling, like she was deciding whether to kiss me or kill me.

Finally, she exhaled. "You can't ask me to sign HR papers, to be your girlfriend, to move in, to tell me you are in love with me, in the same week. It's too much."

"I know, and I'm sorry. But, you need to know something." I stepped in and slid a hand around her waist.

"What now, Theodore?" I leaned in, lips brushing

her ear. "I meant every word. I'm in love with you, and I want you. Today and always."

After she left my office less furious, my cellphone buzzed.

Nico: DID YOU JUST PROPOSE IN A CORPORATE MEETING????

Me: Technically, no.

Nico: "marriage will come whenever she's ready for it."

Bro. That's a proposal with a delayed delivery window.

Me: It was... I— whatever.

Nico: You just hard-launched a marriage like it was a new product line.

Also, Max looked like he was going to throw a chair. I LIVE for this energy.

Thanks for hiring me.

Me: He'll be fine. HR cleared it. Legal approved. And she didn't stab me after, so we're doing great.

Nico: I'm going to need front-row seats to that wedding.

Or at least be allowed to plan your bachelor party.

Vegas.

Fireworks.

Or a camel.

Me: Why is there always a camel in your plans?

Nico: Because you're my best friend and I believe in dramatic entrances. Which you deserve.

Me: I'll let Sam know she should mentally prepare for that.

Nico: She already has. She's dating you, man.

An email from Naomi comes up. That's new.

SUBJECT: RE: THIS MORNING'S MEETING
FROM: NAOMI HAYES (HEAD OF LEGAL)
TO: THEODORE JONES (CEO)
TIME: 9:12 AM

MR. JONES,

WHAT. THE ACTUAL. FUCK.

DID YOU JUST DROP A FUTURE MARRIAGE ANNOUNCEMENT IN A 9:30 A.M. CROSS-DEPARTMENT MEETING LIKE IT WAS A QUARTERLY SALES UPDATE?

I WAS SIPPING MY DAMN OAT MILK LATTE, PREPARING TO TALK ABOUT THE NEW EU COMPLIANCE CLAUSE, AND YOU BLINDSIDE ME WITH "THAT'S COMING WHENEVER SHE'S READY."

YOU'RE LUCKY HR DIDN'T COMBUST IN REAL TIME. AND MAX—OH, MAX—LOOKED LIKE HE HAD AGED THREE FISCAL YEARS.

FOR THE RECORD, I DON'T CARE THAT YOU'RE DATING MY SISTER. I DO CARE THAT YOU'VE TURNED OUR COMPANY'S ALL-HANDS INTO A SOFT LAUNCH FOR YOUR PERSONAL LIFE. YOU'D BETTER BRING DONUTS TO LEGAL THIS WEEK. AND A SIGNED HR FORM. AND MAYBE A RING AT THIS POINT? JUST SAYING.

NAOMI HAYES - HEAD OF LEGAL

P.S. PASCAL IS ALREADY DRAFTING A STATEMENT BECAUSE, APPARENTLY, PEOPLE IN MARKETING ARE PLACING BETS.

- - - - -

SUBJECT: RE: THIS MORNING'S MEETING
FROM: THEODORE JONES (CEO)
TO: NAOMI HAYES (HEAD OF LEGAL)
TIME: 9:15 AM

NAOMI,

I'LL ADMIT, MAYBE THE TIMING WAS... DRAMATIC. BUT IF I HAVE TO LISTEN TO TWELVE MORE WHISPERS, "IS THAT THE HAYES GIRL HE'S SLEEPING WITH?" WHILE TRYING TO TALK ABOUT EBITDA, I'LL LOSE MY MIND. CONSIDER THIS MORNING'S ANNOUNCEMENT STRATEGIC PREEMPTIVE DAMAGE CONTROL.

ALSO, FOR THE RECORD, HR DIDN'T COMBUST BECAUSE THEY WERE PRE-WARNED. HARPER THRIVES ON CHAOS. YOU, OF ALL PEOPLE, SHOULD RESPECT THE EFFICIENCY OF RIPPING THE BAND-AID OFF.

REGARDING THE RING: CALM DOWN. I'M NOT PROPOSING ON THE COMPANY LETTERHEAD. YET. PASCAL'S DRAFT STATEMENT BETTER NOT INCLUDE EMOJIS.

DONUTS ARE INCOMING. LEGAL'S PREFERRED ORDER IS STILL THE OBNOXIOUSLY SPECIFIC BOX FROM THAT PLACE ACROSS THE BRIDGE, YES? WARMEST REGARDS AND ABSOLUTELY NO REGRETS,

THEODORE JONES, CEO (AND APPARENTLY SOON-TO-BE YOUR BROTHER-IN-LAW, ACCORDING TO YOUR EMAIL)

P.S. I'LL START TAKING BETS IF MARKETING IS OFFERING DECENT ODDS.

I had barely hit send when I heard the distinct clack of heels slicing through the hallway carpet like a judge's gavel. The knock was perfunctory. The door opened before I could answer. Naomi stepped in with her phone in her hand, thumb scrolling. "Donuts are incoming?" she read aloud, lips twitching.

I leaned back in my chair. "I figured you'd want to emotionally carb-load before you light me on fire." She laughed, actually laughed, then closed the door behind her and dropped into the chair across from me like she owned the place. Because, to be fair, she kind of did.

"Seriously, though," she said, tossing her phone on my desk. "You just casually drop the marriage line like that?"

"I didn't drop anything," I said, picking up her phone to hand it back. "I answered a question. Max made an insinuation. I clarified."

"You clarified that you plan to marry the

company founder's daughter, your subordinate, in a room full of VPs, assistants, and HR?" I smirked. "Only if and when she's ready for it."

Naomi stared at me for a beat. Then, she crossed one leg over the other and shook her head. "I don't know whether to punch you or write you an endorsement for having the biggest balls in the corporate world."

"Put both in the article, please," I said, grabbing the coffee Harper had abandoned on my desk earlier. She gave me that look again, equal parts exasperated and entertained. "You're serious about her."

"I am."

"And you're not just saying that because she is young, smart, etc?" I raised a brow. "No, but she is all that. Also beautiful and an amazing woman."

Naomi sighed, her face softening just slightly. "Okay, I'll back off. But only if you swear to run the actual company as well as you're apparently running your love life." I raised my coffee. "That's the plan."

She stood up, grabbing her phone. "Fine. I'll review the fallout from the HR announcement and prep legal for gossip damage control."

"Want a donut?"

"Only if you got the lavender cardamom one."

"You're so annoying." She winked. "And yet, I'm your second favorite Hayes." As she left, Harper passed her in the hallway, holding a pink box and a mug that read 'Queen of Compliance'.

I couldn't help but smile.

God help me, I might actually be enjoying this whole Hayes chaos.

CHAPTER TWENTY-THREE

Sam

PASCAL POKED his head through the door like a spy in a sitcom.

"Naomi's here for you," he whispered dramatically. "Should I stall with coffee or make an excuse?" I smiled. "It's fine. Let her in." Naomi stepped into my office with a caution I hadn't seen on her before. She looked less like the Head of Legal and more like just my sister.

Which is bizarre.

Her blazer was perfectly tailored, her expression perfectly unreadable. But I caught the faint trace of a smile beneath all that polish. She shut the door behind her. "You okay?" she asked, no preamble, no sarcasm. I blinked. "Define 'okay.'"

She gave me a look. "Well, Jones kind of proposed in front of a dozen executives, our dad tried to turn it into a press headline, and now HR and Legal are probably running emergency drills in case one of you accidentally announces a wedding date. So are you, okay?"

I snorted. "Yeah, that sums it up. Nope, I'm not okay." Naomi sat in the chair across from my desk and crossed one leg over the other, like we were back in the living room at our childhood house, talking late into the night with wine and whispered secrets. "For what it's worth," she said, "you handled it well."

"By turning the color of a tomato and forgetting how to blink?"

"You didn't run." Her voice softened. "That's progress." There was a pause. A kind of quiet that felt like a mutual breath. I leaned back in my chair. "I didn't expect him to say that. At all."

"Did you expect him to care that much?" Naomi asked, but there wasn't judgment in her tone, just curiosity. I hesitated. "I think… I hoped." She nodded slowly. "I know we're not always the warmest family, Samantha. But I see the way he looks at you. I don't think this is some reckless fling." That surprised me. Not the observation, well, that too, but also the gentleness in her saying it.

"I always thought you hated him," I said.

"I don't hate him. I hated the idea of you being the CEO's secret. Or worse, a scandal for us all. That's part of both my jobs. Older sister and Head of Legal." Her voice faltered just a little. "But I don't want you to be alone in this company, or this family, just because it's easier for everyone else."

And there it was. I swallowed the lump forming in my throat. "Thank you. I really appreciate that."

Naomi gave me a small smile. "Just don't make me be your maid of honor." I laughed. "No worries on that one." She stood, smoothing down her skirt. "Come to lunch with me next week? Just us?"

I nodded. "Yeah. I'd like that." As she walked out, I felt the weight of years begin to shift, just slightly. The distance that had grown between us wasn't gone, but maybe, *just maybe*, we were building a bridge back to something worth keeping.

As soon as the door clicked shut behind Naomi, I reached for my phone and fired off a text to Rose.

Me: You are NOT going to believe the last 20 minutes of my life.

The typing dots popped up immediately. Of course they did.

Rose: Tell me you didn't elope with Mr. tall, broody & inexplicably sexy bossman.

Me: No. But Theo kinda proposed, and Naomi just came to my office.

Like, willingly. And sat down. And asked if I was OK.

Then said she doesn't hate Theo.

And she wants to have lunch. Just us.

Rose: Wait, WHAT THE FUCK?

Is she feeling okay? Any signs of fever? Head trauma?

Also, are YOU okay????????

Me: I KNOW.

It was actually… nice? Like, scary nice. Like she was my sister, not the Head of Legal sent to ruin my life.

Rose: Plot twist: she's been body-snatched.

Either way, I'm proud of you both. And I'm thrilled she didn't passive-aggressively call you a liability.

But, can we go back to the 'kinda proposed' part? I'm lost.

Me: SO, we were in a meeting, and Max made a comment after Theo announced our relationship.

And then he casually mentioned something about a marriage proposal for whenever I'm ready for it.

Rose: OMG!!! Is this the same man who said he wouldn't do this again?

Me: Yup, that same man.

Rose: OMG, I'm in awe.

I'm so happy for you, but also PLEASE MAKE ME MAID OF HONOR.

Me: There's no wedding!!!!!!!

yet.

Rose: YET?!

ME: Bye.

I have to work.

Rose: UGHHHHH!!!!!!!!!!!!

I grinned at the screen, heart still a little tangled but lighter than it had been all week. Maybe this was the beginning of something real—messy, complicated, utterly unexpected, but real.

The rest of the afternoon passed in soft focus.

I wrapped up a few reports, answered a dozen emails, and made edits on a draft Naomi had flagged. I wasn't racing the clock like usual. I wasn't counting the hours. I was just… working. Living. Sitting in my office with a matcha latte that Pascal had made exactly how I liked it.

And at the back of my mind, under the spreadsheets and strategy decks, there was this warm hum of something right. Something that felt like a future I hadn't dared let myself imagine until recently. I caught myself smiling at nothing more than the pale green swirl of foam in my mug.

Maybe it was reckless to feel this way. To feel *safe* and *seen*. But I did. And despite all my defenses, all my past lives, all the reasons I'd built walls so high even I got dizzy near the top, I wanted *this*.

I wanted *him*. I wanted what we were building.

Even if it scared the shit out of me.

By six-thirty, I was packing up my things, folding my coat over my arm, and heading home—to his place. Well, our place now. It still felt strange calling it that, but when I slid my key into the door and stepped inside, I immediately inhaled the scent of him. Cedar and something sharp and clean wrapped around me.

I set my bag down. Took off my heels. Poured a glass of water and walked into the bathroom. I needed a bath like I needed sleep and oxygen.

The water filled slowly, steam curling up the tiles as I added some of the fancy lavender soak. I tied my hair up, slipped into the water, and let it take me under, just enough to quiet the world.

By the time I heard the front door open, my limbs were boneless. The kind of soft that only came after surviving a chaotic, beautiful day.

"Samantha?" Theo's voice echoed down the hallway.

"In here," I called out, too blissed out to pretend I wasn't halfway to heaven in a cloud of bubbles. I heard his steps. Then the creak of the bathroom door. He stood there, loosened his tie around his neck, sleeves rolled up, eyes raking over me as if he had just walked into a dream he didn't want to wake from. "Well, this is one hell of a welcome home."

"Rough day?" I asked, stretching a foot above the waterline with a smirk. He was already undoing the buttons of his shirt. "Not anymore." I bit back a grin as he stepped out of his clothes, climbed in behind me, and pulled me back against his chest. The heat of him soaked into me, wrapping around every tired muscle, every fragile thought. His arms looped around my waist. His lips pressed against the crook of my neck.

For a while, we didn't say anything. And then he whispered, "You didn't hate it, the proposal comment?"

"No," I whispered. "I kind of loved it. Watching everyone's jaws hit the floor was deeply satisfying." He grabbed my head and kissed me. The other hand slipped to my thigh under the water. His fingers felt light on my skin. "Still want this?" he asked quietly, as if he needed to be sure.

I turned fully in his arms, straddling him as the water splashed gently around us. My hands cupped his face. "I do." And then I kissed him, slow and deep. We stayed there until the bathwater went cold.

Theo's hands slid beneath the water, gripping my waist as I moved against him. The tension that usually lived between us, always sharp and electric, shifted into something tender. He let me take the lead for once, his eyes dark but steady, patient in the way he waited for what I wanted to give.

The water moved as I pressed closer. Our skin was slick and warm. I could feel his breath hitch when my hips rolled against his, feel the tight restraint in his fingers when I leaned forward and kissed the corner of his mouth. His response was a low hum against my throat as he trailed kisses down my neck. I held his face between my hands, fingers brushing along his jaw.

Everything about him felt both impossibly familiar and endlessly new. We weren't hiding anymore. No boardroom doors. No dimmed glass.

I lifted myself slightly, guiding him with ease. The water surged between us for one suspended heartbeat, and then he was inside me. Our gasp was shared. A quiet inhale that bound the moment in stillness. He buried his face in my shoulder, hands steadying my hips as we found our rhythm, not rushed or frantic, but slow and certain.

Every movement was a promise; every touch layered in memory and hope and the kind of ache that didn't just belong to lust. His voice was quiet. Rough. "I love you, Samantha." I smiled, forehead against his. "I love you too."

We moved together until nothing else existed but the heat between us and the sound of water lapping gently against porcelain.

Afterward, I curled into him, our skin damp and warm, our breath tangled in the quiet. "I like this version of us," I murmured.

His arms wrapped tighter around me. "So do I."

I woke to the scent of something warm and buttery drifting in from the kitchen, sunlight spilling across the hardwood floors like it belonged there, like I did too.

My body still hummed from last night, from the way Theo had held me like I was something rare. Something he didn't want to let go of. Padding into the kitchen wearing one of his button-down shirts, unbuttoned just enough to be a little bit teasing.

I found him standing barefoot, hair a mess, flipping something golden in a pan. He looked over his shoulder and grinned like I was the sunrise. "You're awake."

"You're cooking," I teased. "Again."

"I'm proving I'm a man of many talents."

"I've... seen your talents." He laughed, low and rough, and handed me a mug of coffee without asking how I take it. He knew now. And maybe that's what hit me hardest. The way he was already folded into my mornings, my rhythms.

"You okay?" he asked after a beat, eyes meeting mine over the rim of his mug. I nodded, then leaned against the counter, fingers playing with the hem of his shirt. "I think I've been waiting for the other shoe to drop. But it's the morning. You're here. I'm here. We're… good."

Theo stepped closer, brushing a strand of hair from my face. "You don't have to keep waiting for things to fall apart. We get to be good."

God, I wanted to believe that. "I think I'm starting to accept that," I said quietly.

He kissed my forehead. "You don't have to rush into believing in us. Let's take it slow." I kissed him back, light, sweet, barely there. "You're making it very easy to believe. But we're definitely not taking it slow." We laughed and ate breakfast standing up, stealing bites off each other's plates and arguing about which pastry place in the city was better. He let me win. I let him think I didn't notice.

And as I got dressed for the office, watching him move around our apartment, our home, I realized something.

This felt like the beginning of a forever I hadn't dared to imagine before.

CHAPTER TWENTY-FOUR

theo

Eight weeks later.

Eight weeks in, and I'm still not used to waking up next to her without reaching out to make sure she is real. She's tangled in my sheets, stealing all the pillows, skin sun-tanned and soft from that weekend we'd spent with Rose and her new man in Montauk.

She'd fallen asleep last night talking about ideas for the next international campaign Hayes could run, her head on my chest and her fingers drawing slow, absent-minded circles over my ribs. I'd never known peace could come like this, quiet and golden and entirely her.

In eight weeks, she has met my mom and stepdad and re-bonded with Elena as if they were long-lost sisters. We've spent a couple of weekends at their house, and by now it feels like she's been visiting them for years.

She knew Nico too well for my own good now. He called her "trouble," and I don't even argue. They are now practically best friends. Which I appreciate.

We'd had dinner at the Hayes compound twice. I sat across from Max and watched him watch me with his youngest daughter, my girlfriend. It wasn't exactly comfortable. But it wasn't war, either. And in this family? That counted for something.

Sam had changed everything. I barely noticed the shift until I was fully in it. Which is why I booked two first-class tickets to Paris, 1A and 1B. A nod to where it started. A reminder that some stories like ours can happen anywhere. Tonight, I'll surprise her.

But for now, she was sleeping. And I was in love with her, with us, with this version of my life that finally felt like it had room for more than work, legacy, and expectation.

It felt like it needed to have *her*.

"No one needs six pairs of heels for a weekend in Paris," I told her. "Bold of you to assume that Mr. Jones," she shot back, tossing one more silky dress into her bag. She looked so damn happy. Glowing, really. And I could tell between her excitement and the way her fingers lingered on her passport cover, that she had missed this.

The airport was buzzing in that way Sam always loved.

She moved through it with ease, like the floor

belonged to her, like she could still slip into that part of herself when she wanted to. I trailed just behind her with our carry-ons, watching every flicker of joy in her eyes. It made my chest feel too tight— in the best way.

First class felt different this time.

We drank champagne before takeoff, "The whole cart, please," Sam joked, clicking her glass to mine. We watched a ridiculous action movie, half-cuddled under the plush blanket. She kept stealing bites of my dessert even though she had her own. I didn't stop her. I wouldn't dare.

When the cabin lights dimmed, and the hum of the plane settled into a lull, she rested her head on my shoulder and whispered, "You planned this whole thing just to see me in a trench coat, didn't you?"

"Maybe. Only if you are not wearing anything under it." She giggled, her hand sliding into mine. I kissed her knuckles one by one, and for a while, we just sat there, flying thirty thousand feet above reality, in our own little bubble.

By the time the plane started its descent, I couldn't tell what felt more surreal, Paris or her.

The car ride from the airport was quiet, Paris blurring past the window, her hand still tucked in mine. Sam didn't talk much, but she kept glancing over at me with that half-smile she gave when she didn't want to admit she was very happy about something.

I'd booked a suite. Floor-to-ceiling windows. A view of the Eiffel Tower that looked like a dream. The moment she walked in, she dropped her bag and just stared. "Oh, come on," she breathed. "You're trying to ruin every hotel for me."

I stepped behind her, wrapped my arms around her waist, and whispered, "Wait until you see the room service menu."

She turned in my arms, already smiling. "You're such a show-off."

"Nah," I said, brushing my lips to hers. "I'm just in love." That shut her up in the best way. We spent the afternoon wandering the Musée d'Orsay. Sam lingered longest in front of the Impressionists, eyes tracing the light, the brushwork, the emotion. I watched her more than I watched the art. There was something about seeing her here, surrounded by the world she loved, that made everything feel even more real.

After, we stopped for macarons and champagne. She made me rank the flavors, even though she already knew pistachio would win. She kissed me in a side street just because the cobblestones were cute. We held hands without thinking about it.

That night, I surprised her with a late-night Eiffel Tower tour. Just us, the twinkling lights, and a few tourists too in awe to care about anyone else. Sam looked up and whispered, "It's stupid how magical this place still is."

I kissed her shoulder. "There's nothing stupid about magic."

She didn't say anything, just leaned her head on my chest and let out the softest sigh. Like she finally let herself believe that all of this, me, Paris, us, might actually be safe to want. She leaned on the railing of the observation area, hair dancing in the breeze, cheeks flushed from champagne and laughter.

"You know," she said, glancing back at me, "this is almost too perfect. Suspiciously so."

I stepped beside her, heart pounding like I hadn't felt in years. "Suspicious, huh?" I echoed. She laughed. "Like, what's next? Fireworks? A flash mob? A hidden violinist?"

"No," I said, reaching into my coat pocket, fingers brushing velvet. "Just this."

She turned fully toward me, teasing, smiling, fading, eyes searching mine as I dropped to one knee.

"Samantha Nicole Hayes," I said, voice low, steady, certain. "Every time I try to think about when it was that I fell in love with you, my mind always comes back here. To Paris. To our last night together."

Her hand flew to her mouth, and her eyes were shining. "Oh my God, Theo…"

"I want to fall asleep next to you and wake up with you by my side. I want to build a life with you. So, I have a question for you…"

I opened the small box, revealing a simple, elegant, and timeless ring, just like her. "Will you give me the honor of being your husband?" Tears filled her eyes. She didn't speak right away, just dropped to her knees too, in front of me, laughing through the tears as she cupped my face.

"Yes," she whispered. "A thousand times, yes."

We kissed under the lights of Paris, her arms around my neck, the ring already on her finger.

Somewhere below, people cheered. But at that moment, it felt like we were alone in the city of love.

And she said *yes*.

We walked back to the hotel slowly, laughing at nothing and everything at once, occasionally stopping for more kisses than were probably appropriate. But we were in the most romantic city in the world. It felt allowed.

She couldn't stop looking at her ring, and I couldn't stop looking at *her*.

Back at the hotel, Paris was still glittering beyond the windows, but nothing compared to her. Not the skyline, not the moonlight, not even the ring now glinting on her hand.

We were barely inside the room when her mouth found mine. Her fingers were in my hair, tugging hard. My hands gripped her thighs, lifting her until her legs wrapped around my waist.

"This dress," I muttered, teeth grazing her jaw, "is coming off."

"Then rip it," she gasped, hips already grinding into me. I didn't hesitate. The zipper went down, and I peeled the silk off her, revealing her soft skin and the lace beneath. She is so beautiful, and now she has agreed to be *mine*.

I carried her to the bed, tossed her down, and followed, pulling my shirt over my head, belt hitting the floor with a thud. She arched up on her elbows. "You gonna make love to your fiancée like a gentleman?"

I shook my head slowly, climbing over her. "No, not tonight."

I gripped her hips, dragging her to the edge of the bed. She gasped as I flipped her onto her stomach, her ass high, back arched. "God, Theo." I leaned over her, lips to her ear. "You want it rough, sweetheart, or do you want it sweet? Tell me."

"Rough," she breathed. "Please."

I slide down her lace panties, and then I was inside her in a single, brutal thrust. She cried out, but I held her. One hand at her waist, the other splayed across her back, grounding her. "Still good?" She nodded frantically, pushing her hips back against me.

"Don't stop." She met me every time, no hesitation, no restraint.

So, I didn't. I thrust into her again and again. She was loud, wild, and unrestrained. Her moans sounded like a symphony of need. I gripped her hair, pulling her up against my chest, one hand around her throat, not tight, just enough to hold her still.

"You belong to me now," I growled, thrusting harder, deeper.

"I've always belonged to you," she cried out. "Theo, fuck… I'm gonna—"

"Let go," I ordered. "Give it to me." She came around me, her whole body trembling, legs giving out as I held her tight. I wasn't far behind. One last thrust, one final groan torn from my chest, and I spilled into her, stars exploding behind my eyes. For a long moment, we collapsed together, tangled in the sheets.

Then she turned to me, eyes shining, breath ragged. "So… you are my fiancé now." I laughed, breathless. "I can't wait to call you my wife." She grinned.

"Come here, Samantha," I said as I walked to the balcony's door. She grabbed the blanket and came to me. "What Mr. Jones?"

"Drop the blanket, hands on the railing." She obeyed without hesitation. Our room had a semi-private balcony. If you don't count the people on the street, no one will see us. I kneeled behind her, spread her legs, and without warning, I pressed my mouth into her. "Fuck Theo, I—"

"Quiet, Samantha, if someone hears you, they're going to look up." She nodded and grabbed the railing until her knuckles turned white. I pressed my mouth into her again and started devouring her. I started to rub her clit with one finger, and she melted right in my mouth. I could feel her trembling, maybe because of the cold, maybe because of my tongue. Either way, she tasted and felt delicious.

"Leg on the chair, now."

I stood up, with one hand grabbing her hair, with the other guiding myself into her. That first thrust was enough to make her legs shake. So much, she almost lost her balance. "Theo, I can't—"

"Yes, you can, open up for me." And she did. She bent over the railing, giving me more access. I fisted my hand in her hair and pulled it as hard as I could while I fucked her right there. She moaned my name in a way that almost undid me.

I kept thrusting her until she couldn't stay on her feet. "Theo, fuck, I'm about to—," I stepped back, and she gasped, "What the hell are you doing?"

"Sit down, open your legs, and touch yourself. I want to see how you make yourself come."

I sat down on the chair in front of her, stroking myself as she sat down and opened her legs. She slid one finger in and started pinching her nipple with the other hand.

To see her like this, so effortlessly sexy, so wet for

me, it almost made me finish before her, but I took a deep breath and kept watching her. Now she's panting, and all I can hear is her wetness and her moans.

I stop touching myself as I kneel in front of her, "Don't stop touching yourself, Samantha." She nods, biting her bottom lip. I spread her legs open even further and put my mouth on her. She gasped and moaned my name. I licked all the wetness of her, while she kept touching herself, but when I made eye contact, I saw how close she was. I slid a finger in, and she gasped and clenched around our fingers. I sucked her clit and bit her hard enough to make her lose it all.

This time, she didn't just moan. She screamed my name. And now, all Paris knew that Theodore Jones, —because she used my whole government name— made her come on that balcony.

"We're not getting any sleep tonight."

She just looked at me with a smile and said, "I wasn't planning on having a sleepover on my engagement night."

The morning came, and I don't recall how many hours of sleep we truly got, if any.

While packing the rest of our stuff, I can see her looking at me with that 'I have an idea' kind of look.

The one that always meant trouble, the kind I couldn't wait to get into. She turned toward me, eyes dancing. "So, I have a fantasy." I raised an eyebrow. "Do tell."

"To do it on a plane," she said, like she was ordering a croissant, casual and composed, while my blood pressure spiked. "A former flight attendant wants to join the mile-high club, huh?"

She shrugged, biting her lip. "I might know someone on our flight's crew who owes me a couple of favors, and knows how to turn a blind eye." I let that sit for a second, trying not to choke on my champagne. "Oh, so you're serious?"

"I'm very serious." I just laughed at her and finished packing.

We made our way to the airport with enough time to stop at the lounge and had a couple of drinks before boarding.

Once on the plane, we get to our seats, and I see her talking to a flight attendant. Sam looks at me and winks. This means she was actually serious about having sex on a plane.

We had an easy take off, we're sipping champagne, and that's when she whispered, "Okay, so in three minutes, you'll walk towards the back lavatory.

Try not to look too smug." She stood up, hips swaying with the kind of confidence that made my sanity slip through my fingers. Her dress clung in all the right places.

I counted to sixty. *Twice.* Then stood, as calm as a man with a countdown to heaven could be, and walked towards the back of the cabin.

Two knocks. The door cracked open, and she pulled me inside with one hand and zero hesitation.

It was cramped, hot, and completely inappropriate, but it was her fantasy, and who am I to say no to her when I just asked her to marry me? "Finish what you started this morning." Oh, I did. I slid my hands under her dress, took off her panties, and grabbed her. Put her on the world's tiniest sink and undid my pants.

She was flushed and gasping already. I teased her and slid into her slowly. She was biting her lip so she wouldn't make a sound, her hands fisted in my shirt, pulling me closer to her. It was fast, frantic, and so worth the risk. When I leaned my forehead against hers afterward, both of us catching our breath, she giggled and whispered, "Oops, turbulence."

I laughed, kissing her hard once more before tucking her hair behind her ear. "Fantasy checked," she said under her breath.

"I hope it's not the last one I get to fulfill," I whispered back.

God help me, I was going to marry this woman.

CHAPTER TWENTY-FIVE

Sam

Two weeks later.

It's been two weeks after Paris, and the ring still feels weightless on my finger, like I was floating with it, not weighed down by it. Which is saying a lot, considering it was about the size of a small planet and had its own gravitational pull in my hand.

We haven't told anyone, not even Rose, who's going to kill me for sure. But I asked Theo to give me some time to really feel all the feels, if that makes sense. It's not because I want to keep this as a secret, God no.

I wanted to scream to the world that I'm engaged to the most wonderful man on earth. But I know that the second we say it out loud, it will become something else, people will have opinions, and right now? Right now, I just want to be happy.

I know this was fast. I know the math didn't make sense on paper, 'met in January, engaged by spring' kind of fast, not literary, but a very close almost. The thing about Theo and me is… nothing about us ever made sense, and it doesn't have to.

We—well, I— decided today is finally the day I'll tell everyone.

So, like a mature woman that I am, I went ahead and created a group chat. My best friend, my sister, his sister. Simple and effective.

I hope so.

Oh, and Harper, because she needs to know.

GIRL POWER GROUP CHAT

Me: Hey, so I didn't want this to be like a huge thing, so I just want to say it…

Naomi: Are you pregnant, Samantha? Do you know there are ways to avoid that, right?

Elena: Is it Theo's? Are you keeping it?

Rose: Oh, you are definitely pregnant.

Elena: I love the group chat's name btw.

Rose: How did that happen? I thought you had an IUD.

Naomi: You have an IUD? Then how? What?

Harper: Do I need to prepare a board meeting about whatever this is?

Oh, nice, the exact reaction I was aiming for.

Me: No, I'm not pregnant. I've been on birth control since I was fourteen, and I've been fucking around since eighteen. I know how to not get knocked up, and yes, I have an IUD.

Which, btw, is none of your business.

What I wanted to say is that…

Theo and I got engaged.

Rose: WHAT?

Elena: Ha, I knew it.

Naomi: How is that better than being pregnant?

Harper: Board meeting, it is. Naomi, gather the legal details.

And this is exactly why I didn't wanna say anything.

Me: First of all, STOP. All of you.

This IS better than being pregnant.

No Harper, no board meeting, or legal stuff needed. Can you please just be happy for us for, like, a second?

Rose: ARE YOU KIDDING? I'm HELL OF EXCITED! My best friend is getting married. You know better, babes.

Elena: I knew it, and I'm all for it. I was just messing with you and following along with Naomi. Congratulations, Sam!

Naomi: Okay, Okay. I'm happy for you. But please be smart and do a pre-nup.

Harper: I can't believe this man proposed again. The second time is the charm, I guess.

Harper: I'm happy for both of you.

Me: Love you guys! And when I say that, I mean Rose and Elena.

Naomi, he already owns our company, a prenup for what? My share?

Harper, she was a bitch. I'm not.

Harper: Still debating on that.

Naomi: Yes, exactly, a pre-nup for your share. See, you are smarter than you look.

I hate them.

Me: I hate you guys.

I put my phone on DND and went to grab a shower.

This is the kind of thing I don't need in my life. A judgy sister, and an even judgier assistant. I know Rose is happy, and Elena seems like it, too. That's all that matters.

Naomi can go fuck herself, and Harper can follow her.

While I'm showering, I can hear voices and glass clinking. But it's way too early for Theo to be home. Nico knows better than to come uninvited.

Am I being robbed? Oh shit, I'm being robbed.

I'm about to die in the shower, and they are going to find my naked body here. That's going to be so embarrassing. Oh no, no, no. No one is killing me here. I turn off the shower, grab my towel, and run to the kitchen. To my surprise, while my apartment has been trespassed, I'm not being robbed.

"CONGRATULATIONS SOON TO BE MRS. JONES" is all I hear in unison.

Now I'm crying, even more than when I saw Theo on one knee. "Oh, girls"

"I know I was a bitch, but I had to keep my personality intact if we wanted this to work," Naomi said with what looked like a real smile on her face. I wipe my face with the corner of the towel, which, by the way, is doing a terrible job because it was NOT designed for surprise-attack-crying. "Naomi," I sniff. She rolls her eyes, but she's smiling, and that's how I know she actually means it.

Rose is already shoving a glass of champagne into

my hand—real champagne, the kind Theo buys without looking at the price tag. "Drink," she orders.

"You look like you survived a horror movie."

"Honey, I did," I say, pointing to my towel. "I sprinted in here naked, thinking an intruder was about to film my final moments." Elena snorts into her own glass. "Honestly? That's very on brand for you."

I flip her off lovingly. "If I had died, I'd come back to haunt all of you." Rose gasps dramatically. "As long as your ghost still has that ass, haunt me all you want."

Harper, of all people, steps forward. She touches my arm lightly. "For what it's worth," she says, "I'm really happy for you. For both of you. You deserve someone who goes feral for you. And he deserves the same."

"Aww," I whisper, "she has feelings."

"Don't get used to it," she mutters, taking a sip. I look around at these women, this beautiful disaster of a makeshift family, and my chest squeezes so hard I might actually pass out. Or it might just be the lack of panties. Hard to tell.

"So," Rose says, eyes sparkling with unholy excitement, "when are we planning the party?"

"What party?" I ask, instantly suspicious. "The engagement party, duh. And the wedding, of course." Naomi hops onto my counter like she pays rent here. "We need themes, outfits, invitations—"

"Nope, nope." I cut in.

"Absolutely not. We are not doing some spectacle. Theo and I agreed we're keeping this low-key." Three sets of eyes look at me as if I just announced I'm joining a cult. "Low-key?" Elena repeats slowly. "You? Low-key? Have you met you?"

"Babe," Rose says gently, "you can't even order iced coffee without causing a scene."

"I do NOT cause a—" Rose cackles.

"Sam, sweetie, you're not low-key. You're barely medium." I groan, pressing my face into my hands. "Theo is gonna kill me if you guys turn this into a circus."

"Oh, please, he knew what he was getting himself into when he decided to start sleeping with you," Naomi scoffs. Before I can argue, Rose throws an arm around me, pulling me into a side hug that squishes my towel dangerously low.

"We're not hijacking your engagement or wedding," she says softly. "We just want to celebrate you."

Elena nods. "You picked a man who worships you. And that's worth celebrating." Naomi lifts her glass. "To Sam. And to the man who is somehow even more obsessed with her, than we are annoyed by her."

"Rude," I mutter, but my throat is tight again. Harper raises hers last. "To the future Mrs. Jones—may she always remember to lock the office doors," I laugh. I cry a little more. I try not to flash anyone when the towel shifts. And just when I think it can't get any sappier, the front door opens.

"Samantha?" Theo's voice echoes at the entrance, and the four women who trespassed in my apartment look at me like hungry wolves. "Oh no," I whisper.

Rose grins. "Oh yes," Naomi smirks, and I swear, right then and there, I considered drying off fully before walking toward my fiancé, but where's the fun in that? He likes me better when I'm wet anyway.

Theo steps fully into the living room, stopping dead in his tracks when he sees the scene: four women, an open champagne bottle, confetti that was NOT here this morning, and well, me in a towel. Dripping wet. He blinks once. Then slowly drags his gaze from my wet ankles all the way up to where the towel is threatening to give up on its career.

"Sam," he says, voice deliciously low, "is there a reason you're hosting a party dressed like you're about to film my favorite kind of home movie?" Rose chokes on her drink.

Naomi fans herself dramatically. "God. No wonder she said yes."

I shoot them a glare before turning back to Theo. "I thought I was being murdered," I say defensively. He raises a brow. "And your plan for dealing with a murderer was… running toward them in a towel still dripping wet?"

"Uhm, yeah?" I snort. "In what universe will that work?"

"In mine!" I snap, pulling the towel tighter as Theo walks toward me with that slow, calculated, I 'm-about-to-do-something-inappropriate stride. He stops in front of me, eyes heated, amused, and entirely too pleased. "I leave you alone for one afternoon," he murmurs, "and you end up half-naked in front of an audience."

I whisper back, "It's not my fault they broke into the apartment like champagne gremlins." Harper raises her glass. "We take offense to that."

"No, you don't," I shoot over my shoulder. Theo brushes a wet strand of hair off my cheek, thumb grazing my jaw, the bastard. "You know," he says softly, "you could've texted me a warning."

"What? 'Hey, babe, come home, I'm naked and terrified for my life?'"

"I would've run red lights."

"Told you," Naomi mutters. "He's obsessed."

"Ladies, if you excuse me," he says to them, but leans in, mouth at my ear, whispering so low I feel it, right down my spine. "When they leave, that towel's coming off." My knees attempt to resign from their job.

Elena claps her hands. "Okay! Boundaries. Let's give them a few minutes to get Sam dressed before Theo combusts."

"Or before I do," I mutter. Theo just smirks, brushing past me toward the kitchen like he didn't just threaten to ruin my life in front of an audience. And God help me, I can't wait for them to leave. I manage to escape into the bedroom, muttering something about 'needing panties'.

The door clicks shut behind me, and I've barely

taken two steps before I feel Theo at my back. "Thought you would like the sight of me wet in a towel," I tease without turning.

"Oh, I do..." he says, voice dark and velvet-smooth. "But that towel needs to come off, you know, so I can have a better view of how wet you might be." Before I can fire back, his fingers hook the edge of my towel, and he pulls it loose.

The towel slips down my skin in a hush, pooling at my feet. I gasp, not because I'm cold, but because he's already sinking to his knees in front of me. "Theo—" I whisper, but my throat goes tight when he places his hands on my hips, thumbs stroking slow, sinful circles that melt my bones.

He looks up at me, eyes dark, full of hunger. He doesn't bother to hide it. "Let me take a moment," he murmurs. "Don't make a sound." His lips brush my inner thigh, and my knees wobble. I thread my fingers through his hair, tugging just enough to make him groan. "You have five minutes."

He smirks against my skin. "Oh, that's more than enough." The rest of the world, the champagne, the chaos, the towel at my feet, everything fades into a blur as he pulls me closer, as my breath catches, and he puts his mouth on me. He licked me once, twice, and I was long gone by the third. One of his hands slid under my thigh, and he lifted one of my legs over his shoulder, giving him better access to, well, everything. "Oh, fuck—"

"Quiet, Samantha, they're going to know what I'm doing to you."

"Oh, let them know that my fiancé is going down on me." He just chuckled and kept going. I was so close already, it was ridiculous. By the time I could breathe again, I was half draped across Theo's shoulder, drunk in that very satisfied, very 'I forgot what year it is' sort of way. He presses one last kiss to my hip—smug bastard—before standing and pulling me up with him.

I pat his chest. "You're a menace." He kisses my forehead like he didn't just obliterate all my motor functions. "You're welcome."

I try to walk. I really do. But my legs wobble like a newborn deer in heels. "Ugh. I can't go out there like this. They'll never let me live it down." Theo slides an arm around my waist before I eat the floor.

"Sam, they already saw you sprint in a towel. The bar's low." I glare up at him. He just laughs. He steers me to the closet, opens the door, and immediately ignores every piece of clothing that is remotely practical. "Wear this."

"That's lingerie."

"I know," He said with a smirk on his face. "Theodore."

"Okay, fine." He grabs a dress, one he likes way too much, and hands it to me with that innocent look that should be illegal. "This one." I step into the dress, but my fingers are still shaky, and I fumble trying to pull the zipper up. "Ugh. I can't—"

"Come here." His voice goes soft. He turns me around, sliding the zipper up agonizingly slow, fingertips tracing my spine. He knows exactly what he's doing. When he finishes, he rests his hands on my hips, squeezing once. "Perfect." I slap his hand away when he smacks my ass.

"Behave." Theo steps in and straightens the hem of my dress. "You look like you've been thoroughly celebrated."

"Oh my God," I groan. Rose asks, "So… getting dressed took a while, huh?" Theo answers before I can lie. "She needed assistance." Naomi cackles while Harper covers her face.

Elena whispers, "We knew it."

"Okay, let's go," Rose says, almost walking out the door already. "She's ours for the night." Theo narrows his eyes at her. "Bring her back in one piece."

"No promises," Elena says. Naomi grabs the keys off my hook like she owns the place. "Let's go, Sam. If we miss the reservation, you're paying the fee."

Rose screeches, "SHOTGUN SITTING NEXT TO THE BRIDE." I turn to Theo, pouting shamelessly. "Save me, now."

Rose yells, "I said we were leaving, not filming softporn."

Elena yells back, "Let them kiss, damn—", I can hear Harper giving orders, "On a clock, people." Theo breaks away last, thumb brushing my lower lip. "Have fun," he murmurs. "I'll try not to get arrested," I whisper back.

"Please don't," Naomi mutters. "I need a break from paperwork for a night." I grab my purse, my dignity, *barely*, and my four personal disasters disguised as friends. As we step into the hallway, Rose links her arm through mine.

"Let's go celebrate the fact that you're getting married to 1A, the hottest billionaire boss you've ever had."

"Christ," I mutter, but my cheeks are hurting from smiling. Harper presses the elevator button. "Ladies, we have one mission tonight."

We all look at her in surprise, mostly. She smirks. "Get the fiancée drunk enough to let us plan the wedding." I groan. "I hate all of you." They all cheer. The elevator doors open, and just as we step inside, Naomi pats my shoulder. "Relax. We'll be gentle."

No, they won't. And honestly? I can't wait.

CHAPTER TWENTY-SIX

theo

After the girls stole my fiancée, I took a long, well-deserved shower, poured myself a glass of whiskey, and I sat at my desk like an abandoned man, staring at the prenup I'd already marked to hell.

Romantic, I know.

It's insane that the very first thing people offer when you say, "Hey, I might propose," is a stack of paperwork thicker than a jet engine manual. Nobody hands you champagne. Nobody congratulates you on finding the one person who makes your blood pressure spike in the best and worst ways. No. They say, "Do you want your prenup in PDF or Docx?"

She's going to hate this. Sam's the kind of woman who breaks out in stress hives if she needs to sign five documents in a row. But this is the world we operate in.

And I'd rather she complain about it now than feel unprotected later.

People get prenups when they have nothing. When the only thing they're dividing is who gets the futon and who gets the cat. But Sam? She has money. Whether she likes it or not. Whether she wants it or not. And she could have even more if she ever worked things out with her father… which she won't. But, I know better than to bet against her stubbornness morphing into a long-term plan at twenty-six.

She has a trust fund she refused to touch when she turned twenty-one. She looked at all that money and said, essentially, "No thanks, I'd rather work", which is admirable, but she's still young, and she might change her mind in the long run, and I need to protect her even from the parts of herself she hasn't figured out yet.

My money? I don't care. She could take every account I have, and it'd be worth it if she still looked at me the way she did the morning after I proposed—sleepy and smug like she owned me. Which she does.

But being a billionaire means you use your damn brain. And this? This is smart.

Annoying, but smart.

INCOMING CALL: MAYLE

"Hey, Mayle, thanks for getting back to me." Mayle has been my lawyer since the day I made my first million—aka the day I realized having money is great until someone tries to take it and you don't know how to stop them.

She's saved my ass more times than I can count,

and I probably owe her a quarter of my money because of that. I wish I could put her on my payroll now, but I know she wouldn't want to work under a family-dynasty-type company. "Of course," she says. "Did you read the prenup?"

"Yes. There's only one tiny detail I want to fix." She stayed quiet for a bit. "What tiny detail, Theodore?" She only says my full name when she's mocking me. Or when she's about to tell me I'm being an idiot. Both are possible here. "I need to add a clause."

"What clause?" Sam is going to kill me for this. Kill me, resurrect me just to yell at me again, and then kill me a second time.

"That she needs to cash her trust fund before we get married," I say. "And that none of that money is allowed anywhere near Hayes International or me." There's silence, then a laugh. "She's going to kill you."

"Well aware."

"I'll work on it," She says, still amused. "Thanks, Mayle."

"Always. I'll send the revised draft soon." She hangs up, and the office goes quiet, too quiet. My brain fills the silence with a thousand thoughts, none of them helpful. Sam is young. She still has time to grow, to change, and to chase things she hasn't even dreamed up yet. Me? I've already lived ten lifetimes in a decade. I've built empires, crashed a few, learned every lesson the hard way. She, on the other hand, is still in the part of life where she discovers who she wants to be. And I'm asking her to anchor herself to me.

She loves me—stupidly, recklessly, beautifully. I know that.

She's in this with both feet. But the last thing I want is for loving me to cost her anything, or in this case, everything. I don't want her to ever wake up one day and think I rushed her into a life she wasn't finished choosing.

I blow out a breath, louder than necessary. I don't want to fuck this up.

My phone pings and yanks me out of my spiral. And when I see the messages, I can't help but laugh, *really* laugh.

Sam: Im hvkf so mhc funnnnn!

Sam: havkl so mjhd*

Sam: having so much fun*

She's adorable. And so goddamn sexy even when she forgets how consonants work.

Me: You are clearly hvkf so mhc fun.

Three dots appear, they vanish, and then they return. Like she's waging war with her thumbs.

Sam: Dont bully me 1A

Me: Never, Mrs. Jones.

I barely get the message sent before she fires back.

Sam: SOON TO BE YOURS!!!!!

My whole body reacts like she just whispered it into my ear while climbing onto my lap.

Fuck, I love this woman. And I'm going to make her my wife.

Me: Keep texting me like that, and I'll go pick you up.

Me: And I'll remind you exactly what happens when you call yourself mine.

There's a long pause. Suspiciously long pause. Then…

Sam: is that a promise or a threeot

Sam: thrat*

Sam: oh my god threAT*

I grin, sharp, wicked, already imagining her flushed and tipsy and trying to tell the girls she 'needs a second'.

Me: Threat. Promise. Same thing when I'm the one putting you to bed.

Another pause. Then a message that has me sitting forward like a starving man.

Sam: ...what if i dont wnt you to put me to bed tonighttt

Sam: I meen yeah put me in the bed

Sam: buut not to bed bed

Sam: like fkihng me type of putting me.

If she keeps going, I'm driving across the city and throwing her over my damn shoulder and bringing her home.

Me: Then you better get your fun out now, sweetheart.

Me: Because when you get home, I will put you in our bed, with your legs wide open for me.

Sam: ohhhhhh im telling the girls u talk like this to me

Sam: actng all mr respectable ceo in public

Sam: but in my phone u a MENACE

I bite back a laugh.

Me: Always for you.

Me: And only because you like it.

Sam: ...maybeeee

Sam: ok yeah i like it

Yeah. No shit.

I drag a hand down my face. She's drunk. She's flirty. She's mine. And she has no idea I'm two seconds from finding her and reminding her exactly what she signed up for when she said, "Soon to be mine."

My phone vibrates again. This time it's a picture. And I think I stop breathing when I see it.

She is in front of the bathroom mirror, her dress is hitched up around her waist, covering just enough. Her panties were in her hand like she had just peeled them off for me and needed evidence. Her thighs pressed together like she's holding back what she really wants.

> Sam: i cant walk out there with thsse on

> Sam: they are soaked becasee of you

> Sam: will you do something about it mr jones???

All of a sudden, she can type perfectly. Jesus. Fucking. Christ. My cock goes hard instantly—painfully, humiliatingly fast.

> Me: Samantha. You're playing with fire.

> Sam: maybe i want to burnnn

I drag in a breath so sharp it hurts.

Me: Put the panties back on, pull your dress down, and get back to your friends before I actually lose my goddamn mind.

Three dots. Then another picture. Her panties are now wrapped around her fingers like some sort of trophy.

Sam: too late 1A

Sam: i already lost mine

Sam: and these panties are soaaakked

Sam: im not putting them back onnn

Me: When you get home…

Me: I'm going to make you tell me exactly what you were thinking while you took that picture.

Me: Every detail.

Me: On your knees, while you touch yourself.

She types, stops, then types again.

Sam: im nt waiting till i get home

Sam: im throbbing

Sam: theo im serious

Fuck.

Me: Are you wet right now?

Me: Why the hell are you wet? What are you doing?

Sam: theo

Sam: im in a bathroom

Me: I didn't ask where you were

Me: I asked, why are you wet right now? And what were you doing?

She's typing, a bubble pops up, then disappears. Comes back. Then, a picture. Now I'm losing my fucking mind. She's sitting on the counter, dress still bunched at her waist, knees parted. I can't see shit, but she has her hand right *there* between her legs.

Sam: i'm sooo wet right now

Me: Sam, don't you dare touch yourself in that bathroom. Let me do that when you get home.

I grip the edge of my desk hard enough to crack it.

Sam: too late

Sam: my legs are shaking already

I curse under my breath, dragging my hands

through my hair because if I had the keys in my hand, I'd be out the door.

Me: Samantha!

Sam: what are you going to do about it huh??

Another picture comes in, and I'm already walking to the door, because I know that what I'm about to see will be enough to send me straight to her. Her legs are parted, and she has one finger in. I can see how wet she is, even from this picture. She's blushing, biting her lip. And when I thought it couldn't get any worse, she sent another text.

Sam: PLEASE come and get me soon bt hs hudnsk

Sam: i'm so wet for you i need you insde of me NOW

Sam: my pussk is rdhy for you

Even with all the typos, this is the dirtiest text she has sent me.

I pull up outside the bar like a man who has been possessed.

The second I step inside, I spot her.

She's trying, *trying*, to pretend she's fine. She's laughing too hard, shifting in her seat too much, biting her lip every time her thighs press together. The girls are distracted, which is the only reason she hasn't combusted yet.

She looks up, and her entire body reacts like she's been waiting for me for hours. Her breath stutters. Her hand grips the edge of the table. Her knees go tight, like she's holding onto whatever torture I left her with. "Theo…"

I lean down, brush my mouth near her ear, and murmur low enough for only her, "Stand up, let's go." She does, shaky, flushed, pupils blown. Rose snorts, "Why does Sam look like she's seeing Jesus?"

"Good night, ladies, I'll have a driver on standby for all of you when you're ready to leave, just so you get home safe."

My hand slides around Sam's waist—firm, possessive, and I steer her out of the bar. She doesn't protest. She practically melts into my arms. The girls look at each other, nod, thank me, and just laugh.

The second the car door shuts, she's on the edge of the seat, thighs rubbing, breath unsteady. I start the car, and she puts a hand on my thigh. And her other hand? It slides down between her legs. Oh fuck. I grip the wheel until my knuckles go white. "Sam," I warn. She looks at me with that needy, drunk, reckless softness that's going to end me.

"I waited," she whispers.

Her voice is a tremor. "But—I can't anymore. It's too much, Theo." Her fingers move under her dress. I can barely see in this darkness, but I see the movement. "You're going to make me crash the damn car. "

"Then don't drive. Do me right here," she breathes, leaning closer, her forehead almost on my shoulder, as her hand starts to undo my pants. "Samantha." My voice is rough, dark. She laughs, opens her legs even wider, one leg on the passenger door, the other by the console, takes one finger into her mouth, then into her. I don't know how I didn't fucking crash on the way home.

But the moment the door closed behind us, she's done, we're done.

I press her back against it, caging her in. Her chest rises fast, desperate. She reaches for me, but I'm done being patient. I grab her hips, turn her, and guide her straight toward the kitchen like I've lost every civilized bone in my body. She stumbles, laughing breathlessly, "Theo—"

"Don't." My voice is low, lethal. "You knew exactly what you were doing the whole way here. Now it's my turn." Her back hits the edge of the counter. I step between her legs, spreading them with my hands until she gasps. I drag her dress up, slow and ruthless, exposing her inch by inch until she's trembling.

"Look at you," I murmur, my mouth hovering over her stomach, her hips. "Shaking and dripping wet for me."

She closes her eyes, head dropping back. I tilt her chin up with a single finger.

"Keep your eyes open," I ordered. "You're not missing a second of how I'll make you fall apart." Then I pull her up to the counter, right where I want her, where she can feel every move, where she knows exactly what I'm about to do without me having to describe it. I kiss her thigh.

She's trembling, and I can see how wet she is right now. And when she whispers, "Theo, please—"

I grip her thighs, drag her closer, and give her exactly what she's been begging for since the first text she sent tonight.

CHAPTER TWENTY-SEVEN

Sam

THEO'S MOUTH is on me, and there's no universe where I survive this.

But I need to remind myself that I caused this. The stupid champagne made me horny, and here we are. Not that I'm complaining.

I would never.

My hands are in his hair before I even realize I've moved. I'm shaking—like actually shaking, because he's not being gentle. He's not being patient, he's devouring me with this single-minded, controlled, obsessive intensity that has my legs trembling against the counter.

"Oh, Theo—" My voice cracks as I'm coming apart. He tightens his grip on my thighs, and the low sound he makes when I pull his hair is obscene. He enjoys every inch of wrecking me.

"Eyes on me," he murmurs against me, and my whole body jumps. I tried. God, I tried. But he drags another sound out of me when he slides a second finger in, one that echoes in the kitchen, and my head falls back against the cabinets with a thud. My vision blurs, my knees weaken. I'm already too close, and he is feeling it, because he's not slowing down. He pins my hips, like he's inside my head and telling me without words, 'You're not going anywhere. Not until I'm done.'

I came so hard, I swear I left my soul on the kitchen counter.

When I finally collapse forward, panting, he stands, wipes his mouth with the back of his hand like he just tasted something he intends to worship, and lifts me with ease. My dress falls back over my hips, useless and wrinkled, as he carries me down the hall like I weigh nothing.

"Round two," he says, low and certain. "Bedroom." He looks at me like I'm the center of the goddamn universe.

He lays me on the bed and climbs over me like he owns every inch of me, because he does, and I let him. His hands are everywhere. On my hips, my waist, my breasts, my throat, my thighs. He is claiming, guiding, teasing me right up to the edge again. I'm still sensitive, still pulsing, still dizzy from the kitchen. "Theo, I can't—"

"Yes," he practically growls. "Yes, you can." I arch into him, helpless. My whole body wants him. I'm so needy for him. I gasp when I feel two fingers sliding into me. I swear I have no air left inside of me.

He yanks the dress, exposing my breast, and starts licking and biting my nipples. I fall apart again, faster this time, like he has my body on a string he's tugging with *lots* of precision. My vision goes blank. I stop remembering my own name. I don't even get a full minute to recover.

Theo pulls me onto his lap, pressing me against his chest, and the filthy, reverent praise he whispers into my neck has my whole body lighting up again. "Look at you," he murmurs. "You look so wrecked, and you are mine to wreck over and over." I gasp loudly because that phrase hits every nerve I have.

He guides himself into my entrance, slow at first, teasing, then deeper, and his hands slide down my back, keeping me exactly where he wants me, moving me exactly how he wants me. And I'm gone. I can feel the stretch, every inch of him. I'm shaking, clawing at his shoulders, moaning into his neck as he thrusts up into me with a controlled, devastating rhythm that makes me dissolve all over again.

"Round three," he whispers against my ear, dark and triumphant, "and you're still so needy for me. You're going to kill me, Samantha." I came all over him. So hard that my legs gave out. Theo looks down at me and smirks like he's proud of what he's done.

"We're not done, you said no sleep tonight," he murmurs. My laugh is a pathetic, breathless little sound. "I can't move."

"You don't have to." He flips me gently onto my stomach, kisses down my spine, and pulls me back against him with this slow, possessive tenderness that makes me melt all over again.

He's softer now, but every thrust is deeper, and I can feel him in my entire body. By the time I come again, quietly, helplessly, barely able to breathe. I'm shaking in his arms. He pulls me onto his chest, covering us both with the blanket, one hand stroking slow circles on my hip.

My body's still trembling in little aftershocks. "You okay?" he asks softly. I manage a hum, barely a whimper. Something that means I'm alive but barely. He chuckles, low, smug, unbearably sexy.

"Good. Because I meant every word I said tonight." His hand tightens on my hip.

"You drive me insane." Another kiss. "You're mine." Another. "And when you send me pictures like that?" He laughs quietly. "I lost my mind for you, sweetheart. Every damn time."

I curl into him, exhausted and warm and stupidly in love. "Theo?"

"Mm?"

"If this is what being your wife-to-be is like…" I nuzzle into his neck. "I'm not surviving the first month of marriage." He tilts my chin up and kisses me slowly and deeply.

"Oh, you'll survive," he murmurs.

He pulls me tighter, holding me like he's never letting go. And I fall asleep on his chest, completely ruined, completely safe, and completely *his*.

I groan as I move around the bed.

Oh no, *Oh no*.

I wake up and immediately regret having a body.

Every muscle in me protests. My thighs feel like they've been on a CrossFit retreat. My hips ache in ways I didn't know they could. I try to roll over—oh no, bad idea. Pain shoots down my legs like I've done a triathlon. "What the fuck," I croak.

Then I smell bacon, and I hear soft humming. And I realize two things. Theodore Jones absolutely wrecked me last night, and he is currently in our kitchen making us breakfast.

I try to stand up.

Nope, nope, *nope*.

My body basically said, 'sit down, you slut'. So I limp, *limp* to the bathroom, splashing water on my face. I look like someone who barely survived a very pleasurable natural disaster.

As soon as I get to the kitchen, Theo sets a plate in front of me—eggs, bacon, fruit, a stupidly sweet kiss on my forehead— and whispers, "Eat, baby. You're going to need the energy."

After breakfast, or my best attempt at nibbling food while my entire body throbs, Theo sits next to me, and he runs his hand down my thigh, gentle, soothing. I melted into him out of instinct.

Then he clears his throat. And I know that sound. I freeze. "Don't you dare break the mood," I whisper dramatically.

"Sam," he says softly, brushing hair from my face, "we need to talk about our prenup." Every molecule in my body screams no. I drop my head on his shoulder. "My legs don't work. My voice is gone. I am freshly fucked and deeply dehydrated. You're picking a BAD time to be a responsible adult."

"I know," he murmurs. "But I also know you. If we don't talk about it now, you're going to spiral later." Ugh, I hate this man.

"Okay, talk," I whisper. He exhales, thumb tracing slow circles on my hip.

"There's a clause I wanted to add, well, I added it already," he says. "About your trust fund." Of course. My stomach twists a little. He continues before I can react, "I want you to cash it before we get married."

What. The. Fuck. I blink. "What? Why?"

"Because," he says, cupping my cheek, "I want it separate from Hayes International. Completely protected. Completely yours. I don't want it tied to my life, my company, or my name. I want you to be safe from your father. From anyone." I stare at him. "So, you want me to use my trust fund… to protect me from my trust fund?"

"Yes, essentially," he says, unapologetically, like it's the clearest logic on earth. "Because you're young and stubborn. And maybe one day you'll want options you can't see right now. I'm protecting your future." My throat tightens. "You don't care about that money, so why?" I whisper. "No," he says immediately. "But, I do care about you."

I sigh. "If I weren't so sore, I'd be arguing harder. But I'm exhausted from all the… *things* we did last night." I smack his chest. He catches my hand and kisses it while looking at me like asking for forgiveness. I groan. "Fine, I'll talk to my lawyer and my accountant."

He smiles like he just won the lottery. I look at him, groggy, ruined, loved, overwhelmed. "Thank you for always looking out for me, even when I don't see it that way," I whisper.

"Always"

Me: Hey, can we meet? I need a lawyer.

Naomi: Why? What happened? Are you okay? What did you do, Samantha?

Me: Nothing, I'm okay, just need to talk about some things.

Naomi: Okay. That's not vague at all.

I arrived at the coffee shop near the office, and Naomi was already there, laptop closed, coffee untouched. She looked up the second she saw me, eyes flicking over my face like she was running diagnostics.

"So," she said, folding her hands. "Talk to me." Not hello. H*ow are you*? She was in full business mode.

"Theo wants me to cash out my trust before we get married."

"Okay, that's smart. But why?" she asked slowly. "He says he wants to make sure it's mine," I said. "That he doesn't want it tied to the company. I think he wants to protect me. He keeps saying he wants to take care of me, that this way the money can never be used against me." Naomi let out a slow breath, rubbing her thumb against the edge of the table. "That's not a casual request, Sam."

"I know," I whispered. "That's why I wanted to talk to you. I never wanted that money, but it is mine."

"You'll inherit it anyway when Dad dies, so it will be yours sooner or later." I hate this conversation so much. "I cashed mine out right at twenty-one," she said. I looked up. "You did?" That doesn't surprise me much. Naomi has always been the smart and calculated one. She softened then—really softened. "This is your life," she said. "And on this one, I'm on Theo's side. This is your money, and it should be only *yours*. There are other accounts where you can put it under your name and your rules. I can help you cash it, and then open those accounts."

I hesitated. "You really think this is the right move?"

"I think you're marrying a man who wants you protected," she said. Then, quieter, "And that matters."

"How much is it?" She asks like I have a clue. "I don't know, I texted Lauren on my way here, she said she'll send the papers via email, but I haven't opened it."

"You coward," Naomi said affectionately. "Give me that." She takes my phone out of my hands and stares at me. "Not bad, it is a bit higher than mine, but you're cashing it a few years later than me, and Dad put some interest accruals and clauses to those accounts. That makes sense."

When I finally saw the number, I almost choked on my drink.

$26,650,000

I hate my family.

I hate my dad.

I hate Theodore.

And somehow, impossibly, I still want to marry him. I swallowed. "I'm scared." Naomi smiled faintly. "About the money, or about getting married?"

"Both?" She laughed softly. "Everything will be fine, you're making the right decision, and you have a man who cares for you." I nod and smile. We finished our coffees and walked to the office.

"Hey Harper, is Theo there?" I ask her to signal the office door. "Since when do you ask for permission to enter his office?"

"I'm trying to set boundaries," She looks at me, confused.

"He is in a meeting, but I'm sure he won't mind if you step in." That's suspicious. "Thanks." As I enter, I can hear him say, "Yeah, I'm sure she will sign it, but she just needs more time—" He looks up. "Give me a second." He puts the call on mute. "Hey, I'm glad you are here. You should be part of this conversation."

"Yeah, Harper insinuated that. What's this about?"

"I'm on the phone with Mayle, we're discussing the prenup and the trust fund." I take an exaggerated breath in. "So, about that, yeah, I'll sign it." He looked surprised, but please. "You're cashing it?"

"Yes, I talked to Naomi this morning, we discussed my options, and she advised me on some accounts I can open to keep that money safe, but available." He's looking at me like he is so proud of me. That makes my heart melt.

I know that sometimes, he sees me like this, a twenty-six-year-old who fell in love with this sexy and obnoxious older man, and she just lost her mind, and maybe I did. And I still do, especially when his tongue is on my pu— the point is, I need to show him and everyone that I can be a responsible adult.

"You look like you are about to combust. What's on your mind?" Fuck that doesn't help.

"Well, I was thinking about how I made this responsible adult decision, but then got distracted thinking about your tongue." He smirks now, "My tongue where?" He asks, grabbing me and pulling me to the edge of the desk. "Here?" He asks, sliding his finger up my thigh, I shake my head, "I was thinking a bit higher." He keeps sliding his finger up until he reaches the hem of my panties. "Here?"

"You are dangerously close, but higher." Then he pulled the edge of my panties, pulled them to the side, and with his thumb, he pressed on my clit, and I gasped. "Here?"

"Yes, right there." He rearranged his chair so that he was seated right between my legs and pulled me closer. My legs were on either side of his chair now. I'm seated at the edge of his desk, and he just pushed me backward. As soon as my head hit the desk, his mouth was on me. I saw stars. The way this man can stop whatever he's doing just to taste me, to provoke me, to—, FUCK THE CALL.

I stand up and close my legs, "What's wrong, what happened?"

I hit unmute on the phone pad, "Hey Mayle, yes, I will sign the prenup. You'll have it on your desk by EOD, nice talking to you, bye-bye." And I hung up.

He is just looking at me in awe. “Okay, now.” I resume my position and let him devour me right there on his desk.

The rest of the day was uneventful until we got home.

CHAPTER TWENTY-EIGHT

theo

I THOUGHT RUNNING a billion-dollar company would prepare me for anything.

But it did not prepare me for Samantha Hayes with a Pinterest board. And her "bridesmaids" who are sending packages and text messages at any given hour of the day. I thought Harper and Elena would have more respect for me, guess I was wrong.

I'm standing in our kitchen watching my fiancée with her laptop open, a legal pad full of bullet points, sitting cross-legged on the counter in an oversized sweatshirt that says *BRIDE* in gold letters—that I know for a fact she didn't buy, but immediately fell in love with it when she opened the package.

Elena and Rose have been pampering her in a way that I didn't expect. Well, not from Elena anyway. She was never like that with my ex-wife. I bet she even hated her. So seeing her like this, giving so much love to Samantha, has really shown me a side of my sister that I truly appreciate.

She's holding her phone in both hands, eyes narrowed. "I hate it," she declares. I glance at her screen. "That's a bouquet."

"It's a *statement bouquet,*" she corrects. "And it looks like something a Victorian ghost would carry into battle after her husband died defending their country."

"It's… white flowers."

"It's *too* many white flowers." I take a sip of coffee and pretend this is normal. "Okay. No Victorian widow battle bouquet. Noted." Sam smiles like she's won a war. "Good."

I reach across the counter and brush my thumb over her knee. "We don't have to do anything big. You know that."

"I know," she says, softer, smiling at me. "I just… I want it to feel like us."

"It will." She studies me for a second like she's trying to figure out if I'm being sincere or CEO-sincere. The problem is I'm both. I'm always both. But with her, I'm trying—actually trying, to be only one thing. Not Theodore Jones. Just Theo. Her fiancé. She moves my way, giving me space between her legs as she plays with my hair. "Okay. So. Here's what I want."

I tilt my head. "I'm listening."

"I want a small ceremony," she says. "I don't want any press there. I know you are the CEO of Hayes

International and all, but no. No Hayes spectacle. No 'legacy family moment', nothing like that. This is not about our jobs. This is just about us."

"Agreed."

"And I don't want it at the Hayes estate. I'm so over my family's home."

"Also agreed." She looks relieved enough that I feel like a sharp knife just twisted in my chest. It's like the idea of that place still feels like a cage to her, even when it's dressed up in marble and money. Which is sad, but I completely understand.

"What about your dad? Is he coming?" I ask carefully. Sam's expression tightens a bit. She's not angry. Not really. She's just… tired. Of him, of everything related to that name. "Yes, I invited him. I don't know if he'll be there. Probably will be," she says. "Because Naomi would kill me if I didn't invite him. And because he'd make it a whole thing if I didn't too, so."

I nod. "Okay, he should be there. You are his daughter despite everything."

"And your parents?" she asks, suddenly a bit nervous. "Are they like, really excited about this?" I smile. "You know they are. My mom even cried when I told her." Sam's eyes widened in such a soft way. "She did? Really?"

"She said, and I quote, 'Finally. A woman with sense will be joining the family. Thank God.'" Sam laughs, bright and startled. "Your mom likes me, right?"

"She loves you." Sam's smile falters just a fraction,

like she doesn't fully trust that kind of unconditional approval. Like she's waiting for the fine print. I lift her chin gently. "She's already too obsessed with you, I'm afraid."

"Great, I'll take that." Sam grinned.

"You're collecting them," I say, deadpan. "It's like a hobby." She rolls her eyes, but she's smiling again. "Okay. So for the ceremony. I was thinking something very intimate. Obviously romantic. Like… maybe a garden? Or a rooftop? Something that looks warm and cozy, but still elegant."

"I like the rooftop idea," I say instantly. Sam squints at me. "Why do you say that like you already chose?" I shrug. "Because you like the sky. You like being on top of things."

"That's not entirely true." I raise a brow. Sam sighs dramatically. "Fine. It's true. I like being on top of things. Like on top of you, for example."

"That I know. So rooftop," I repeat. "Small venue, around sunset time. Just a few of our closest friends and family. With good wine, good music—"

"And good food," she adds immediately.

"Of course."

"And no speeches longer than three minutes," she says. I smile. "That's clearly directed at Naomi."

"That's directed at everyone, but yeah, especially at Naomi," Sam says, and I laugh. She steps back, grabs my legal pad, and starts reading my list. "Venue, officiant, guest list… okay, wow," she says, impressed. "You made this sound like a business plan."

"It's how I cope." She taps the paper. "What's this?"

"Ring insurance." Sam looks up slowly. "Theo."

"What?"

"I'm wearing it on my finger," she says, holding up her hand like evidence. "It's not like we are getting married on a yacht or something." I tilt my head. "It's just a safety measure." She stares at me, then laughs so hard she bends at the waist. "Oh, my God. You think I'm going to lose it."

"I think you're going to do something impulsive, and it might fall, or you're going to put it somewhere safe, and it's going to disappear." I correct. "Which is different."

"I'm not impulsive," Sam says, as if she didn't once disappear from a bar and let me carry her out over my shoulder while she yelled, *I AM A FUNCTIONING ADULT.* I keep my face neutral. "You're right." She narrows her eyes. "That tone was suspicious."

"I'm being supportive of your statement," I say, and she throws the legal pad at my chest. I catch it easily, grinning. "Ow."

"You're insufferable."

"And yet," I say, stepping closer, "you're marrying me."

Sam's gaze drops to my mouth. "Unfortunately." I slide my hand to the back of her neck, tugging her in just enough to make her inhale sharply. "I'm going to be so good to you."

Her eyes soften. "You already are." That hits me harder than it should. It's simple. Honest. Like she doesn't even realize what she's giving me when she says it. I kiss her slowly, carefully, like I'm still learning how to love her without scaring her.

When I pull back, she's smiling. "Okay," she says, breathless. "Small rooftop wedding. Sunset hour. A simple dress. And no chaos." I raise an eyebrow. "No chaos?" Sam's grin turns wicked. "Okay. Minimal chaos."

I nod. "That we can promise." She leans into me again, whispering like it's a secret. "But I want one thing."

"Anything." She looks up at me. "I want it to feel like the first night we met." My chest tightens. I immediately thought of Paris and how we shared those bottles of wine. Her mouth, her laugh. The way she looked at me. "Done," I say, voice low. "We'll do it our way."

Sam exhales like she's been holding her breath for months. Then she presses her forehead to mine and whispers. "Okay." And for the first time in my life, planning something doesn't feel like pressure. It feels like peace. "Now, can I do something my way?" I ask, spreading her legs open.

She just stares at me. I grabbed one side of her panties and pulled them to the side, as I knelt in front of her. She leans back on the counter and spreads her legs wider. "You can do this, in whatever way you prefer, Mr. Jones."

"Oh, I will." I pressed my mouth into her and licked her, just once. Then, I started to rub her clit with the wetness from my tongue as I slid one finger into her. That made her melt, moan, and desperately grab me closer to her. But when we made eye contact, that was it. I knew what she needed.

"Theodore, fuck me, NOW."

As I stood up in front of her, I kept touching her while I freed myself, teasing her entrance. With the other hand already covered in her, I kept rubbing her clit. She gasped and clenched around me. "Like this, Samantha?"

"Yes. Oh fuck, yes."

She lost her mind, and I lost mine.

But this woman was going to be my wife in 72 hours, and I couldn't wait.

CHAPTER TWENTY-NINE

Sam

Three days later.

I wake up on my wedding day with the kind of calm that feels illegal to have.

I don't feel anxious, I don't feel the infamous cold feet the brides talk about. I'm not even overthinking anything. There's no sudden urge to flee the country and live under a fake name. I just feel *calm.*

And then, the calm slips away when Rose bursts into my apartment like the FBI on a raid. "WAKE UP," she screams, throwing open my curtains.

"IT'S WEDDING DAY!"

I sit up so fast my soul leaves my body. "Jesus Fucking Christ—Rose! I'm awake, and if I wasn't, trust me, I would be now."

She's already holding two coffees and a garment bag, as if she's running a tactical operation. Which she is. My life is a constant tactical operation, or used to be. Behind her, Elena strolls in with a bottle of champagne at nine in the morning like she's a French widow with a secret lover. I've seen her future, and it's bright like that.

Harper follows, carrying a clipboard. Of course she is. And Naomi—well, she walks in last with the expression of someone attending court. Nothing strange there. She looks at me in my robe and messy hair and smiles faintly. "You look happy," she says.

"That's one of the nicest things you've ever said to me."

"I'm learning how to be a sister," she replies. That makes me smile because she really has been trying to be my sister. Rose claps her hands. "Okay! Timeline check! We have hair, makeup, dress, and an emotional breakdown scheduled at—"

"I'm not having an emotional breakdown," I say.

Naomi lifts a brow. "Don't lie on your wedding day, it's bad luck." That's definitely not a thing. I glare at her. "I'm truly not lying. I'm okay." Elena pours champagne into a coffee mug because she has no respect for early mornings.

"To Samantha," she announces, raising it like a toast. "The woman who actually stole my brother's heart and made me gain a sister. Sorry, Naomi, she's mine now." We all laughed, and I could hear Naomi muttering "All yours" in the background.

Harper, without looking up from her clipboard, added, "I'm happy he has you now."

"Harper, that was actually sweet!" I gasp. Harper finally looks up, expression completely calm. "I can be sweet." Rose snorts. "Okay. Everybody breathe. Sam, do you have your vows?"

"Yes."

"Do you have something borrowed?"

"I borrowed Naomi's emotional stability." Naomi doesn't even blink. "That doesn't count. Here." She says as she gives me a pair of beautiful, elegant earrings. "I need them back intact. They cost more than our trust funds together."

"What?" She laughs, "It's a joke." We all laugh, and I realize something terrifying.

I'm happy.

Not performatively happy. Not 'smile for the cameras', or 'be a Hayes', 'be fine', happy.

Really *happy*.

And that's all because of *him*.

I get my makeup done while Rose narrates every step like she's filming a documentary called *How To Marry The CEO Of Your Dad's Company*. Naomi sits on my couch, sipping coffee, watching the chaos like she's on a jury. "You're quiet," I tell her.

She shrugs. "I'm observing."

"So, judging?"

"Always." Elena leans over the back of the couch, her curls perfect, her eyes sparkling. "So," she says, "are we excited?" I swallow. I think about Theo's hands. Theo's voice. Theo's steady calm. Theo showed up for me in a hundred ways I didn't know I needed. "I'm… yeah, I actually am," I say.

That makes Rose tear up instantly. "Oh, my God."

Harper sighs like she's irritated by feelings. "Don't start crying, please. We don't have time to redo our makeup." Naomi's gaze softens. "Good," she says quietly. "This is the right kind of environment I need to be in." We all get ready together, and our dresses are perfect. I'm not a bridezilla, so I let them choose their own dresses.

Naomi is wearing a deep green dress with enough cleavage to set a boardroom on fire. Harper looks stunning in a burgundy dress. Rose always loved pink, so we settled on a dark one. And Elena is wearing a golden mustard dress that makes her look amazing.

I love these women.

A few hours later, we are all in a small rooftop garden, with warm lights, soft flowers, the city behind us like a quiet witness. With no spectacle, no press, and no performance.

Just us and the people we actually care about and love, besides my father and Susan.

Theo's parents are here, his mom holding tissues like she's already crying, his stepdad looking proud in that quiet, solid way. They're warm, easy, and when his mom sees me, she grabs my hands and whispers, "You look beautiful, sweetheart," like she's known me forever. I blink fast and smile. "Thank you."

Theo is waiting at the front.

And the second I see him, everything else blurs.

He's in a dark suit, no tie, as I ordered and he agreed. Everything looks so simple, he looks so relaxed, so happy, so *him* behind closed doors.

I'm so glad people can finally see the man I fell in love with. His eyes lock onto mine, and I swear the whole city goes quiet. No more hums, no more traffic noise, just quiet. Rose squeezes my hand before she walks me forward. "Don't run," she whispers. "I'm not going to run," I whisper back.

"You ran from commitment for twenty-six years."

"That's not—okay, yes." Naomi steps closer on my other side, her voice low. "You're okay."

I nod, throat tight. "I'm okay."

While I appreciate my father being here, I didn't want him to walk me down the aisle. Not because of our work-in-progress relationship, but because I wanted to do it myself. I've been independent my whole life, and if I was going to enter into marriage head over heels in love, I wanted to do it on my own.

When I start to walk, Theo's gaze never leaves my

eyes. Not once. When I reach him, he takes my hands as if he's been waiting his whole life to do it. And maybe he has. I see his eyes shining. I hope he doesn't cry because I will lose it.

The ceremony is simple. Romantic, but not in a cheesy rom-com type of romantic. No dramatic speeches, no overdone metaphors.

When it was time to say our vows, I was calm, happy, and excited, and then Theo said, "I choose you, in this life, and in any other to come." his voice broke slightly. And I'm gone. No more calm, cool, collected, I'm a mess, and when it's my turn, my hands shake, but I don't let go of him.

"I spent most of my life running," I say, voice soft. "Not because I didn't want love. But because I didn't think I deserved something that would stay with me." Theo's eyes shine, and I want to cry and laugh at the same time. "But you," I whisper, "you don't feel like a trap. You feel like *home*."

His thumbs stroke over my knuckles as he whispers, "You are my home, Samantha."

When we kiss, the whole rooftop erupts into cheers like we didn't just do the most intimate thing two people can do in front of a small crowd.

Everything was perfect, and I just got married to the man of my dreams.

When we walk into the reception, I'm in awe of how warm it feels. And I'm not talking about temperature.

There are candles on every table, there's good food, even better wine, and music low enough that people can actually talk and enjoy themselves.

I decided to change dresses because, while I wanted a small, intimate wedding, I also wanted to wear fashion statements and signature pieces. This dress is short, silky, and expensive, but I deserve it, and he deserves what's underneath.

I'm halfway through my second glass of champagne when I see Nico. He's leaning against the bar, smiling like trouble, and he's watching Naomi like he's decided she's his next hobby. I can see that happening.

Good luck to him, though.

Naomi, naturally, looks like she'd rather swallow glass than flirt at my wedding. Nico slides up beside her, smooth as hell. "You look beautiful tonight." Naomi doesn't look at him. "I look expensive. There's a difference."

Nico grins. "I like expensive things." She finally turns her head, giving him the kind of look that has ended men. "Are you hitting on me at my sister's wedding?" she asks. "I'm appreciating you," Nico corrects. "There's a difference." Naomi's mouth twitches. "That's bold even for you."

I cover my mouth to hide my laugh. Theo appears behind me, arms wrapping around my waist. "What are you laughing at?" he murmurs. "Your best friend is trying to get himself killed," I whisper back.

Theo hums. "Nico's been trying to die since 2012."

Naomi says something sharp enough to cut diamonds. Nico laughs like he likes it. And I file it away in my brain because I know what this is. It's a spark. But it is not my problem.

I start doing some rounds around the tables, thanking people for being here. Thank God there are only like six tables. His mom hugs me so tightly I almost cry again.

This night was exactly what I wanted.

Back in the apartment, the second the door closes, Theo's composure cracks like a dam. His hands are on me, his mouth on mine, like he's been holding back all day out of respect, and now he's done being respectful. I laugh against his lips. "Hi, husband."

Theo groans. "Don't say it like that."

"Like what?" I tease. "Like you want me to lose

control." I slide my hands up his chest, slowly unbuttoning his shirt. "Oh, I do."

His eyes go dark. "Samantha." I tug him closer. "Theodore." My back hits the edge of the counter, and he steps between my legs, spreading them open. "You are getting too close, sir."

"You are *mine* now, Samantha. You are *my* wife," I nod and kiss him again.

I feel him drag my dress up, exposing my tights, as his hands reach my waist. He grabs the hem of my very expensive, very carefully chosen lingerie and tries to take it off. I stopped him right there. "Uh uh, sir. This lingerie was very expensive, and it deserves recognition." He put his arms up and laughed at me. "Okay, turn around then." I do, and he unzips my dress, letting it fall to the floor. I step out of it and turn around.

"Let me see you, Sam." I just stood there, in my shiny white lingerie, as my husband watched me.

He started tracing all the hems of the bra, the straps slipping down my shoulders, one nearly exposing my nipple. He started kissing me, then my neck, my shoulder, my arm, my stomach, and he paused right before my waistband. He looks up at me and grabs one of my legs, putting it on his shoulder. He started kissing my knee, my thigh, and he landed right on the spot that made me clench my legs, and so wet I think I just ruined these panties.

He grabbed the other leg and put me exactly where he wanted me, on his face.

He licked and bit me. "You are ruining my panties."

"I'll buy you new ones." I chuckled as he set me on the counter and took a step back.

"What?" He is looking at me like a starving man.

"You look so sexy, Sam." I'm stupidly blushing right now. It is so strange how this man can be between my legs at any given moment of the day, anywhere, and I'm okay, but when he looks at me like that, I'm gone.

"You still have so many clothes on, *husband*." He nods and starts undressing, and I just watch. When he is down to his briefs, I can see how hard and ready he is for me.

For *his wife*.

I hopped off the counter and walked towards the bedroom. He just followed me without a word. I sat on the bed and spread my legs. "Do you remember back in Paris when you told me you liked control, surrender, and that you liked it when someone asked for what they wanted?"

"I do," he says, studying me.

"Then come on, control me, do everything you ever wanted to do with me. I'll surrender to you," I tease, but I truly want to see what he hasn't given me so far. I want to see that side of him.

"You don't know what you're asking for, Samantha." His eyes go dark.

"Then show me," I tease again. He takes a deep breath, and I can see the shift in his eyes.

"Spread your legs wider, and stay there." I obey, watching him walk towards my nightstand. He grabbed my vibrator, a bold move. "Open your mouth," he said as he walked my way with the vibrator in hand, and put it in my mouth. "Suck on it, eyes on me."

Okay, now my panties are really ruined.

He started pressing and pulsing on my clit with his hand while I played with the toy in my mouth. "This is going to feel deep," he said, pushing the toy all the way back to my throat. I gagged, but kept playing with it. "Good job."

He took it out, pulled my panties to the side, and slid it into me. A low moan escaped me, and my legs closed. "Uh, uh, open up." He's playing with the toy and playing with me. With his other hand, he unclasps my bra, freeing my breasts, and cups one into his mouth. Licking and biting my nipple hard enough that it hurts—in a good way.

I'm losing it, and I'm so close. "Theo fuck me, please."

"No," he said in the calmest way and kept playing with the toy.

He turned it on at the highest setting, and I felt how my soul left my body. My orgasm consumed me. I moaned, gasped, and screamed his name.

"I did what you wanted. I showed you what you wanted to see. Can I tell you what I want now?" I nodded.

"I want to spend the night making love to my wife," I laughed, "After making me come like that?" He nods and starts kissing me, slowly, deeply, and I melt right into his arms.

He took his time now, I swear he kissed every inch of my body, traced every scar, and counted every freckle. He worshiped me. And I have never felt something like this in my entire life.

"Can I take these panties off now?" I nodded, laughing, "You already ruined them, so yeah." I felt electrified when he slid them down my legs. He grabbed my ankles and put them on his shoulder, and he slid into me. His movements were so different now, so slow, so controlled, sweet even.

I lost count of the positions we did, and the times we did it that night.

"You know, when I first met you, I thought that you were sent to distract me. I needed a distraction, and somehow life knew to put a quirky, sexy as hell flight attendant on my flight."

"I did distract you, but it was your fault."

"How so?" he said, looking at me with such curiosity in his eyes. "You kept talking to me, and then you invited me to share a wine bottle, and you almost invited me to a threesome."

He laughs now, really laughs. "I have a question about that,"

"Yes, I would've joined you two that night."

"You would've?" He arched his brow, looking

really surprised. "Look, when a hot man is flirting with you, and a hot bartender insinuates a threesome opportunity, in a foreign country, you think you will never see those people again, so you say yes."

"You sound experienced, Samantha," I laugh. It is refreshing being able to talk to him like this, about everything and nothing at the same time. "That wasn't my first layover in Paris, Theodore."

"You are full of surprises, aren't you?" He pulled me closer to him and started kissing me behind the ear. "How many threesomes have you had, Mr. Jones?"

"Isn't this the type of questions we're supposed to ask on our first date, rather than on our wedding night?" Another kiss, and I can feel his hand going down my spine. "Fair point, but we have never followed the right order, so." I can hear him laugh in the back of my neck, his hand getting dangerously close to my ass. "I've had a couple."

"Men or women?" I start sliding my hand up his thigh. "Both," he whispered in my ear, giving me another kiss.

I gasped dramatically, "Theodore Jones, you dirty bastard."

"We were all friends, we all wanted to experiment, so we did." I slid my hand a bit more, getting closer to his length. "Did you kiss the guy?" I grabbed him now and started touching him slowly.

"Sorry to disappoint you, but no, I didn't kiss the guy." I stopped touching him and mimicked a cry.

"What a turn off," he just laughed and kept kissing my neck and rubbing my ass. "You're not going to ask about me?" he didn't even flinch.

"I don't care. You had a life before me, and I'm sure you had a lot of fun." I started teasing him, touching him again. "I have had more than a couple, and I had one with two men."

"Greedy. Is that why you enjoy having me play with your toy?" He wrapped his arm around my waist and turned me toward him. I nodded, "You can say that." He grabbed the toy back from the nightstand, "So let's see. Do you like this?" He pressed the toy against my clit, the pulsing sensation vibrating through me, and I jumped, nodding at him. "And this?" He slid one finger in and kept rubbing the toy against my clit. I moaned into his mouth and nodded again.

"What about this?" He slid the toy in, and one of his fingers—he just sucked on, up my ass. That made me squirm, clench, and scream. "Yes, I like that."

He kept playing with me, started licking and biting my nipples. "And what about this?" He said as he guided himself to my entrance, without taking the toy out.

"Can you take this?" I nodded, hungry for him, hungry for more. He entered me, and that stretch made me gasp. I felt so full, it was borderline painful in the most exquisite way. I could feel his finger, the toy, I could feel him. "Fuck Theo—"

"Shh, relax," he said as he started moving his

finger, slowly, in and out of me, while the toy and his cock stayed steady inside. He grabbed my hand and put it on the toy. I was kind of in control now.

He started thrusting slowly, and I followed his pace with the toy. I could feel the vibration on my entire body. With his other hand, he cupped my breast and started biting my nipple. "I'm going to speed it up now." I nodded.

And when he did, the whole room started spinning for me. It all felt so tight, so wet, so perfect. "You take me so well."

He took the toy out, rested it on my clit, and started thrusting me deeper, with his finger too. "I'm about to come, Theo."

"Good, come for me then," and I did.

We stayed there restless, still throbbing, shaking, but happy and full. "Is that something you still want to repeat?" He said out of nowhere, and while he was looking at the ceiling, I could see the wheels on his head spinning. "What, this? Absolutely."

"A threesome, I meant." He didn't look at me when he said that. "I mean, I don't know. I could be open to it. Do you want to?"

"Honestly, no. I don't want to share you with anybody, let alone a man. But, I understand that you are still young, and that there can be some things you still want to experience." He looked pissed, but in a 'I'll do it for you' kind of way, and I will never allow him to feel like that just to do something for me.

"Hey, look at me," I said, cupping his face in my

hands, "I don't need to experience anything else. The way you fuck me on a daily basis is more than enough. And honestly, a lot better than anything else I've done in the past. So no thank you." he laughed and kissed me.

"Good, because if a guy ever touches you again, I' d have to kill him, and that would ruin the company, and our marriage." I crack a laugh. "You won't kill anybody, and you won't ruin anything, but me."

"Another thing that I need to ruin is this night," I stood up and looked at him, "Why? What happened?"

"Well, it is 4:48 a.m. and our flight leaves at 7:45 a.m, so if we want to catch it, we need to shower and get ready, like, right now," I growl at him.

"Theodore Jones, you booked our honeymoon flight in the early morning after our wedding?" He looks at me like I'm saying the stupidest thing in the world. "That's how honeymoons usually work, you finish the wedding, and then off you go."

"I mean, yeah, but have you met us?" I say while I grab a blanket and stand up from the bed. My legs are still shaking, I swear I'm dripping, and I'm pretty sure that my makeup and my hair are so ruined that I need a blowout and a makeup artist to fix me.

"Well, that was the point of having a sunset wedding, sweetheart."

I rolled my eyes at him, "Yeah, but I bet you didn't count on having sex for six hours straight. Right?"

"Well, that's your fault," he says, laughing at me as

he stands up, slapping my ass on his way to the shower. “Are you joining me?”

“If you want to catch that flight, absolutely not.”

CHAPTER THIRTY

theo

This time, going to Paris feels completely different.

When I brought her here to propose, I was feeling nervous, hopeful, but nervous as hell, and I think I was in some kind of haze. Now, I feel complete and genuinely happy. Now, there's no haze. No doubt.

I feel complete.

Sam stands at the hotel window in nothing but panties, hair a mess, sunlight spilling over her bare legs like it's worshipping her. She's holding a croissant in one hand and coffee in the other, like she's lived here her whole life. Like she belongs here.

The sight hits me in a way that's almost painful, a quiet kind of ache that spreads through my chest. The kind of feeling you get when you realize something is too good to be true, and then you remember it *is* true, because it's *yours*.

Because she's *here*.

Because she chose *me*.

I watched her for a second too long, memorizing the curve of her shoulder, the way her hip leans into the window frame, the small content hum she makes like she doesn't even realize she's doing it.

She turns her head and catches me. "What?" she asks, suspicious. I smile, and it's impossible to stop. "You're real." Sam squints, like she's trying to decode me. "You're being weird."

"I'm married to you," I say. She laughs, bright and unguarded, like she can't help it. She takes a bite of the croissant, chewing slowly like she's savoring the moment on purpose. "Okay, well, stop feeling married so loudly. You are scaring me." I laugh under my breath, like I've been caught doing something embarrassing. Like loving her too openly is a crime.

I cross the room and slide my arms around her from behind, pressing my mouth to her shoulder. She's warm from the sunlight, skin smooth beneath my lips, and I swear my whole body relaxes just from holding her. "I can't help it."

Sam leans back into me, relaxed, like she was always meant to fit there. "Yes, you are married to me." I bite her shoulder lightly. She squeaks. "Theo!"

"It's our honeymoon," I murmured, lips brushing her skin. "I'm allowed to do whatever I want to you and with you." She turns in my arms, eyes bright, cheeks flushed from laughter and sunlight and maybe me. "You did that last night, all night long."

I lift a brow, trying for casualness, but I can feel

the grin pulling at my mouth anyway. "So what?" I asked. She just laughed at me.

"There's something I want to talk to you about." The words come out before I can second-guess them. And the second they leave my mouth, I feel her body go slightly still, like she's bracing for impact. Her eyes narrow immediately, instinctively. "No, Theo, don't start killing the mood."

I wince, not because she's wrong, but because I hate that her first reaction is defense. Like she's expecting me to drop something heavy on her. "You might like it. I promise." She tilts her head, still suspicious, but curiosity sneaks in. "Try me, but if I get mad, you are taking me shopping *and* drinking later." She says it like I won't do that, regardless. A laugh escapes me. I'm relieved now. "I'll still take you shopping and drinking, but deal."

She takes another sip of coffee, steadying herself. "Okay."

"There's an opportunity for me… well, for us, as Hayes International, to spend some time here in France. There are some clients who want us closer. The contract will be around six to nine months, but we'll need representation here during that time. And, who is best for it, than the CEO and the International Business Strategist?" I watch her face while I say it, tracking every shift. I expect hesitation. I expect her to worry about logistics and to question whether it's too fast, too much.

But her expression transforms so quickly it almost

knocks the air out of me, like someone opened a window in her chest and let the light in. "You are saying that you want us to move to Paris?"

"Well, not exactly Paris, and not move, move, but live here for a while, and—"

"Yes, Theo. Absolutely yes." The words slam into me in the best way. There was no fear on her face. She didn't hesitate, and she didn't even seem worried. She just said, yes. My heart stutters, stunned by how easy she makes it. By how she doesn't make me beg for permission to want things with her. "Are you—, really?"

She steps closer, eyes shining, and the look on her face makes my throat tighten like she's about to say something stupidly emotional that will ruin me. "I want my life with *you*. I like what I'm doing in the company, and I absolutely love France. This is the best case scenario possible." Yes, she did.

"In that case, do you want to go see your new potential home?" She blinks. "Did you look for an apartment already?" I clear my throat, suddenly feeling twelve years old and caught hiding a gift behind my back. Which was exactly what was happening right now. "Well, not exactly."

Her stare sharpens instantly. She points the croissant at me like it's a weapon. "Leading with 'not exactly' is never good." I kiss her forehead, because it's the only thing I can do that feels steady. "Trust me on this one."

She makes a noise that says she doesn't trust me at all, but she trusts me with her life.

And the whole time, my pulse is too loud. Because I know what's coming. And I know her. And I know she's either going to melt or murder me.

Probably both.

The compound is about 45 minutes outside the city, away from the noise and tourists. The drive itself feels like slipping out of one world and into another. Paris was fading behind us, elegant buildings and crowded sidewalks replaced by open space and green stretching endlessly. Even the air changes here. It's cleaner, and quiet enough that I can hear Sam's soft little breaths beside me, the occasional rustle when she shifts in her seat.

She keeps glancing out the window, eyes wide, like she's trying to imprint every detail. Her knee bounces once, then stills, then bounces again. When we turn down the long private road lined with trees, her head snaps toward me. "This looks expensive."

"It's France," I say, like that explains anything.

When we get to the house entrance, I can see Sam's eyes almost watering at the sight. The moment the gates open and the property reveals itself, she goes completely silent, like her brain is buffering. Her lips part. "This is not an apartment."

"No, it's not." Her shoulders lifted on a sharp inhale, and her voice cracked on the next words, like her emotions were piling up too fast. "And there's a vineyard in here."

"Yes, there is." She turns slowly, staring at the rows of vines like they're a hallucination. Her hand lifts, hovering in the air like she wants to touch the scene just to confirm it's solid. "This place is huge, Theodore. Who owns this?"

My chest tightens. This is the moment. The one I've been holding back, the one that's been burning on my tongue since this morning. "We do."

"Wait, what?" Her voice is so small, so startled, that it makes me want to gather her up and shield her from her own shock.

"I bought it this morning as soon as you said yes." Her face changes in real time. Joy flashes first, then panic, then disbelief, then that familiar Sam fury trying to claw its way to the surface because she doesn't know what to do with how much she feels. "Wait. You did what?"

"I bought it under both of our names, and I thought we could have our honeymoon here instead of in a hotel room." For a beat, she just stares at me. Like she's trying to find the catch. The trick. The hidden clause.

She steps out of the car, taking her sunglasses off, and when she looks back at me, I can see her eyes shining. She laughs once, sharp and breathless, like she's about to cry and scream at the same time. "Theodore Jones, I love you, but I hate you."

Relief hits me, and I grin, stepping closer, hands sliding to her waist. "I can work with that." She shoves my shoulder lightly, but she's smiling through it. "You're insane."

"About you," I say, and the words come out too honest to be anything but true.

Her throat bobs, and she looks away fast, like she refuses to let me see how much it gets to her. "And I have another surprise for you, one I really hope you'll like." Her head snaps back. Immediate alarm. "Oh God, what now?" Before she can spiral, I step back and throw my arms wide like a showman.

"SURPRISE," I can hear Naomi, Elena, Harper, and Rose screaming from the top of their lungs and clapping like little kids. And I'm glad Elena brought Nico, because I'll need all the manpower if we're going to be here with all of these women for a week.

The second she hears them, her whole body jolts. She whips around so fast her hair flies. Her face goes through five emotions in one second: shock, confusion, delight, outrage, and then something so soft it makes my chest ache.

"You brought them here?" Her voice wobbles, caught between laughing and crying. She presses a hand to her mouth like she's trying to physically hold her feelings in.

I step beside her, close enough that she can lean

into me if she wants. "Even though it's our honeymoon, I thought it would be nice to have them here for your birthday."

She turns to me, eyes glassy, furious in the most loving way possible. Like she wants to yell at me for making her happy.

"Scratch the 'I hate you', I absolutely love you, Theodore Jones." I laugh, breath shaking out of me, and pull her into my arms before she can change her mind. She melts into me instantly, fingers clutching my shirt, forehead pressed to my chest. For a moment, the world is just the sound of her breathing and the feel of her against me.

And in that moment, with the sun high, our friends laughing behind us, and an entire life stretching open in front of us, I made myself a promise.

I will spend the rest of my life making sure she never doubts that she belongs anywhere she wants to be.

Especially with me.

"I love you too, Samantha Jones."

between departures

acknowledgments

Thank you to my readers. Those who took a chance on my first book and stayed, and those who found me here. You are the reason I continue showing up at the page, even on tough days.

To my husband, thank you for your patience, support, and for letting me escape into my fictional worlds without judgment.

To those who helped by reading the book, catching typos, and fixing all the commas I missed, thank you for keeping me sane—you three know who you are.

And to myself, for finishing this book, pushing through fear and doubt, and choosing this dream again and again. I'm proud of you.

With love,

K.V. Thorn

also by k.v. thorn

Never Not Yours

Coming Next:
Love In Transit Series,
Book 2, Book 3, Book 4

about the author

Writing has been a journey for me.

From my first journal at nine years old, to school projects, to endless journals, .docx files, and notes no one saw growing up, to my debut 'Never Not Yours,' and now my second book.

I'm just a thirty-something woman writing about romance, love in all its many forms, and everything in between.

I love writing about female characters who haven't had an easy life but figure it out, and male characters who are troubled but perfect in their own way.

With love,
K.V. Thorn

between departures

LOVE IN TRANSIT SERIES

K.V. THORN

THORN PUBLISHING HOUSE

www.ingramcontent.com/pod-product-compliance
Lightning Source LLC
LaVergne TN
LVHW100510110826
845146LV00002B/586

* 9 7 9 8 9 9 3 8 3 0 8 4 1 *